EXILED FROM HELL

EXILED FROM HELL

BOOK I OF THE
"THE WAR OF SOULS"
TRILOGY

David Gearing

AKUSAI
PUBLISHING

For information contact;

www.akusaipublishing.com

Book and Cover design by Kevin Johnson

ISBN: 978-0692268759
First Edition: August 2014

10 9 8 7 6 5 4 3 2 1

Dedication

To my summer writing group.

Chapter One

Just a normal day in Hell, really. The skies ran dark, the celestial bodies above glimmering rays of light that barely touch the surface.

"You want me to do what?" Erigan's red claws scratch the back of his curly, black hair. "Why would I want to go to the Seventh Circle of Hell *again*?"

Erigan stands just outside of his office building, waiting to get past his boss, who blocks his entrance inside. He's dressed for his usual day of hauntings and mere annoyances.

It's the primary job description at the Terror Division of Hell. A small job, really, but only because they don't trust this ex-god with too much responsibility. His bosses have seemed to learn better in the past two-thousand years.

The office building, like everything else in this quarter of Hell, is ashen gray and slightly off tilt. Much like a Salvador

Dali painting. This particular one towers nearly sixty floors up into the skies of Hell.

This is not impressive by Hell standards. The citadel that houses Lucifer and his armies stretch out nearly five point five times that much, and only twice as wide. Rounded at the tip, it always made Erigan smile when he flew into the City of Dis.

Not as beautiful as Mount Olympus, of course. But impressive nonetheless.

"Because I told you to." Ba'al twists his arms around the door and thrusts his large, body into the doorway. "You're not coming in until you've fed the harpies."

"Feed them with what?" Erigan pulls up the sleeves of his black suit, punctuated stylishly with a red tie and slate gray button down shirt. "My arms?"

Ba'al raises a hairy, black eyebrow. "Tempting, but no."

Ba'al's shoulders appear wider than they are. It's a spell, they say behind his back, to make him appear more godlike. More powerful. Something to be feared.

But it's hard to fear someone after you read what they say about you in the bathroom stalls.

Ba'al tucks in his midnight blue tie into his gray jacket. "It's tempting," Ba'al says with a smile. "But no. Take this."

He tosses a burlap bag of round pellets onto the ground. Dark green pellets with specks of red and blue. "What is this?"

"You do not want to know," says Ba'al. "Now hurry up or you will be late for work."

Eerigan blinks and raises an eyebrow. Was that a threat?

"But I'm already at work," says Erigan.

"And now you aren't." The door closes and locks. Ba'al stands at the front of the doorway, behind the glass, and crosses his arms. Seeing that Erigan isn't moving anywhere, he shooshes him away with his closed fingers.

Erigan looks into the bag and closes it again. It smelled like rotten wood. Down here between the Fifth Circle and the Sixth Circle, that's not a bad thing by most standards.

The wings on Erigan's feet take flight and push him forward and up at the same time. Erigan clicks his sandals together and they pick up speed toward the gates downward to the Seventh Circle of Hell.

Down below him, something catches his attention.

"What the fuck do you mean, I can't get in? I'm not drunk. You're drunk." A tall, muscular man with wide shoulders chucks another guy inside of a building and the door slams shut.

That door belongs to The Pentagram. Where many of Erigan's friends and family from another lifetime hang out and chat about old times.

"Dammit, Herc," says Erigan. He lands onto the ground and pressed the door in. "Behemoth?" he says.

The large man smiles through his thick, close-cropped beard. His brown hair, once in tight curls, is now sopping wet with sprayed beer and liquor everywhere.

"What are you doing here?" says Erigan. He comes to the bar and rests the bag of harpy food on the counter. "Hey, Behemoth, I have a job. Let's go."

Behemoth takes a sip of someone's beer and tosses it clear across the table. "But I'm drinking."

Dio, a young boyish-looking demon stands up. His dark, crimson red skin gives off a soft, youthful, and baby-ass smooth sheen. He push back a lock of his hair, shoulder-length and dirty blond. Beyond that, he looks remarkably human.

"Yes, please. Get this hairy beast out of our tavern." He stands pushes Behemoth off the counter with a thud. "I love you dearly, brother, but you have to keep friends like this on a tight leash."

Erigan steps forward and grabs Behemoth's bearpaw of a hand. "He's our half-brother, too, remember?"

Dio scoffs. "Not on my half," he says. He slides his empty glass to the cowering bartender, whose horns are stuck in the dark wood of the shelving behind him. "Any time you're ready, I'd like another drink. Just saying."

Behemoth slaps down Erigan's hand and stands up. He dusts himself off and brushes back his curly hair. Realizing it's wet, he sniffs his hands and licks the beer off of them. "Where are we going?"

"Seventh Circle," says Erigan. He heads for the door. "Again."

"Again?"

"Again."

"But why do you always get the shitty jobs?"

"Because someone in Hell hates me and our kind," he says. "Now hurry up, or I'll be late for work."

Chapter Two

Curiously, he had been sent here several times with orders from Ba'al to feed the harpies.

Not just a few days ago, but time and time again.

Just through the fiery sands of the Sixth Circle flows the Phlegethon River. Boiling blood and all.

After that, the wailing trees of the Seventh Circle, the Circle of eternal punishment for suicides. It was God's will that they suffer for their crimes against their bodies, so harpies come out and feed on these trees.

The trees, being people. Or their souls, of course.

"This is always so weird," says Behemoth. He pushes aside the branches of the trees and steps through to the center of the circle.

"Please," says one of the trees. "Listen."

Behemoth shivers. "That is always creepy."

"Listen to our story," cries out a tree. Its voice is ghostly, faint, a call on the warm winds that cross over through the blood river. "Listen about my husband."

Erigan digs his hands into the bag of feed and tosses it out into the spaces between the trees.

He had learned through common sense—and by that he means trial-and-error—that sending the feed onto the ground in the open parts was much easier than listening to the screaming of those black feathered bitches with wings, getting caught thorns of the living trees.

"Please, listen. My husband is a powerful man."

Erigan rolls his eyes. "We're in Hell, honey. There are lots of powerful men here."

"He wishes himself a god," the voice says.

"Who doesn't."

Another handful of feed hits the ground.

A flock of harpies comes from the trees on the outside of the circle. They caw, a shrill voice that calls out to their sisters that feeding time has come early today.

"He wishes himself a god," says the woman tree. "He was once chained to the underworld, but shamed me by fooling the gods. So much shame."

Erigan pauses. He pretends to not listen, but he really is. The story sounds familiar.

"You know of him," says the tree. "So much shame. So much shame. I killed myself, I could not bear it."

Erigan nods. "Sisyphus?" he says.

"Yes," she cries out with a muted excitement. "You

know my husband. My shameful husband."

Erigan nods. "Ya, I know the bastard." The other gods got tired of being tricked by him, so they called in Erigan—going by the name of Hermes back then—to chain down Sisyphus himself. The bastard still somehow made it out of Tartaros.

The flock of birds gets too big for both Behemoth and Erigan to stand in the same space.

"Should we move back?"

The area is soon flooded with a flying feathers and a piercing, blood-curdling shriek from a pissed off harpy.

The feathers fly and one of the harpies takes to the sky, but bumps into Erigan.

Erigan feels his grip on the rocky floor slipping. "Behemoth, a little help."

Behemoth turns his back on the mess of feathers and food. He covers his eyes, shielding himself from the ruckus. "Fuck me, you'd think they never eat."

Erigan tries to break his fall by turning to his side, but it doesn't work fast enough. He falls backwards into the thorny branches of the talking tree—Sisyphus's wife.

She breaks his fall but when Erigan pulls himself back up by using the seemingly stronger branches, he falls back onto the ground with a twig, a thorny and bleeding twig, in his hand.

The tree screams in pain, shrieking and screaming louder than the mass of harpies.

The shrill is enough to scare away most of the flock to their homes on the outer edge of the Circle.

Rustling footsteps trample through the trees behind them. "Who's here?"

"It's the minotaur," Erigan whispers.

Behemoth stands up to peek.

"Get the fuck down here," Erigan whisper-screams at his friend. He grabs is friend's bear paw and tries to pull him down.

Behemoth listens and kneels down. "Now what?"

"I think we go. Now. Fast."

"Did you do what you were supposed to do?" says Behemoth. He adjusts his hair and pulls up his hood, a lion's head slain from a time long, long ago.

Erigan looks at the half-eaten harpy kibble on the floor. "Good enough, I guess."

"Good," says Behemoth. He starts running in a direction that, Erigan is sure, isn't even close to the path back to the city.

"Where are going?" says Erigan.

Behemoth, too far to hear his friend, cannot answer. Running with that much muscle always takes too much effort.

Unless you have wings, like Erigan.

He takes to the air and follows the trail of wailing, broken trees left in Behemoth's wake.

He finds the hidden path to the gate, the secret crossing just north of where the Minotaur typically guards from strangers.

It was a dangerous path, to slide over the river and not go through the Minotaur first. He was known to be a charge-first, ask-questions-if-you-survived kind of guy.

Erigan did not want to test that theory, however. So he follows Behemoth through the gates and back into the city.

Or at least that was the plan.

What he runs into is the strong muscular back of Behemoth.

His arms are up, bent at the elbows. The lion's tale from Behemoth's cloak tickles Erigan's nose. The smaller demon peers around Behemoth's surprisingly thin waist.

A bull-headed man, nearly as muscular as Behemoth, holds a spear, clad in a black shiny armor that glistens in the celestial light above. The thick black fur on the bull's head sheens like it got wet, sweating. The lips curl upwards into a snarl, showing wide, powerful teeth.

"Where the fuck do you think you're going?" he says and then snorts something onto the ground.

Chapter Three

Seeking only temporary refuge to catch his breath, Erigan steps into the shadows of the strong walls of Dis, City of the Dead. Armored and fearful fallen angels typically guard the walls that encircle the city. But at the moment, they're too busy chasing after Behemoth as he runs around its wide, circular borders.

Erigan rests his hands against the cold stone of the walls. His scrawny chest—not merely as impressive as the aptly-named Behemoth's—heaved up and down. He isn't used to this running bullshit.

Fading from shadow to shadow. *That* he could do. But running? That was for the dumber, strong demons.

But in the omnipresent lighting that keeps Hell lit like a bug zapper, finding a shadow dark enough to fade into is rather difficult.

"All the better to watch you with," the jokes went.

But even so, the truth was evident—even Lucifer the Lightbringer didn't trust his fellow demons in the darkness of Hell.

Erigan's claws trace along the sturdy, gray stones only to find a bit of dust in his hands. His hands dig further and deeper until something moves at his fingertips. Erigan's smile reveals sharp and yellowing canines in his lower jaw thanks to his underbite.

"You clever son of a bitch," he says. Erigan digs his claws dig deep into the stone and pulls it out. The rock itself is hollow.

"What the hell is this?" A trick right out of his own playbook.

Erigan throws the rock over the cliff just behind him. Someone had sealed the entrance. Removed the trigger brick with another fake one.

He twiddles the branch around between his fingers. The thorny branch scrapes along his smooth red skin. Not drawing blood but leaking it from the broken edge.

Erigan tucks the twig into his tunic and turns to peer down the broad alleyway.

His friend Behemoth, a demon of animal strength, races like white lightning down the road. Lion's skin flaps against his shoulders and back.

"How you doing there, buddy?" asks Erigan.

Behemoth doesn't turn his head, only runs forward. "Why do I let you talk me into these things?"

Erigan smiles and then steps back into the shadows. The flapping of wings precedes a shout from down the alley.

"Here!" shouts a fallen angel in a blood red leather uniform. The uniform looks disheveled now from the chase, maybe even a bit dusty. Lucifer would be pissed if he caught sight of this.

Erigan hides into the shadows, shifting his own skin color to blend in with the darkness.

The flood of flapping leathery wings and uniformed boots stampedes past him.

When the coast is clear, Erigan takes the twig out of the pocket of his tunic and takes a look at it. "All this for that?"

The wings of Erigan's ankles begin to flap as he runs around the opposite direction. He knows it will only be a matter of time before Behemoth comes racing around again.

Though he could never beat Erigan in a footrace—even without his wings—Behemoth was a helluva runner. One of the best, that big lug.

"Erigan!" Behemoth voice thunders around the corner. His bearded smile reveals a hint of enjoyment as he passes by Erigan once again. "When do we get to fight them?"

Erigan prances along with Behemoth's pace. "Not yet, buddy. Soon."

"But you said," Behemoth says, but they are interrupted by the tooting of horns.

"Aw hell," says Erigan. "Cavalry."

Behemoth digs his heels into the ground, pulling up

the ground and digging narrow six-inch deep gashes into the dark maroon dirt. "What?"

"Oh, come on, it won't be so bad this time."

"This time?" says Behemoth. "I swear, there had better not be a *this time*."

"You worry too much," says Erigan. He holds out the twig and hands it to his big, burly buddy. "Hold this for me?"

"What the hell is this?" Behemoth pushes out of his view the lion's head that sits on his head. "You stole a twig from the Seventh Circle?"

"You say that like it's a bad thing," says Erigan. His eyes stay fixed on the onslaught of black leather that heads his way. The black cloud of angry fallen angels seems to grow as it comes around the horizon.

Erigan holds out his hand, extending fingers as he tries to count them. Needing his other hand and maybe some toes to keep track of the numbers, he decides to quit.

Behemoth holds the twig out to Erigan. "What is this, exactly?"

"Nothing, buddy. Promise."

"But it's bleeding," says Behemoth. He licks the slick red liquid that leaks from the broken, frayed edge. "It's human," he says. He smacks his lips and licks it again. "Female. Young." He shoves the twig back into Erigan's face. "Why do you have this?"

Erigan pushes Behemoth's thick, strong hands away from his face to keep an eye on his would-be killers.

"We're a little busy, don't you think?"

"That?" Behemoth says. He smashes his hands together and flexes his shoulders and triceps. "Bring them on. I do not fear a battle." His dark brown beard stretched along with his burly smile.

"That's the old god I remember."

Behemoth peers down at the much smaller demon Erigan, who is suddenly and painfully aware of just how difficult this battle could be.

"We should get going," Erigan says and grabs hold of the wall's rocky surface. Peering back down at Behemoth, he says, "Coming?"

Chapter Four

The glowing darkness, this ephemeral light that can best be described as "daylight" for most humans, gradually beams around the corners. The red-orange sunset colors beam across the horizon in little rays that overshadow the large army that stomps toward Erigan and Behemoth.

"I knew you'd fuck up eventually," a voice growls. It belongs to Mam'mon. Ex-archangel. Followed Lucifer to the ends of the earth, then ended up getting tossed out on his ass by the Lord himself.

"Ya, well, you know. Old habits die hard." Erigan snorts with pride.

"Listen, it's just a misunderstanding, right, Erigan? Just something of a game we were playing, right?" Behemoth nods at Erigan, nudging him again with his elbow.

The look on his face says, "Please save me." But Erigan steps forward.

"And what are you going to do now?" he says.

Mam'mon snorts, wipes his lizard-like muzzle and grins. White teeth that glisten with fresh saliva catches Erigan's eye.

"I was hoping you'd say that." Mam'mon turns around and snaps his fingers as he walks away.

Two others, a massive minotaur and a centaur, grab hold of Behemoth by the shoulders and drag him out of the shadows of the massive walls of Dis. The air smells stagnant to Erigan, a little bit hard to breathe.

He's not sure if it's the tension or if the two thousand years of being in this Pit are finally getting to him.

"Get your hands off of me, by the Gods!" says Behemoth. With a mere shoulder shrug, he tosses the centaur and minotaur off his shoulder and adjusts the lion's head that sits on his head. "If it's war you want, war you get."

The battle begins with Behemoth grabbing the minotaur's face with his massive hand and tossing him into the walls.

Bits of the wall crumble to the floor as Erigan sidesteps the destruction.

He takes short but quick steps to the other end of the walls. He knows there is another entrance nearby. A small crevice, if he remembers correctly.

"Just where the fuck do you think you're going?"

cries out Mam'mon. His clawed hands pull Erigan up off the floor by the tunic.

There Mam'mon dangles the little demon in the air between his index and thumb, laughing. "Runt," he says.

Erigan looks up with a smile. Bodies of winged and leathery demons fly into the air. He remembers that Behemoth was a warrior in his past life. A deadly one at that.

Twelve tasks couldn't have taken him down. What makes them think an army could?

"You're losing," says Erigan.

"Momentarily," Mam'mon jests.

Erigan smiles, then winces.

Mam'mon holds Erigan closer to his face and sniffs him. "You were down there for a reason, weren't you? You smell like human blood."

Erigan, still wincing and bracing for something, just shakes his head. He points behind him.

And Mam'mon turns his head to view behind him. A winged projectile, courtesy of Behemoth, comes bolting at Mam'mon.

The view fades to darkness as a winged harpy lands in Mam'mon's face, clawing and scratching to be freed.

Mam'mon's grip on Erigan frees up, giving him freedom to run.

He finds refuge in the shadows along the wall. He holds his feet still, trying not to let his sandals twitch nervously in the red clay beneath him.

"C'mon, buddy. Let's get going," says Erigan.

Mam'mon stands tall once again. The harpy, however, did not fare so well. Its body lay broken and twisted along the floor at Mam'mon's feet.

Erigan shrugs. It's only a momentary setback. There are always hundreds more coming into Hell every day. Always more soldiers.

"Stop messing around and seize him!" commands Mam'mon.

Meanwhile, the lizard-faced commander searches underneath his feet and around the large protruding boulders for Erigan. "Where are you, you whelp?"

Erigan presses himself up against the walls and takes larger, silent steps toward the other end of the walls.

"Sorry about this, old buddy," he says.

But the demons, they pile on more, almost to the same height as the city's walls.

Erigan knows his friend will be freed once they realize it was his plan all along. They won't frame Behemoth. He's too useful and too stupid.

Erigan is the real prize.

He peers off into the valley and watches as the army finally overcomes Behemoth. His own strong, calloused hands reach into the air for help, as if gasping for breath.

Chapter Five

Dust settles in the horizon and at long last, Erigan reaches the edge of the walls. The crevice he had looked for, it wasn't here.

His eyes traced a thin line that led to the edge of the path around the city. The city of Dis itself was built upon a cliff of bones and rock.

The rock appeared sturdy enough, but the cliff kept it free from being attacked by angels in The Rebellion.

It was all for naught, however. The angels never dared to enter Hell. They never had to, they felt. In Hell, we'd all destroy ourselves.

"It's my day off," Erigan mutters. "I'm not even supposed to be here." He takes the chance to step out of the shadows. Along the ex-battle field, he sees only the army, now shadows and silhouettes against the lighted backdrop of Hell's eternal sunset.

The army marches off in the opposite distance.

Mam'mon apparently gives up his search for Erigan. Erigan smiles and presses his hands against his chest in thanks.

He pauses for only a second, however, paranoid that maybe he has been sighted.

Along the skies, a flock of human birdlike creatures flap in thunderous unison. Harpies. The sentries and lookouts.

More shadows grow around him. The ex-angel sentries return to their ledges along the thick stone walls.

Erigan looks down at his winged sandals. If only, he thinks. He'd never be able to get far if he flew anywhere now. Strictly grounded.

"Where do you go, little trail?" he says.

Erigan braves another step out of the shadows. If he acts fact, he can make it to the ledge. If it goes where he thinks it does…

Erigan drops to his knees and crawls to the ledge of the road. Then, grasping tightly along the rocky ledge, he peers over. A darkened hole.

"I take back everything bad I ever said about you, Herc," says Erigan. With trepidation he puts one leg over the ledge and reaches around for the hole. It's big enough for him to fit into, if only he could get in there safely.

Sure he could fly, but how far would he go before he lands down there, amongst the frozen lower levels of

Hell? He can't slum it down there just yet—he still owes Judas money.

When Erigan feels enough solid ground to rest his foot, he turns around and lays face first onto the ground. He tries to take in a deep breath and hold it, but takes in the musty dirt and shit through his nostrils.

But then Erigan pauses. He hears flapping and chattering up above him. "Goddammit," he says. "Fucking angels."

Erigan goes for broke, pushing himself down while letting his left leg flail. He can't find the ledge anymore, as if it just disappeared.

"Where the hell are you?" he whispers. His lips are so close to the ground that he accidentally kisses the shit-tasting ground.

At long last a smile comes to Erigan's face. He's found the hole and both feet are firmly held inside.

"Here goes nothing," he says.

Erigan lets go of the rock and pushes off. He flips backward and closes his eyes. Though he could fly in his past life, he hasn't gotten used to the feeling of falling.

Because he's a sucker for punishment, he opens his eyes to see two angels settle themselves on the ledge. Their wings pull tight against their body and all he can see is black uniforms and medal buttons along their coats.

"Did you see that?" one of them says to the other.

Erigan feels his eyes widen. They might have seen him. He'll have to act fast.

Using his hands to hold himself steady, he slides his ass further into the hole. His arms, however, they shake from the strain of holding his own body.

He's got wings on his shoes, for crying out loud. He's never had to even run.

"This is bullshit," he says to himself and then smiles.

Of course! Wings!

He clicks his heels together and holds his breath.

"Wake up, damn you," he says. He clicks his heels together again. The wings finally wake up and flap madly to pull him into the hole.

"That! Over there!" shouts an angel.

He jumps from his post and runs to the rocky cliff. "Is that him?" the angel says.

"Sorry guys, but I'm late for work." Erigan feels the cold air of the tunnel envelope his body and smiles. "Bye bye," he says.

"It's him! Go get Mam'mon!" shouts the angel.

The smaller of the two disappears into the sky, flapping away. The larger one, however, reaches out with both hands, trying to snatch Erigan's tunic by the shoulders.

"Come here!" he growls.

"Can't do that," says Erigan. "But maybe next time you'll catch me," he says and extends not one, but both middle fingers to the angels before being sucked in.

Chapter Six

Once again, the office smells like sulfur mixed with farts. This time, Erigan thinks, it might be his own fault.

An occupational hazard when you work in the Department of Minor Infractions, also known as the Terror Division.

In Hell, everything is run by special committees and bureaucrats. Boy, does Hell love its bureaucrats.

The Terror Division is no different. When they aren't trying to kill your will to live, they're looking for someone to blame for something, anywhere.

This is why Erigan often feels it necessary to entertain himself.

Hence the smell.

Leading the Flatulent and Gluttonous out of the Third Circle might have been funny at the time. But leading them into the office using chocolate-covered

Brussels sprouts?

Even Erigan currently second guesses that decision.

The glass doors–brand new as of last month–close behind him. The office is set up into cubicles, gray industrial partitions against the red velvet backdrop of the walls. The true mark of Hell.

Erigan smirks and approaches the wall to clock in for this evening's shift.

He looks into his wallet for a rose red credit-card sized plastic badge. He only keeps it safe because he's only issued one to clock into work.

The last guy who lost his card went through the ringer–literally. In Hell, the bosses don't take insubordination very well.

The gray metal box takes his first swipe of his badge, but not the pin number.

"What the fuck?" Erigan mutters beneath his breath. He looks up, pokes his horned head in both directions of the hallway, then curls his fist. "Take the fucking number!" he whispers to the box then hits it with his hooked, bony knuckles.

"Easy does it there, Erigan," says a voice behind him. It growls a little bit as he makes the "r". "Don't make us charge you for another one."

"On my shit pay? You'd maybe get a third of one of these." Erigan looks over his shoulder and smiles at his boss, Ba'al.

He looks particularly tall this morning, taking up just over the first half of the hallway with his impressive wingspan. The leathery wings outstretch across the halls then wrap tightly around Ba'al's body. This gives him something like the effect of wearing a thick Halloween cape.

"Listen, smart ass," says Ba'al. "Keep it up and you'll be canned like the other guy."

"You're not going to find very many other people who can do what I do," says Erigan. "And certainly not as well as I do."

"You young guys always say that," says Ba'al, "and you know what? We always find a replacement."

"I've been around for two thousand years, Ba'al. You're not getting rid of me that easily. Trust me." Erigan smirks and punches in the last number of his four digit PIN.

"You're an ass, Erigan. And an arrogant one at that. That's the worst kind." Ba'al snorts something up through his nostrils. A forked tongue peels his lips apart, licking them and pushing the phlegm around the back of his throat.

As Erigan walks past him, Ba'al shoots the lugey damn near Erigan's foot.

Erigan pauses and contemplates today being the day he gets fired. Tearing someone's head off is usually a good way to go out.

But he shrugs and walks away. Not like he'd win, anyway.

"You fucked up your last assignment, whelp," shouts Ba'al. "Next time and it'll be your ass on a pitchfork."

Erigan extends his hand slowly as he walks away, extends his middle finger and whistles into the next room.

The sound of Ba'al's deep belly laugh follows Erigan to his chair in the cubicle. Erigan turns on his computer, flicks through the endless number of neon Post-Its on his desk.

His cubicle, his home away from home, is littered with memos of minutia and reminders. Nothing overly important. This is, after all, where all of the bad managers end up.

And each and every one of them ends up higher on the totem pole than Erigan. Erigan's pointed tail flicks at the garbage near the entrance to his cubicle. For a second he almost knocks it clear across the room, but remembers his anger management training.

"Breathe in," he says.

He rests his ass against the soft fabric of his chairs. Made in China and as soft as anything you'd ever find in Heaven.

In Hell, everyone splurges on comfort. Only the best.

When the computer clicks on, he surfs though his email and peers over the cubicle wall. The email is a link to something outside the intranet. A no-no according to company standards.

Still, Erigan clicks anyway.

Lights flash in the computer monitor and a minotaur wearing nothing but a banana hammock flaunts his stuff in Erigan's face. He stares, measuring himself up against the man-bull and then closes the email.

Typical Behemoth.

"Erigan! Get in here!" Erigan recognizes the voice as coming from behind him. The manager's office. Not Ba'al's, but a secondary manager. She's much, much worse than anything Erigan could dream up even in his worst nightmares.

Erigan draws in a steady breath and stands up. He peers up past his eyebrows to what little of his left horn still remains. He wonders today if he's going to lose the right one, too.

Chapter Seven

"Yes, Lilith?" says Erigan. He tries to force the twinkle, but it doesn't go anywhere.

Lilith's office sits behind a glass window that can overlook the entire floor. All ten cubicles oriented around each other in a big X from wall to wall.

He'd be lying to himself if he didn't sometimes peek at Lilith "hard at work" in the office in between email and phone calls.

The rest of the office smells of burnt roses, the herbal smell of something roasting in the microwave behind her desk. Maybe road kill. Maybe human. Too hard to tell.

"Don't swish your tail at me, boy," says Lilith. She stands up and walks in front of her desk. The black streak in her otherwise white hair curls around her head and falls along her shoulder. Erigan's eyes follow its smooth line to the tips of her breast. "Eyes up here."

Erigan averts his eyes completely and stares out the window into the pits of Tartaros.

"We have an assignment for you," she says. She licks her lips—a dark red, not unlike dried roses—revealing a glimmer of sharpened canines.

"Good," says Erigan. "I've been a little bored down here."

"That's not what I heard," she says. Lilith rests here ass along the edges of her desk and rests her hands behind her. This makes her tits pop out like two heads of the Hydra eager for a feast. "Don't get too excited," she says.

Lilith nods toward a dark wood shelf that lines the northern wall. This shelf doesn't house books, but clay pots and urns. Relics nearly a millennia old, possibly longer.

Rumor has it there were juices from the Tree of Knowledge in them.

"The manila folder," says Lilith. Her voice caresses Erigan's red, pointed ears. His legs shake with anticipation when he reaches for the folder and opens it up.

Immediately, he feels Lilith's sharpened nails gently scrape along his neck.

"Careful," says Erigan. "It's a new suit."

Lilith pulls him around and rips his shirt open. Erigan's raw, darkly red chest exposed in the office. She claws at the bristles of black hair that swirl in a tight pattern between his pecs. "You shaved," Lilith says with a smile.

"I hope you did, too," says Erigan. He takes his hands and slowly moves them down lower and lower until he realizes that he's grabbing her thigh near her crotch.

"What are you afraid of?" she whispers.

"Afraid of getting bit," he says.

Lilith scoffs. "Please, I can control it if I need to."

Erigan smiles and withdraws his hands. He politely steps back and smiles while buttoning up his shirt. "Same time tomorrow?" he says.

"You're a helluva pig," she says. Lilith reaches for the folder on the bookshelf and tosses it at him. Erigan barely catches it. Photos pop out; photos of a little human boy. White, maybe eight years old, wearing blue robes.

"You're kidding me," says Erigan.

"Your mission," she says.

He flips through the pages and notices no addresses or explanations. Just pictures.

"How the hell am I supposed to find this place?" he snarls.

"You should have thought about that before you went all celibate on me," she snarls back.

Erigan smiles, grabs his folder and tucks it up under his arm. "Glad to see you too, bitch."

Lilith runs her hands through her white hair, fingering a few curls between her index finger and her pointed thumb. Her fingernails are so sharp Erigan swears tiny slivers of hair fall to the ground.

"You don't have to be so shy," she says. "He will never find out."

Lilith reaches out and takes Erigan's shirt by surprise. Once again, she pulls the buttons apart and rubs her hands along his chest and shoulders.

Each stroke pushes more of his shirt out off his body.

Erigan braves his conquest. "This is really what you want to do?"

Lilith responds with a playful bite on his neck. She points a razor-sharp fingernail to the chair opposite her desk. "Sit down," she says.

Erigan does as he commands. His eyes stay fixed on the windows out into Tartaros. Souls burn in eternal damnation, each one wishing they could be in Erigan's shoes right now.

"Let's make this quick," says Lilith. "But not too quick."

The door slams to offer them privacy.

Chapter Eight

Erigan escapes Lilith's office with his tie still sitting loosely around his neck. Erigan isn't prone to sweating usually, but something makes him itch under the collar.

The bright fluorescent lighting just above his horned head begins to flicker, but just subtly so.

Not an outright lightning flash—ah, Zeus, how much he missed him—but that annoying flicker that he gets out the corner of his eyes.

"I hate this place," Erigan says. He steps into his cubicle one more time, peeking at the reminders that have littered his desk.

Literally every inch of his desk. These notes tell him about happy hours with the friends and reports due in the next few days.

Everything he does not want to make time for.

But in Hell, if you mess up, you get Hell-fired.

Erigan considers for a second to not file his last report.

"Fuck 'em," he mutters to himself and shuts down his computer. The computer screen goes blank and he lets out a long sigh.

He looks down at the folder still in his hands. A little boy needs haunting, apparently. Who better than the trickster and messenger to go get a little haunting done?

Having been a part of senior staff for half a millennia, he wonders why he is now handed out a minor haunting. In the past he's started wars and gotten his exorcisms filmed for cameras.

Today, he's hunting down a bright blond-haired boy with big blue saucers for eyes. The picture has him smiling and holding something of a soft teddy bear.

He looks up, peeks at the bright orange Post-It on his desk.

Happy Hour for Lunch with the boys?

"What the hell," he mutters and turns around for the door.

The haunting? It can wait. Right now he just needs a drink.

Or three.

The floor begins to shake as he walks, but Erigan isn't so stubborn to think that he's the cause of the quakes.

"Behemoth!" Erigan stretches out his arms for a giant hug. "I told you they'd let you out," Erigan says with a smile.

"You're an ass, Herm," the giant demon shouts back. Because of his large size Behemoth catches up with Erigan's pace in only a second.

"And you're none the worse for wear," says Erigan.

Behemoth shoves his huge muscled arm across Erigan's path. "Why did you set me up?"

"You said you wanted to come with," Erigan says. "It's an occupational hazard, getting caught."

"You didn't even try to get me out," Behemoth snorts.

"I didn't have to," says Erigan. He rests his hands along the rough stubble of Behemoth's cheek. "You look great and it's only been, what? A few hours."

Behemoth removes his fist and grasps for Erigan's horned head. "You let me take the fall for what? A twig?"

Erigan places his little fingers into Behemoth's vest and pulls out the twig, safely kept in the pockets. "They didn't look very hard, did they?"

"I had to hide it," says Behemoth. "But why? Who is this for?"

"No one, buddy. Promise."

"Stop calling me that!" Behemoth growls. "We are no longer buddies as long as you keep using me as your shield."

Erigan keeps his eyes set straight forward. "I'm meeting the boys for some quick drinks before my next case," he says. "Coming along?"

"Case?" says Behemoth. "What case?"

Erigan tucks the twig back into his own tunic.

"Something stupid," says Erigan. "Why are you so eager to know?" Erigan turns his head to face his friend. "Are you so eager to return to interrogation?"

Behemoth's lips let out a snarl, showing his sharpened teeth. His shoulder muscles flex as he stands solid as a statue in the flashing fluorescent lights.

Erigan feels the rage fuming from Behemoth's body. That look on his friend's face. Erigan knows it well.

"Come on," he says. "The first round is on me."

Chapter Nine

The air tastes stale and dry in Erigan's mouth. The nice part of being an ex-god turned demon is he gets to leave on his haunting missions.

The downside is getting to smell this shit day in and day out when he comes back.

The streets in Dis are busy in the way that supermarkets on Earth are busy on paydays: Not impossible to get around, but most of the time Erigan finds himself surrounded by fucktards who just don't know where in literal Hell they are going.

Behemoth trails behind Erigan in short strides. But only because the side streets don't really allow for the two to walk side-by-side.

Poor city planning, Erigan used to complain.

By definition, Hell itself *has* to get bigger. Why wouldn't the Powers That Be plan for that?

The cities were built with plenty of buildings. Wooden doors and thick, solid white bricks make up the buildings. The bricks offer a warm glow in the ephemeral "daylight." Sometimes this makes them looks like ghosts. Other times, it just makes them look like they are cooking their inhabitants.

Hrm, houses that cook people, Erigan thinks. Maybe he should run that up to senior management sometime. They do so enjoy a new haunting idea now and again.

"You always take the backroads," says Behemoth in his deep voice. "You could cut your time in half if we took the main roads. Grendel Street isn't that bad this time of day."

Erigan adjusts his tunic and peers down both sides of the street before crossing it.

He turns to shush his companion. "I'm still in hiding," he says. "Remember this morning?"

"How could I not?"

In Hell, there aren't any cars. The inhabitants of Dis walk everywhere. The hustle and bustle of modern human city life means nothing to most of these demons. They've got an eternity to get anywhere.

At least until the next regime change.

Judging by the silence around town, Mam'mon and the soldiers that chased the pair still wander about. No doubt wondering and hoping that Erigan will show up again.

But his friend, Erigan knows, his friend is simply too tall to hide. So, he doesn't bother to hide him at all.

"Do I have to wear this uniform?" says Behemoth.

"If you look like one of them, then they won't second guess who I am," he says.

"Can I at least keep the lion's skin?"

Erigan turns to face his large friend. Behemoth's barrel chest stands a nose-length's away from Erigan's face. The large man is a bruiser, a fighter, a warrior.

Even as a child, a killer of snakes and destroyer of women. Not that all of that was his fault to begin with. Jealous goddesses are quite dangerous.

"You look like quite the lady killer," says Erigan. He takes the black button-down shirt and adjusts it. "Tuck this in," says Erigan. He points to the shirttails with his left claw. "You don't want to look like an amateur."

"Lady killer, huh?" says Behemoth. He presses his thick hands into the tops of his pants and adjusts the shirt. "Better?" he says.

Erigan looks his friend up and down. He barely fits into the uniform he stole only moments ago. Even the biggest of the demons don't quite match Behemoth's size.

Still, he looks presentable.

"Dashing," he says.

Behemoth beams with pride.

Erigan steps across the street and toward The Pentagram, his destination.

The door creaks open. Erigan stands at the doorway, staring down the bar for his friends. Golden candelabras line the walls and offer enough light to keep the main of the room quite visible. Erigan smiles to the barkeep, a lowly black demon with a pale blue face.

"You still have those damned things?" says Erigan pointing to the candelabras. "They're what? A thousand years old?"

"Meh, the boss likes them." The barkeep pulls a stone stein from the shelf behind him and fills it with a light yellow liquid. "Here."

The stein slides along the bar to Erigan's hands.

"Stole those from King Louis VII of France when he and his wife left for the Crusades," says Erigan.

"We know, we know," says one of the men at the bar. "Drink up. The faster you get drunk, the faster we won't have to listen to your damned yapping."

"And I love you too, Dio." Erigan holds his stein up into the air. The three other half-drunken demons at the bar raise theirs as well. "To the old ones," says Erigan.

Together, they chant, "The old ones!" and slam their beers.

"I'll have one, too," says Behemoth.

The barkeep wipes his brow with the backs of his hands. His face looks worried and his words stammer. "I-I-I don't think I can do th-th-that."

Behemoth bends over the bar. His face is so close to the barkeep's that Behemoth's breath pushes the barkeep's hair out of his face.

"And why not?"

"Easy there, you big lug," says Erigan. "If you scare them off, we'll never get service."

Behemoth sits on the dark wooden stool and rests his head in his hands. "I never get service anyway, so..."

Erigan taps Behemoth's shoulder and points to the wall behind him. Specifically the splintered and cracked boards that stretched out from the wall like the fingers of a twisted old witch.

"I told you that's not my fault," says Behemoth. "If you didn't make that bet, I wouldn't get mad."

"You're the one who said you could out-drink me," says Erigan. "I can't help it if you can't hold your liquor."

"You cheated, Erigan. You cheated and you know it." Behemoth continues to rest his head in his hands.

"Don't go making no googley eyes at me, boy," says the barkeep. He tosses a piece of jerky to a four-foot long rat at the end of the bar. "You'll be getting no drink from me. You're lucky you get entrance."

Behemoth's hands move slightly and his head drops to the bar.

"My Lord, I think he's weeping," says Erigan. He chuckles then sips his beer.

"You know, this type of stuff wouldn't have happened if we had only kept Zeus around," says Dio. He sat firmly in his chair. Dio, the old god of drunkenness and revelry. And wine. And grapes. And anything else that could make alcohol.

His hefty waistline did nothing to keep the old god looking young. His perpetual red nose and bloodshot eyes had begun to age Erigan's brother these past millennia.

"Where is our foolish father, anyhow?" says Erigan.

"Who the hell knows?" says Dio. Takes another drink. "Probably bedding his fair share of men and women."

"Dad always loved sex," says Erigan. He offers his stein for cheers, but Dio ignores the offer.

"More than us, it seemed."

Erigan empties his mug and slams it on the bar. "One more, then I gotta go," he says.

"Back to the office?" says Dio with a smile.

"No, back to Earth realm," says Erigan. "I have a case."

"A haunting or a reaping?" says Dio. He burps then wipes his mouth. "Blah, not like it fucking matters anymore."

"What happened to the god of drunken revelry?" says Erigan.

His mug comes sliding to him with fresh beer frothing over the top.

"In our day," says Dio, staring off into the bottles that lay beyond the bar, "in our day, we used to be gods. We ate ambrosia. Drank nectar. Fucked whoever we wanted to."

"That's whomever," says Behemoth.

"Didn't have a name badge," says Erigan, adjusting his own still hanging on his lapel.

"Could drink whenever we wanted to," adds Behemoth. His voice remains muted against the bar.

"Those were the days."

"Those were, old buddy. They definitely were." Erigan drinks the beer and drops the mug against the hard cobblestone floor. "Thanks for the swill, my good man."

Dio raises his hand up as if to say goodbye. "I'll tell the others you said hello."

"Would you?"

"If I can find them," Dio says. He shakes his head and taps at the bar. "One more, please."

"Have they gone missing? Probably on vacation," says Erigan. "That Apollo, always loved his music. Check Coachella."

"You just don't care, do you?"

Erigan's eyes narrow. "Yes, well, I'd love to sit here and wallow in your sorrow, but, well. You know. I don't want to. Tell everyone Mercury says hello, would you?"

"Aww, you too?" says Dio. He pushes the mug away from him. "Even you're taking the Roman name?"

"What? I like the ring of it."

"Your name is Hermes, brother. Not Mercury. Not Erigan."

"Not since the regime change, Dionysus. Get with the times." Erigan carries a strong smile for his poor brother,. "Everything will be fine," he says though he didn't know how much he believed it himself.

Chapter Ten

The glow of daylight meets them both as they leave for The Pentagram. No people hustle, bustle, or otherwise on these shadowy streets.

No one in an immediate hurry to get anywhere. Winged guards rest along the corners of the street. Watching, wielding spears and chatting amongst themselves.

The winged angelic guards like to harass wandering, lost souls. Hence the silence. An angry dark angel is a deadly dark angel.

The tall white buildings tip over to the side as if trying to pull themselves from the roads they stand on.

Erigan chuckles to himself. Even the buildings want to get out of Hell.

Erigan takes a careless step off the somewhat modern concrete sidewalk and into the old fashioned cobblestone roads.

"I will have to leave you behind, I think. This is a pretty small case," Erigan says. Erigan takes out the photo and glances at the picture. "It should not take much effort, I don't think."

Behemoth lumbers near Erigan as they walk across the streets, still following him.

"I could kill whoever I wanted," says Behemoth.

"That's *whomever*," says Erigan. "Not whoever." He pats him on the back. "And we have been done with that conversation for a few minutes now. Try to keep up there, buddy."

Behemoth snaps out of his daze and follows him to the other side.

"Sorry," says Behemoth. "Just thinking."

"Stop when it starts to hurt," says Erigan. He smiles and grabs Behemoth's lion hood. "Oh snap out of it! It's just a beer. You can get a beer anywhere else."

"But you guys like going there."

"Yes, yes we do." Erigan takes the big lug's hand in both of his and marvels at the size of his knuckles, about the size of his own palm. "Damn you're big."

Behemoth withdraws his hands and then grabs Erigan and snatches him up into his arms in a giant bear hug.

Erigan struggles, squirming, but Behemoth shrugs his shoulders together, having the effect of muting Erigan's screams. He tries to pull his head back from Behemoth's strong pectoral muscles.

No good.

Erigan begins to struggle for breath. The first time he's felt his own heart race this much.

To be honest, he is more surprised that he has a heartbeat.

Erigan throws his hands into fists and beats with every ounce of his strength into the giant beast's chest.

"Lee-ah-eee-oww!" he screams.

Behemoth's own heartbeat—Erigan can hear it in his ears—slows down, then comes to a calm rhythm.

"Good evening," Behemoth says.

Erigan stops struggling. What did he just do? Greet someone?

Erigan's body goes limp.

Save your energy, he thinks, in to later give a surprise kick to Behemoth's groin.

Limp. Calm.

For now.

Behemoth's breathing slows and eventually he lets Erigan drop to the ground.

Erigan bounces on his ass. Holding himself up, he looks around and scratches his head. Erigan says, "Where are we? And what was that for"

"Soldiers," says Behemoth. "I tried to hide you."

Erigan looks around the alleyway. The darkened roads that ran behind the building. Just off the main road.

"Well, thanks, then. I guess." Erigan scratches his head.

Behemoth smiles. "See? I can do good."

"You did great," says Erigan.

The two pick up their pace and walk down the road.

"What made you think to hide me in a bear hug?" says Erigan. He pats his own chest, still feeling some of the shock and fear.

"I had to hide you and keep you quiet," says Behemoth. "Nothing will ever keep you quiet, except these." Behemoth strikes a pose, hoisting his arms up into the air and then flexing them. The mountains that he calls biceps bounce playfully as Behemoth grins.

"Put those away," says Erigan.

Behemoth laughs, his voice roars through the streets.

The demons up ahead, poor lost souls condemned to search the streets of Dis looking for a drink of water, they hold onto the buildings and cry out "Earthquake."

Behemoth smirks.

"You like doing that, don't you?" Erigan comes down the center of a dark alleyway and continues to the dark end. Up above, something glimmers in the ephemeral glow.

"What are you doing?"

"Roofs, my friend," says Erigan. He stretches as tall as he can go but can't reach anything. "Help?"

Behemoth reaches up above and with the flick of his finger, drops the metal ladder down to Erigan's reach.

"Thank you. With the soldiers wandering all over the place—and because I like to breathe—I need to take the high road."

Erigan puts his first foot up on the ladder and hoists himself upwards. "You can come if you'd like to. Either way, we need to get to the Gate soon."

"Isn't it easier to take the main road?" asks Behemoth.

"Soldiers, remember, dummy?" Erigan continues up the steps, all twenty three steps and then comes to the top of the roof. He peers upwards and is greeted with the sudden *whoosh* and an explosion of dust.

Behemoth bends over in front of him and grabs Erigan by the shoulders. With his giant hands, he pulls him up.

"You're welcome," says Behemoth.

"What strong legs you have," says Erigan.

"All the better to—" he pauses. "How does it go?"

Erigan shakes his head. Memory like a fly, that Behemoth.

They survey the roofs.

Erigan spots the glint of the dark blood-red metal gate to the far west. He takes a quick running start and leaps over the first roof.

"I can carry you, you know."

Erigan measures up the distances between the roofs. "You could, couldn't you?"

Behemoth nods. "Come here," he groans. He hauls Erigan on his shoulders without much effort.

The jumps between buildings appear effortless to Behemoth. Each jump covers nearly three-quarters of each building. The red Gate at the edge of Hell.

The Gate itself stands tall. It's connected by design to a mountainous cavern that blocks the view as far up as the eyes can see. A genuine eternal wall of stone and mourning.

If Erigan squints hard enough, he can see the bones of scoundrels past. Those rabble-rousers who were too difficult for even Lucifer to deal with.

He hopes that his father, Zeus, isn't somewhere up there.

With each jump, it gets closer and closer until finally, the two are at the edges of Dis just beyond the walls.

In between the Gate and the pair stands a stone table. The officer in charge of allowing passages to and from the realm of Hell.

Part of Hell's eternal commitment to all things bureaucracy.

Erigan doesn't bother looking for his badge. He knows that it wouldn't matter otherwise.

His job mandates that he leaves Hell, but his boss's bosses want him for interrogation. The little demon smiles. This is the life.

Erigan measures the distance between the desk and the Gate.

"Think you can make it?" says Behemoth.

"Of course I can make it. As long as I have these babies."

The wings on Erigan's ankles flitter and kick up enough dust to make Behemoth's breath visible in front of him.

"Ready?" Erigan says. He nudges toward the ground below him.

Chapter Eleven

Behemoth adjusts his lion's head helmet, pushing off to the back to better his view. The ephemeral glow of daylight gives the rocky walls in front of them a reddish glow, like the clay he used to play with when he was only a demigod babe.

Erigan's feet feel cold against the white stone of the leaning building he's perched upon. But his blood pumps, ready for the inevitable struggle that's about to come.

Behemoth's breathing sounds calm, patient. A born warrior, Erigan couldn't have picked a better companion in life.

Everything Erigan lacks, Behemoth has in spades. Brawn. Size. Looks.

Okay, scratch that. The ladies—and men—have often chased after Erigan.

And if anything, Erigan loves to give chase.

Peering downwards, Erigan nods and grins at Behemoth.

The beastly demon quickly tosses his head back and forth, cracking every vertebrae in his neck. "Whatever you did, Erigan, you pissed someone off bad."

"I was just following orders," he says. Then he leaps off the building. He lands softly thanks to his winged sandals between two soldiers, each facing toward the gate.

The soldiers don't move.

Behemoth does not have to wait for orders. He leaps downwards and lands with a thud.

Both soldiers land on their asses.

And Erigan takes this as his cue.

This commotion is enough to get the attention of the angel sentinels that sit amongst the walls of Dis. They begin a quick descent toward Behemoth, brandishing their sword and spear directly at the pair.

Behemoth grabs their black feathered wings and crunches them in his hands. "Run!" he yells.

And Erigan follows orders. Going at his sandals' top speed, Erigan crisscrosses through his foes toward the gate.

An alarm—much like the sounding of a horn—blares through the thick, humid air.

"Stop!" commands the scrawny and four-eyed bureaucrat who monitors the Gate at his stone desk. "You must first show me your pass."

Erigan shrugs as he flies toward the unsuspecting and skinny demon.

Such a small target, Erigan figures he should be able to dodge him and escape through the gate with little trouble.

"Erigan!" shouts the bureaucrat. "You don't have proper clearance!" The bureaucrat holds up a metal clipboard with a raft of papers attached in different colors. "You have to fill out form 1034B dash 89A."

"Don't have time, Aragiel, sorry," says Erigan, already passing by the stone table.

"This will not do!" The bureaucrat shuts the gate and blocks the lock with his body. "You'll have to get through me."

Erigan, a smaller demon than most, flexes what he laughingly calls his muscles. "Get out of the way or I move you myself."

Aragiel gets out of the way, his legs shaking in his black pleated pants and dusty black jacket. He lets out a wimper and then scrambles to behind the desk, his hands covering his head.

Erigan says, "I thought so." He tries to crack his neck the way Behemoth does but fails miserably.

While making these epilepsy-like movements, he turns around to see off in the distance his friend going hog wild in battle.

Behemoth grabs the two angels again as they attempt to fly away. He crunches their heads together and tosses their limp bodies to the side of the walls.

"Good luck, old friend." He tips his imaginary hat and turns around to grab the lock of the gate.

But oddly enough, he finds it barely cracked. As if it was opened for him.

"This is almost too easy," says Erigan. He rests his hand on the gate. It feels cold to his touch, even welcoming.

The thunder of flapping wings and stomping boots echoes in the alleyways behind him.

"Damn damn damn," says Erigan. He opens the gate just a bit and looks for his friend Behemoth.

Limp bodies of dark-winged angels and feathered harpies fly into the air and splatter along the ground at his friend's feet.

"Thanks again, buddy!" screams Erigan. He waits only a short second for a reply but gets none.

His friend is too busy—too entertained—by his current predicament.

A voice nearly makes Erigan jump out of his padded sandals. "Arrogant whelp. I knew you'd be in trouble."

"Mam'mon." Erigan smiles. "How are the wife and kids?" He nudges the door open with his fingertips behind his back in hopes that Mam'mon is none the wiser.

"Cut the bullshit," says Mam'mon. "You owe me something." Mam'mon's snout lets out a huff of smoke and one of his cloven hoofed feet stomps impatiently.

"Listen, I'd really love to chat, but I'm busy. Gotta wash my hair. I'll catch ya later, though, okay?" Erigan thrusts the door open and leaps into the gateway.

Mam'mon stands there, arms crossed. His shoulders look massive, his minotaur-like body so firm it could have been carved out of stone.

Erigan waves back at Mam'mon without turning his head backwards.

"You can stop the fight now," says Mam'mon.

Erigan listens to the words echo down the dark, rocky hallway. Erigan rests one foot into white hole that leads to earth when he hears Mam'mon's echo say, "We've got him."

Chapter Twelve

The trip is never an easy one, traveling from Hell back to Earth. Erigan always felt it something like getting shot into the air without one of those "airplanes".

Not unlike him flying with his winged sandals.

He emerges in a darkened closet. This is supposedly where he needs to be. But in the haste, who even knew what the Hell happened.

Erigan moves the soft clothes that fluttered along in his face. He pushes them slowly and carefully down the wooden pole that presses along the top of his head. Waking anyone would be the last thing he needed to do.

Erigan's fingers traces the edges of the doorway to look for the handle.

An electric light flashes on in a blink.

Erigan freezes, holding his breath. He turns his head slightly to get a better view through the cracks along the edges of the door.

"Good night, Mommy," says a little voice.

A young voice. Is he here already here for the boy?

Erigan's heart beats with anticipation. He looks forward to getting back into the swing of things at Hell. Turn in the kid, write up his report and get the Hell back into more trouble.

"Good night to you, too, dear."

The bedroom's light flickers off. Sheets rustle. The boy is finally back in his bed.

"Here we go," he whispers to himself.

The sheets rustle again.

"Who's there?"

The light flash on and Erigan finds himself frozen yet again.

"Just go to bed, boy," he mutters.

"Me?" says the boy.

Erigan smiles and cracks the door open.

Rule number one of haunting: let the kids to the dirty work. Doing too much of the work yourself only makes you look friendly.

Fuck Casper. Fuck friendly ghosts.

"Who is that?" says the voice again.

Erigan listens to the soft fleshy tapping of his footsteps—small and gentle footsteps—toward the closet door.

For special affect, Erigan fades into the shadows, only allowing his own yellowish eyes to peer into the doorway.

The handle rustles from the outside.

Erigan waits, bated breath. The sooner he can capture this damned kid and move on the better.

"What are you doing up out of bed?" The bedroom door flings open and slams against the wall.

The child's mother comes into the room. Her voice growls as if she's angry, but not pissed.

Not yet.

"I told you to get to bed, sweetheart." The bedsprings squeak from the weight of the woman's ass.

"But, Mom, I was hearding something," the child says.

Erigan rolls his eyes. This shit is already getting old.

A typical snatch and grab turning into a ceaseless stop-and-go endeavor.

And being stuck in a closet. Embarrassing.

As potential senior management, he shouldn't have had to slum it in dark closets. Not for kids.

Erigan listens to the smacking sound of a wet kiss on the child's head. He pauses, rests his hand on the door once more.

The bedroom door shuts tight an the light flicks off.

Game time.

Erigan creaks the door open slowly at first. His eyes are already adjusted for the darkness, but his ears were elsewhere, listening for human footsteps outside the room.

"Hello there, boy," says Erigan.

He peers around the bedroom door and damn near

swears in front of the child.

There on the bed sits the child.

And not a boy, but a girl. Sitting up. Staring at Erigan.

"Who are you?" she says.

"Aren't you supposed to be in bed?" he says.

"Why are you in my closet?"

The bedroom glows with the soft pink of the painted walls. A little pony nightlight illuminates the room's southern half. The blinky, fuzzy light clearly needs to be replaced sometime soon.

Along the bed sits an attentive little girl along with twenty or thirty of her favoritest stuffed animals.

"Go to bed," Erigan says.

"But you're in my closet," she says. Suddenly her eyes widen. A smile overcomes the lower half of her face. "Are you Santa?"

Erigan grins. "Yes, honey. Yes, I am."

He snaps his fingers and steps out of the shadows of the closet. He feels his stomach feel heavy, shifting its shape and size, and jiggle as he walks to the edge of the bed.

"Where's your beard?" asks the girl.

Erigan snaps his fingers again and grow an instant beard. "Better?" he asks.

The girl nods in silence. Her mouth falls open. "Wow."

"Why, thank you," he says. He polishes his fingernails against his red Santa coat. "I am pretty good."

"Well duh," the girl says. "You're Santa."

Erigan keeps his eyes on the crevice between the bedroom door and floor.

The girl gasps. "Are you watching me while I'm sleeping?" she says.

Erigan shakes his head, the thought absolutely disgusting to this demon's mind. "You're not Brad, are you?" He pulls out a manila folder and flips it open. He fingers through the file. "Um, Brad Herner?"

"Who's that?" says the girl. "My name is Noelle."

"Fuck."

"You shouldn't swear," she says. She sits back on her bed and the smile just won't leave her face. "You're scarier than I remember."

"I get that a lot," he says. "Do you mind if I use the front door?" Erigan points at the girl's bedroom door and begins to walk toward it.

"But I thought you used chimneys."

"Do you have a chimney?" he asks.

The girl sits for a moment looking confused. She forces her tiny white feet into the sheets of her bed. "No."

"Well then. How can I travel up one if you don't have it?" It was never a problem for Erigan to feel smug about outsmarting anyone. Even if it was a tiny five-year-old girl.

The girl shrugs. "Am I a good girl?" she asks.

Erigan nudges the door open and pauses. "Sure. Why not? Maybe I'll get you a pony."

The girl's eyes beam and Erigan leaves the bedroom, fading into a shade when he gets into the house's hallway.

In this form he flutters by the edges of the mother's vision as a glimmer, a shade.

He slides across the wooden paneled floors smooth as black silk. His form takes the corners and edges with the silent flow of water running along the walls.

Soon, he's just underneath the front door and standing outside.

Chapter Thirteen

The only thing that illuminates the dark earth sky is the sparse twinkling of stars.

The streetlights block out most of what you could see in the open darkness of the nighttime sky.

Most human eyes, anyway.

To his trained godling eyes, Erigan pinpoints the exactly location of planets. He watches the bright orange glow of Saturn and Jupiter and sighs.

If Zeus were only here.

Three thousand years ago he would never have had to hide his form. He was a proud godling. Fast. Quick-witted.

Now he is forced to hide amongst the shadows and skulk about like the beasts of Tartaros. Stupid angels and Gods with their rules.

Shameful.

For fun, Erigan shifts his form into a solid human. A short, slender youth with curly hair. It was Erigan's favorite form back in Greece. Back in the days that he was allowed to travel freely between realms.

Back when the old realms still existed.

"Oh my God!" A voice catches Erigan's ears and makes him turn his head across the street.

A group of teenagers walking along down the street.

"Dude, you're naked!" shouts the tallest boy.

"Trust me," says Erigan. "God has nothing to do with this fine specimen." Erigan flexes his muscles and poses. He stares off into the distance and allows the stars and moonlight to glimmer off of his smooth and pale skin.

"Fucking fag!" shouts another one of the boys. "Get some clothes you freak!"

"Fine," says Erigan. He snaps his fingers and feels the magical warmth of threads hug his torso. "Better?"

The kids stand frozen, staring at Erigan.

"Dude, is this some kind of movie or some shit?"

Erigan smirks. Humans. Never did want to believe.

He snaps his fingers and feels the weight of his horn grow from his forehead.

He growls and takes only two steps toward the teenagers.

They screech in chaotic fear, stumbling to beat each other to the end of the street.

Erigan smiles and pulls out the file. His forehead feels lighter as the horn gradually disappears.

"Now where were we?"

He flips through the file.

"Brad Herner," he says to memorize the name. "Got it."

Erigan continues down the street toward the glowing streetlamps of downtown Saraday, South Carolina.

Tall wide-leafed trees mix with needle-leaf evergreens along the sides of the road. Along most blank spots of the town, where buildings and roads don't take up space, is almost always a tree.

Erigan takes quick steps down the street's incidental decline. The weight of gravity pulls Erigan down the road almost as if by magic. His feet feel heavy, slapping along the road just to keep himself from falling down.

This human body, it's going to take some time to get used to it again.

With any hope, he won't have to stay in it for long.

Erigan takes in the thick pine and herbal smell of the trees that wafts into his nose. In Hell most everything is thick and reeks like mold.

Depending on where you are, the lower levels of Hell have a thin cold air, like icicles cutting into his nostrils.

The key in Hell is pain. Everything must bring pain. Physical or otherwise.

Remembering the pain of breathing in Hell, Erigan stops along the wide windows of a street side shop. He takes a look at himself and smirks. His own face reminds him of a youth or two he may have chased down in Greece a few thousand years ago.

His name has slipped Erigan's fading memories,

but he remembers the days of running amongst the tall grasses of the low rolling hills. The nights cuddled up amongst the mountains and flocks of sheep. The warmth of having a body near him. The smell of light sweat mixing with the local flowers.

Erigan feels something swell up inside his pants and he adjusts slightly with a tuck and pull up under his belt.

Did human bodies always get this out of control so easily?

Erigan wanders further down the streets, passing by the fading street signs and darkened abandoned buildings of the dying city. Each of the buildings looks built from wood, probably only a few hundred years old.

Young by immortals' standards.

But now the entire town feels the sudden throes of poverty.

Erigan looks over his shoulders and realizes that nearly half the street, the main street at that, is vacated and abandoned.

Even towns cannot escape the cruel reaches of death.

Erigan turns his thoughts to finding the boy. It's nighttime so he puts to rest the idea that he's going to find the boy wandering the streets.

If he's anything like normal humans, his parents have already put him to sleep.

He'll have to track him down and find him tomorrow. Maybe at school.

But first, human food.

Chapter Fourteen

Erigan follows a young couple into the only restaurant he can find open this late at night.

The door opens with a bell chime, jerry-rigged with a real piece of string that connects the door to a bell on the wall. A simple human device.

Erigan walks into the restaurant and is immediately greeted with the smells of salty pork and beef. The walls are lined with dark wooden paneling. The people walk upon a carpet that looks maybe it was made when Hannibal crossed the Atlas Mountains.

Though the smell enticed him, the simple thought of eating such filthy animals struck him as atrocious.

Why would anyone want to eat anything that bathed in its own shit and urine? Or anything that moved that slow?

In Greece, the growing of cows for eating was of little

importance. They had little room to grow large cattle. This simply meant the Greeks had to tend to smaller livestock, namely sheep.

Erigan felt his human stomach grumble.

Now sheep. That was the freshest of meats. Lightly seasoned with mint and garlic and sage. Simply amazing.

Erigan searches the small number of customers that sit in the booths. Not a single plate seems to be populated with the likes of lamb meat of any kind.

Still, Erigan does not let this get him down.

"Hi," says the waitress. Her golden blonde hair is cut short like a man's. Erigan eyes her face as she talks. Her lips move like a woman's. Red lips. Blushing cheeks.

But that hair. If she had grown it out, she would make for a beautiful mistress.

"What can I get for you?"

Erigan stares into the distance, surveying the crowd.

"Hello?" she says again. "Sir?"

"What do you want?"

The waitress takes a step back, her mouth open.

Erigan says, "I'm sorry. What can I do for you?"

The waitress's mouth remains open, confused. Her eyebrows go up, then down, then back up. "I was, um," she says.

"I'm looking for someone," says Erigan. "Maybe you can help me find him. It's a little boy. By the name of Brad Herner?"

The waitress looks up as if looking into her own memories. "I don't think so," she says. She tries to gain control back over the conversation. "Did you need a table then or...?"

"Or what?" asks Erigan. He takes a long time to finish the word "what", taking after the waitress's pronunciation of "or."

"Or did you just want to take something to go?"

"Take what?"

The waitress points to the glass counter that rests the cash register. Inside the glass sit pies of different colors and flavors. The one that catches Erigan's eye the most is a bright green pie. Almost radioactive in its coloring.

"What is this?" he asks.

"Key lime," she says. "Can I get you a slice?"

Erigan smiles. "Of course, that would be very nice of you."

The woman gives an awkward smile and then disappears down the aisle and into the kitchen across the building.

Erigan looks around at the paintings that hang from the walls. Tall green vases against a blue and green backdrop. Inside the vases, yellow flowers, ones that look unfamiliar to Erigan's untrained eyes. They never had flowers like that in Greece. And certainly not in Hell.

The waitress appears behind the counter again with a white box. "Just one slice?" she says and rests the pie on the counter.

"Not unless you'd let me take the whole thing,"

Erigan jokes.

The woman looks as if she's considering it for only a split second. Then she begins to giggle.

"Oh my, you are a funny one."

Erigan nods once and leans in on the counter. From this distance, his nose catches a whiff of the sweetly sour smell of limes and sugar from the pie.

The sides of his mouth tingle and fill with saliva. "That smells really, really good."

"It should," says the mannish-looking woman in a thick southern accent. "We made it just this morning."

And the pie is boxed with Erigan's hands on them , ready to take it out, when the woman rests her own hands on the box.

"That'll be five dollars and twenty-seven cents, sir."

Erigan looks down at the pie. "For this?"

The waitress nods.

"Can't I just pay you later?" Erigan grabs the pie and holds it up under his armpit. "I mean, I'm good for it."

"I'm sure you are, hun, but you see, I can't let you walk out of here with that. I'd get fired for sure!" The woman smiles like she wants to rip Erigan's head off.

"Listen you disrespectful bag of flesh," says Erigan. "I will shred you to pieces and feed you to the hounds of Hell if you do not let me have this pie. Why, pray tell, why the fuck would you offer me the damned pies and then make me pay for them? What kind of hospitality is that?"

"This is a restaurant, sir," says the woman after she

manages to shut her gaping mouth. "We sell food."

"Well Demeter herself could teach you a few things about manners. Hell, even Hera could teach you a few things about how to be a woman."

The woman's eyes remain unmoved.

"You know, goddess of women? Juno?"

The waitress's eyes light up. "Oh! I love that movie, with the pregnant girl?"

Erigan rolls his eyes. "Movie? What?" He runs his left hand through his hair—what soft and silky hair!—and then snaps his fingers. "I don't have time for this shit," he says.

When the snap completes its echoes through the restaurant, the woman disappears. All that remains is a pile of her clothes.

Erigan leans over the counter and watches as a spider comes crawling out of the white blouse's neck hole.

"Next time, treat your betters with more respect," says Erigan. He tucks the pie up under his arm again and leaves the building.

He knows the main rule of being back on Earth is to never make a scene.

But not knowing who Hera is? That's just unacceptable.

Since Lucifer and God came into town and took over the earthen realm, things just haven't been the same.

Erigan's leather sandals sprout wings and flap furiously to lift him up into the air. He lands on the roof of the Little Teapot Café.

He sticks a key lime pie-covered fingertip into his mouth and relishes in the sweet, somewhat bitter goodness.

"Where were you two thousand years ago?" he says to the pie and then shoves the rest of it into his mouth.

When he looks down and checks out the streets, he considers for a second that he might not know the way around town. Maybe he's in over his head.

If he had only fucked Lilith, he would have the whole damned file instead of being completely powerless.

Why must the most evil women be the most beautiful?

Erigan considers for a second that the term "evil woman" is a bit redundant when his thoughts are silenced by the ringing of the bell down below.

A man and woman come walking out of the building. They hold hands and walk slowly side by side.

"Are you sure it's okay to just leave the money there?" says the woman.

"I don't see why not," says the man. He holds the woman closer to him in a hug. "I didn't see anyone else who could help."

There's a bit of silence and then they stop walking.

"Are you sure you don't want to come on over?" says the man.

Erigan watches along the rooftops. The rest of the buildings appear loosely scattered across the town. Its roots lay mostly rural but at some time must have tried to entertain the idea of an urban sprawl.

It didn't get very far from what Erigan could see. From end to end, it had to be only a few miles wide and about three times as long.

If he counted the entirety of the settled areas, this area would be just under the size of the early settlements of Rome.

"I'm sorry, Carl," says the woman. "I have to get back to my son."

The man named Carl leans over and kisses the woman on the lips and then steps away. "Very well, then. You tell Brad I said hi, will you?"

Erigan's ears perk up. "Well fucking jackpot."

Chapter Fifteen

Erigan follows quickly and quietly behind the woman as she walks down the somewhat vacated streets of Saraday. The trees cast long, thin shadows across the grass and sidewalks.

As Erigan dances in shade form from shadow to shadow, the trees begin to look like crooked fingers grasping for the human woman.

The skies above were clear and black, almost blue-black. Definitely one of the things that Erigan loved the most about being on the surface of earth. The nighttimes and beauty of the skies.

Clouds illuminate and cast wispy shadows on the ground when they pass by the moon's nearly full face.

Erigan nods his head toward the moon's face. Come to think of it, it had been forever, it seemed, since heh ad seen his half-sister Artemis.

The woman's trip back home is short, leading Erigan to the front of a large brown building.

Apartments, the humans call these buildings.

The long, thin panels that line the building's outside walls don't look like natural wood to Erigan's eyes. Certainly textured to look like wood. Maybe plastic?

The woman takes keys out of her purse and opens the door.

The black screen door opens up and Erigan sees his chance to gain entrance without any worries.

Keep the woman in his sights while checking out the scene.

The woman enters the hallway and is met with bright fluorescent illumination.

Erigan, seeking a safe place to hide, glides along the wall as a shadow.

The woman pauses for a moment, pushes back a lock of her yellow blond hair and peers at the wall.

She doesn't make any movements, no questions. Just caution.

For fun, Erigan keeps his shadow up against the wall for only a split second.

When the woman blinks, he's gone across the hallway and hiding amongst the shadows of the doorframe.

The woman holds her breath. She walks, cautious, across the doorway and enters the stairwell.

Three flights of stairs later, and she unlocks the door to her apartment.

Erigan watches, slithering along the sides of the wall

just behind the woman's field of view.

Again, seeing his chance to sneak in, he slithers into the apartment before the woman can close the door.

An electric light illuminates the apartment. The light brown paint on the walls make the rooms look smaller and darker than they really are. Various pictures of the woman and a little child hang on the walls, some tilted and ready to fall off.

Almost too dark for Erigan, who begins to feel like it's his old cubicle in Hell. Shadows take over nearby hallway as a trace of light glimmers below a white wooden door.

"Brad," the woman says, "I thought you'd be in bed by now."

She rests her head against the door and waits to hear the click of the lamp.

Instead, the door clicks open.

Erigan, keeping his shadowy existence a bit longer, hides along the shadows of the hallway.

The bedroom door cracks open and Erigan's eyes meet his target assignment for the first time.

Brad looks like a boy of only eight years old, bright blond hair like his mother. His hair sits rather carelessly on his head. Pieces stick up on the back.

"I was waiting for you, mom," says the boy.

"Bradley, you should be in bed," says the woman. She looks around. "Where's the babysitter?"

"Monica said she had to leave," says Brad. He wipes something form his eye with the back of his hand.

Erigan smiles amongst the shadows. There is something about the boy that reminds him of someone else. Who is it?

The mother lets out a sigh and covers her son's ears. "Shit," she mutters and then pulls her hands away from her son. "You didn't hear mommy say that."

"Say what?" says the boy. He smirks.

The mother pats Brad on the head with a smile. "Good boy." She turns him around. "Now get to bed, it's late."

"But I want to sleep with you."

"Not tonight, buddy."

The mother ushers the boy into his bedroom and leaves the door cracked.

The woman takes her shoes off without bending over, heeling them off with her toes. She kicks the shoes near the shadowy form of Erigan and then flops down onto the worn leathery couch.

She sighs and looks across the room at the blank flat screen television set. Erigan, firmly nested in the walls—blank with the exception of one narrow bookcase—stares back at her. Her eyes draw his focus. The bright green flecks scattered about her irises seem to glow especially well in the electric yellowing light.

The woman turns her head to the sideboard. A wine glass with pink lipstick still smudged along the ridge. The woman closes her eyes and shakes her head.

"You better not have drank it all, bitch," she mutters to herself.

Erigan's shadowy form takes a human shape and he steps out of the wall. For a second he allows himself to appear wispy and faded through the lamplight.

The woman stops with her hand on the wine bottle. Monica did not, apparently, drink it all.

"Brad?" she says. "Are you still awake?"

Erigan answers the woman with a light kick to the sideboard. He always loved this part of his job.

The woman rests the wine bottle back on the counter and steps out of the kitchen. She stops at the doorway, peering down the hallway where Brad's bedroom lies. "Brad?"

The door remains slightly closed. No lights.

"Bathroom, maybe?" she says.

She returns to the bottle and pours herself a glass. The red liquid smells fruity but bitter to Erigan's nose.

He wonders if Dio had ever tasted this new stuff. He reads the label but forgets the name as soon as his eyes shift to watch the woman rest her ass back on the couch.

Erigan watches for a moment. Though pretty, he felt bored watching this woman do absolutely nothing.

So he wanders into the hallway and creeps into the bedroom. The blue light of the moon outside filters in through the horizontal blinds. Erigan looks upon the sleeping child with both contempt and a strange feeling.

Is it pity? Affection?

Erigan takes a place for himself at the foot of the bed. There he sits, cross-legged and staring the boy. He holds his head in his hands and smiles.

"All this trouble just for you, huh? Who are you?"

Erigan's crawls along the bed, holding himself up just over the boy's face.

With a clawed hand, he gently traces the side of the boy's cheek. "Wakey wakey," he says.

The boy stretches out and then pries his eyes open.

His bright blue eyes meet with Erigan's and Bradley begins to scream.

In response, Erigan decides to scream as well. If there's anything he loves, it's chaos.

The lamp at the boy's nightstand clicks on. "What's the matter, Bradley?"

Brad sits up on his bed. His eyes keep focused on Erigan, who sits at the end of the bed, invisible and taunting.

He knows what the boy sees that the woman does not. Bright yellow eyes. Toothy smiles. Dark red skin. A face with sharpened, burned features.

"Don't scream now, Bradley, we've just begun," he whispers.

Brad covers his ears and eyes.

"Honey, what's the matter?" says the mother. She sits on the bed next to Brad and takes him into her arms. She pats his hair down on the back of his head and whispers.

"A monster," says Brad.

The woman smiles shushes her son. "It's okay, dear. I promise. Nothing to worry about."

"That's right, Bradley," says Erigan. "Nothing to worry about."

Chapter Sixteen

Being the good demon that he is, Erigan followed his prey to its elementary school. The building is one of the largest red brick buildings not attached to anything else in the town. People and children scatter across the play yards outside, screaming, tagging, and yelling at each other.

Erigan crawls into the classroom and sits in a small desk that forces his own knees to hug his pointed ears.

A bell screeches overhead and the classroom floods with the energies of twenty-five little ones, each one screaming and yelling. Again.

Erigan grits his teeth. He had only come inside to get away from the such screaming.

He looks around the room to remember faces of the screamers. He will look forward to making these little shits crap their pants some night in the near future.

But for now, he watches as Bradley takes his seat up near the front of the class. He looks to be a good student, resting a pad of paper and some yellow pencils along the side of his desk. He crosses his hands across his chest and waits for the thick-waisted teacher to adjust her glasses and stand before the class.

"So how was your weekend?" she asks.

The class looks around at each other, then the words "good" come trickling out of their frightened little mouths.

"That's great, class," the teacher says. "So who remembered their homework?"

"For fuck's sakes," says Erigan. Still in shadows and invisible to the students, no one reacts except for one student in the front row—Bradley.

He turns around and his eyes open wide. "Um," he begins to say before Erigan rests a pointed finger to his lips.

"Shh," he whispers.

"Miss," says Bradley. He raises his hand. His eyes are wide open, sweat nearly trickling down his forehead. "Miss," he repeats again.

"What is it Bradley, did you remember your homework?"

"I have to go to the bathroom."

Erigan grins. He says nothing but thinks the boy is dumber than he looks. Separating himself from the herd is one of the worst, most suicidal things he could do right now.

"Very well," she says. "Take the pass and be quick, okay?"

Bradley nods and stands up. He tries not to lock eyes with Erigan, who enjoys this game of cat and mouse.

Erigan taps his fingers together, watching the boy take the blue sign that hangs on a short red string. Bradley hugs the pass close to his chest and opens the door, disappearing behind the wall.

Erigan counts to three before standing up and trotting off behind the doorway. He searches left, then right and listens for the pitter-patter of little frightened feet.

Listening, he catches the squeaking sounds of a door and then the muffled echoes of feet to his left.

"Finally, you little shit." His ankle wings take flight and carry him to the bathroom. There, he listens to a stall door slam shut.

The boy has cornered himself into a locked room. This is almost too easy.

He walks into the boys' bathroom. The blue lights give the medical green tiles an almost irradiated glow. He hears the humming of the lights above along with the frightened tapping of shoed toes along the tiled floor.

The electric humming, however, is hard for the demon to tune out. In Hell everything runs on light and magic. This arrogance of man, harnessing the powers of Zeus for their own gain, both fascinates and disgusts Erigan at the same time.

And the smell. Do these boys not know how to flush?

The stale waters of the River Styx can barely compete with this stench.

"Bradley," Erigan whispers.

The room grows silent, the tapping ceases.

"I know you're in here."

The boy doesn't answer but rather shifts his balance on the toilet seat.

"Still haven't figured out that I can find you, have you, boy?"

"Leave me alone," Brad shouts. His voice wavers. Nerves, Erigan figures. Good. He likes them nervous.

"Just come on out," says Erigan. "I promise I won't hurt you."

"You're going to eat me?" Brad starts to whimper, almost crying into tears.

"No, of course not. You're not worth any nutritional value."

The boy's whimpering stops. He asks, "Huh?"

Erigan shakes his head. "Never you mind. Tough crowd," he says.

Erigan falls to his hands and knees and crawls toward the last of the three stalls. No shoes or feet visible from down below.

The boy is standing on the toilet seat now. Smart, but not enough to save him.

"Please don't make me work this hard," he says. "I just need to nab you and head back."

"I don't wanna go."

"You're assuming you have a choice," Erigan shouts.

Using his winged ankles, he hovers over the floors and slams open the first stall.

No one there.

His wings carry him to the next stall.

"Just come out, will you?"

When Erigan rests his hands on the next stall, he hears the shuffling of feet in the stall next to him.

He smiles, and moves to his left. With his right hand, he presses the right stall open just slightly to keep the boy's attention.

The boy's whimpers begin to get louder, almost as if he's crying.

Erigan grabs the handle of the stall door and stays his hand. He grins first, then allows his body to take on a twisted, deer-like shape. His one horn grows from the top of his head and his body feels heavier, denser.

His voice turns high-pitched and goat-like as he says, "Heeere I come."

He slams open the door. The boy screams and jumps in terror. When he lands back on the seat, he slips and falls along the space between of the wall and the toilet.

Bradley's feet stick up into the air. His hands cover his face.

Erigan snatches the boy's shoes and drags him out of the stall. The boy screams, high-pitched like a woman. Erigan would have expected someone to have come in and rescue him by now.

But to his surprise and pleasure, no one comes in.

"Okay, boy, here we go."

Erigan tugs on the boy's shoes to fling him closer to his body. Still hovering in the air, he snatches the boy's legs and hauls him over his head.

"Okay, buddy, off we go."

Erigan's wings begin to flutter hard. The boy stops wailing, his attention caught by the fluttering wings on his captor's ankles.

"Cool," he says.

Erigan's wings flutter harder and he looks up. "Any time now," Erigan says.

But nothing happens.

"Where are we going?" says Bradley.

"Shut up and let me concentrate," Erigan growls.

He looks upwards at the ceiling and commands his feet to fly up. With any luck, he'll just need a running— uh, flying—start.

But as his feet begin to lift him higher, he notices that the tiles come closer and closer.

"Damn it, Aragiel, you had one job to do!"

The boy begins to kick and scream. The back of the boy's shoe kicks the one horn that Erigan has left on his head.

"Knock it off brat or I'll eat you."

"You just said you wouldn't eat a human."

Erigan growls and the immediately the boy's kicking stops.

He closes his eyes and concentrates on going home. The darkness. The stale air. The smell of piss and farts.

Home sweet home.

But his wings, they take him nowhere.

"Damn it to Hell," he says.

The boy's body begins to go limp.

Voices come from the other side of the door. "What's going on in here?" It's a woman. An elderly woman.

"Great," Erigan mutters to himself.

Chapter Seventeen

Erigan grabs the boy's torso and twists him around so he can speak to him face to face. "Listen, kid, it doesn't look like we can go anywhere just yet."

Brad's soft red cheeks look patchy, irritated from the crying and tears.

"You got that?" says Erigan.

Seemingly confused, the boy nods his head and Erigan puts him down.

"Do me a solid and do not tell anyone I was here."

Bradley scowls at Erigan and looks upward, thinking. Making a decision.

"Please?" says Erigan. "I cannot have another screw up here."

The boy still hesitates.

"I'll be your best friend?"

Erigan begins to barely make out a smile in Bradley's

lips.

"Okay," says Bradley.

Erigan drops the little boy to the ground and pats him on the head. "Good lad," he says.

Bradley smiles and the door opens.

A rather skinny woman pops her head into the bathroom. Her white hair is striped with black strands that stretch from her temples to the tight bun in the back. Seeing that no one else is in there, she takes a step into the bathroom.

"Are you decent?" says the woman.

Bradley puts his hands behind his back and smiles. "Yes, Mrs. Jacobs," he says in a sing-songy tone.

"Who are you talking to?" she asks.

Bradley looks behind him and points. "To my new friend." Bradley smiles.

Erigan cracks his knuckles. The brat said he wouldn't tell anyone.

The woman looks straight through Erigan's ethereal body to the wall behind him. Mrs. Jacobs nods. "And who would that be?" she says with a smile.

"His name is, um," Bradley stops and turns around. "What is your name?"

Mrs. Jacobs turns her head to Bradley's field of view. "Who are you looking at, dear?"

"My name is Erigan," the demon mutters. "Now can we get on with it, please?"

"His name is Erigan," announces Bradley. "And he says we should leave."

"Is that what he says now?" Mrs. Jacobs nods and takes Bradley by the hands. "It looks like you got a little scraped up."

"I fell off the toilet."

Mrs. Jacobs chuckles but tries to hide it from Bradley. "We'll just have to take you to see the nurse and get you taken care of."

Bradley and Mrs. Jacobs leave the bathroom.

Erigan looks at the ceiling, then the floor. "Okay, you bastard, why aren't you letting me go home?"

Chapter Eighteen

Erigan sits outside another red bricked building, this one just smaller than the schoolhouse he had left only moments ago. A local wooden sign, strong and probably as old as the town, identifies it as the Saraday Local Library.

The library itself sits atop one of the few hills this town seems to have. From this height he can see down the steep and sloping main road, out to the wide river that most likely leads out to the Atlantic Ocean.

If it weren't for the sudden feeling like his afterlife is going to Hell in a hand basket, Erigan would probably feel like he was right at home.

This time he sits in his plain human form, casually dressed. The key here is to be as obvious as possible.

For this disguise he chooses plain blue jeans, white button down shirt. He thinks it will allow him to at least pretend to blend in the natives, should he have to stay any longer than he'd like.

For only the second time today he's already felt fear. Fear of not going home. Fear of being cut off. Fear of relying on the assholes in Hell he only occasionally calls his "friends".

"C'mon, Behemoth, where are you?"

"Right here."

Erigan turns to his left to follow the source of the voice. "Where?"

"Up here," the deep, burly voice says.

Erigan peers upwards into the tree just three feet from where he sat. Sure enough, Behemoth lies in the tree, wrapped around a tree branch. Somehow he's managed to defy gravity. His strong thighs hug the branch, giving Erigan a slight view of his bare ass.

"Again with the lion's skin? And how does someone as big as you get in a tree that small?"

Behemoth snarls at Erigan. "Sorry, not everyone can be as skinny as you are." He adjusts the lion's cowl. "And women like the lion's head."

Erigan looks at his frame and stands up. "I am not that skinny."

Behemoth jumps down from the tree and crosses his arms across his massive chest. "You're as thin as that twig you stole from the Seventh Circle."

"Why can't I go home?" Erigan stares Behemoth directly in the eyes. He knows he can't compete with size, so he tries with attitude. "What happened back there?"

"Boss man doesn't want you back." Behemoth's matter-of-fact tone makes Erigan take a second to reconsider his words.

"Does not want me back?"

Behemoth grabs Erigan's head and pulls him closer to his face. With one eye closed, he peeks into Erigan's ears. "Have you been up here too long?" he says. "Human wax buildup?"

Erigan frees himself and stands arm's length away from the strong brute. "What is going on? Where is Aragiel?"

"Aragiel has been pulled from his station."

"Pulled?"

Behemoth winces. "Thrown into the ninth circle? Kinda. More like it."

"Who did that? Lucifer doesn't fucking care that much."

"Who do you think?"

"Mam'mon?"

Behemoth nods and looks around. "Rumors is he is pissed. Well, beyond pissed off. Enough to keep you locked out of Hell."

For a brief moment, Erigan feels a smile coming on. Most of the poor, worthless souls would kill—again—to be in Erigan's shoes. He should know, he's had offers made.

"Indefinitely?"

Behemoth shrugs. "Or until he gets what he wants."

"And just what might that be?"

Behemoth shrugs again.

"You are not a lot of help there." Erigan turns to sit back down on the steps in front of the library. An elderly couple come up the stairs and nod to Erigan.

He extends a middle finger and turns to his invisible friend.

"What do we do know?"

"Make the most of it, bro." Behemoth sits down beside Erigan and smacks him on the back. Behemoth, still wearing his lion skin cloth that now drapes over his wide torso and next to nothing else, looks comical as he tries to sit like Erigan. A puzzle of muscles bundled up into this awkward position.

Well, awkward but solid as stone.

"So I live here until I can return?"

"Or until he hunts you down."

"I could always count on you to be the optimist," says Erigan. He stands up and adjusts his button-down shirt. "I suppose I can stay human for a while. It has been a while since I have been allowed to roam free on the surface."

Despite sitting down, Behemoth's head still comes to Erigan's chest. "I'm almost jealous of you, Herm." He stands up.

And because he remains invisible, doesn't block out of any of the sunlight coming directly into Erigan's eyes.

Erigan squints and shades his eyes. His powers to return back to Hell have been revoked and he finds himself on the run from one of Lucifer's biggest generals.

Erigan has always heard humans talk about having butterflies in his stomach. For the first time, he think he knows what that feels like.

"Ya," Erigan says with a gulp. "Jealous."

Chapter Nineteen

Erigan's decision to go to the bar seemed like the only logical one he could make. So there he sits in this dusty bar, facing a mirror surrounded by colorful bottles of every inebriating elixir known to mankind.

Many of these Erigan doesn't think he's even heard of before, but the pretty colors catch his attention. As does the pretty blond that sits at the other edge of the bar. She looks to be reading something while sipping on something clear.

Judging by the woman's demeanor, Erigan decides she's just drinking water and scoffs. "Why bother?" he says aloud.

The woman looks over at him and turns smiles, but only to be polite. Then she turns her barstool the other way.

Erigan's little brother Dio used to have a saying:

"When the going get tough, the goes drinking."

Erigan figures now's as good a time as any to put that to the test.

Despite the white sign that tells the bar's inhabitants that there's no smoking, plenty of people have lit cigarettes near the ends of the bar. Erigan shrugs.

The smells are only slightly less toxic than what he's used to. Slightly more pleasant, too.

"Barkeep!" Erigan says and snaps his fingers. He leans across the solid wooden bar and gets a glimpse of a wall of animal heads.

The disgusting heads, each one looking less than dignified attached to wooden panels and boards. If Artemis were here, she'd have this guy's head on the walls as well.

Erigan takes a special note in the memory box of his brain: definitely tell Artemis about this place. Should be fun to watch.

He grins to himself and waits for the pale white bald man to listen to his pleas.

"I'm not a 'bar keep'," the man says. His voice grates at Erigan's eardrums like boots on gravel.

"My apologies, my good man. I'll have that stuff, over there." The liquid glows a bright yellow-green. A color that seems to be chasing Erigan around.

Thinking that it'll taste like the pie he had only twelve hours earlier, it seems as tasty as it will be effective.

"You sure 'bout that?" The man's eyes narrow. He

studies Erigan's blue eyes and curly hair. "You wanna be messin' with that stuff this early in the morn?"

"Is it early?" says Erigan. He leans over the bar, only inches from the barkeep's head.

The man's face is not entertained. "Yup."

"Then I'll have that. Seems like a wonderful way to start the day." Erigan slaps the bar with his hand and searches around for recognition.

Only two other people sit in the bar, each at opposite ends of the building. One plays pool with the other stares at the muted television news program.

The barkeep slams the shot glass down and pours the liquid. This does not smell like limes.

"Again, you sure about this?" says the bald barkeep.

Erigan nods and sniffs the glass first.

Big mistake. It makes his jaw clench tight at first.

"Nothing ventured, nothing gained, right?" He opens his mouth and shoots the drink past his tongue and into the back of his mouth.

It burns at first, but tastes oddly familiar. Liquorice, he believes, and some herbal spice Erigan hasn't smelled in at least a millennia.

"Ooh, that is some good concoction," Erigan says. He drops the glass on the bar and waves for more.

The barkeep shakes his head and looks over Erigan's shoulder. "Must have been a messed up day," he says.

Erigan nods. "You do not know the half of it," he mutters and downs the next shot. He feels every muscle in his face pull toward his lips as he swallows. That one lasted longer on his tongue than he would have liked.

Erigan smacks his lips together. His tongue begins to feel a bit numb. Even coated with a thick film.

"Do you humans always drink this stuff?"

The barkeep shoots Erigan a glance and returns to his work counting small sheets of paper with little black and purple numbers on them.

Erigan considers standing up when his legs strongly disagree with him. He feels them shake at the knees. Wherever he thought he was going certainly will have to wait.

"That'll be ten bucks, sir," says the barkeep. He now has the time to pay attention to Erigan's needs.

"I'm just going outside," he says. "I'll be back."

"And if you want to be going outside, you'll need to give me ten dollars."

Erigan had heard of this stuff before—dollars. Something like currency. Money. The root of all evil if he were believe some humans.

Erigan grins. "We did not have this stuff on Olympus."

"You ain't making no sense, boy." The man grabs for a shotgun underneath his bar. "Shitfaced or not, you gotta pay your tab."

"Shitfaced?" He sits back at the stool and rests his elbows on the bar. "I rather like that word. Shitfaced. Shitfaced." He grins, then chuckles.

"It's fine, Gerry, I got it." The blonde woman at the end of the bar comes over and stands near Erigan.

And it's her. Bradley's mother.

"Listen," she says. "I'll cover it."

"You ain't got to, Sophie," Gerry says. He motions the barrel of the gun to the doorway.

"No, it's fine. I've got this." She shoots Gerry a glance. "You've shot enough people in your lifetime. One more deadbeat loser won't make a difference."

Bradley's mother slaps the ten dollar bill on the bar. As she does so, she locks eyes with Erigan. He notices a brief glimmer, a playfulness about her.

Before he can say anything such as "Thanks," she returns to her seat.

"You're a lucky guy," Gerry says.

"Luck rarely has anything to do with it." Erigan catches Brad's mother's attention with a wave and a nod. He finishes another drink and stands up with his hands up.

"That's it," says the man. "I'm calling the fucking police."

"Fine," says Erigan, "if you wish." He holds his hands up and stands at the bar.

"The police? Law enforcement? Why do you have to go and scare me like that?" Erigan maintains his smile at the bar. He holds his hand out in front of him, his middle finger and thumb prepared to snap.

No, too easy.

He notices the grimace on Gerry's face, the way that his jaw clenches tight when Erigan's lips begin to move.

Just where he wants him. This type of shit, this is

what Erigan lives for.

His feet don't touch the ground, instead hovering only an inch above the floorboards. He floats backwards at a crawl's pace.

"Excuse my departure, but now I have to run away and save myself," Erigan quips. He keeps his hands up, but flashes a wink at Sophie.

The man cocks his gun and points it at Erigan's curly human head.

"The woman paid for your drinks. Now git goin'."

Erigan bows out, but not before pointing at the bell that hangs from a steel bar above the cash register. He points his index finger and shoots imaginary bullets at it.

To everyone's amazement, it chimes. Everyone turns their heads toward the bell.

"Just how the hell—" Gerry begins to say but his words are cut off by the closing of the door behind Erigan.

Chapter Twenty

Erigan decides to walk to Bradley's apartment building. The streets are nearly empty. Black asphalt almost as fresh as the day it was laid down. Thin laurel oak trees with their flat, oval leaves lined the streets.

If anything, it was a beautiful day out.

Trekking up to the apartment building, Erigan notices that there are more trees than people walking around.

School? he thinks. Maybe some festival going on around now?

The sun beats down warm and Erigan begins to feel a sensation he has not known before now.

He scratches along this forearms and back, reaching into the neck of his collared shirt to get between his shoulders. His skin feels damp. Sweat?

His body was more human than he gave himself

credit. It was a wonder that Behemoth ever found him to begin with.

Erigan stops at a corner store which stops at a fork in the road. If he were to go right, he'd head into more one and two-story houses.

Small for a god's expectations, but well suited for the area.

Right, and he'd end up along the main road and to the apartment.

But something catches his eye as he begins to walk toward the store's giant glass windows. Erigan finds a spot that isn't covered with bright red or yellow beer advertisements and checks himself out.

His face is clean-shaven, his eyes blue at the moment, but that could change if he needed to. His hair falls in tight curls on his forehead.

But something about it looked unnatural. Just not interesting.

Closing his eyes, he focuses on his chin and then looks at himself. Stubble.

Clean shaven was for women. With stubble, he now had a man's face.

Erigan smiles with pride and continues up the second street on the right. He comes to the conclusion that if he's going to hide, he might as well hide in plain sight. A somewhat clever disguise, and learning how to live like a human should be all he needs to keep from standing out.

But being human. The thought of it made him almost excited.

But if he was to be a human, he'd have to do as humans do. This meant a home first. Always find shelter. Then be productive.

Behemoth was right: it had been many lifetimes ago that any of them have had the chance to stay on the surface for a while and enjoy the humanity.

His situation did have a silver lining, he had to admit. A forced vacation, all the women he could meet, and absolute freedom. And it all smelled like piney South Carolina air.

Erigan reaches the stairs of Brad's apartment building and stops for a moment. This place seemed as good as any.

He enters the apartment building and walks to the front office near the inside set of glass doors.

"Hi," Erigan says. He tries to force his voice to sound low, manly. "I would like one apartment, please."

The woman behind the counter, she turns her head slowly at first, then stops to gaze into Erigan's blue eyes. Her facial muscles freeze. She smiles, maybe even enamored at the sight.

Erigan sees this and smiles. He leans onto the counter, shifting his weight onto one shoulder. "So you have something I can have?"

The woman giggles and adjusts her hair. "I think I have something, mister uh," she says.

The woman's face is plump, lips lined with a dark liner and a bright rose red elsewhere all over her lower lip. Her brown hair is cut short to her shoulders, like curtains falling off her head.

"Mr. Erigan." He smiles. "Hermes Erigan."

"What an interesting name," she says. "Are you Mexican?"

"Greek, actually." Erigan flashes his brilliant white smile once more.

"Well my name is Peggy, Mr. Eric. A pleasure to meet you."

When Peggy comes out of her office, she takes a stop and grabs for her chest. "Oh my, you are a handsome fella," she says.

Her southern drawl comes crawling out of her mouth thick and slow.

"Thank you," says Erigan. He follows Peggy's sloppy steps up the staircase. Each of her steps stamps down on the stairs. Each foot echoes into the silent, dirty white staircase.

"Here we are," Peggy says two flights of stairs later. "Apartment 1D."

The door swings wide open. The burnt orange paint on the walls gives the room a fiery glow. A wide glass door and windows seem to take up the entire wall on the other side of the living room. If he hadn't known that the apartment was up for rent, he would have thought someone still lived here.

"And the furniture is also available?" he asks.

"Do you like it?" she says. "The apartment just came vacant only a few days ago. Some old man lived here. Moved out suddenly." She pats the back of an armchair.

"If you're like it, you can have it. All of it."

The view from the windows catches Erigan's eye and he steps into the room, breathless.

Erigan takes in the stretching green scenery. Trees and rolling hills as far as his eyes could see. Rivers traced the bottoms of the hills like veins on the back of his hands.

"It's beautiful," he says.

"Isn't it though?" she says. Peggy comes into the room and stands next to him. Through his peripheral vision, Erigan can see that Peggy isn't enjoying that same view as he is.

She's admiring him.

"I'll take it."

"Good choice, Mr. Eric." Peggy takes a step back.

"That's Erigan."

Peggy leans her head toward Erigan's shoulders and takes in a loud amount of air through her nostrils and then lets it out in a quick huff. "If you'd like to follow me, we can get some paperwork started."

"Paperwork? Not here, too." Erigan turns around.

"Well I don't know how they do things in Greece, but here in America, we need to fill out paperwork. You know. For security."

Erigan sighs. "Fine, paperwork it is."

The two climb down the stairs and as he does so, he spots two familiar faces coming into the hallway.

"But Mom," Bradley says, "he's not imaginary. I promise."

Chapter Twenty-One

Brad's mother carries on upstairs with her son in tow. She holds her son's hand when she realizes that other people are coming near her. "This is what I get for teaching you to read," she says.

Brad huffs and scowls. "Yes, mom."

Erigan sidesteps the two as they squeeze by.

"Excuse me," he says. "You're that kind woman who helped me earlier."

Brad's mom appears to blush. She swipes her hair to one side and then pretends to smile. "Yes, I think so. Hi, how are you doing?"

She doesn't offer him a hand.

Brad raises an eyebrow and points at Erigan. "Who's that?"

"Just some drunk Mommy helped out earlier today."

"He doesn't look drunk," says Brad.

"And how would you know what drunk looks like?" Brad's mother sighs. "That's it. Babysitter's fired."

"I wanted to thank you again." Erigan takes a closer step to the boy.

His mother reacts by pulling him closer to her. "So you live here?" she says. "That's, uh, that's great." She fakes another smile.

"Not yet, dear," says Peggy. She giggles. "He just needs to fill out paperwork."

"Well don't let us keep you," says Sophie. She pulls Brad in front of her and continues up the stairs. As they turn the corner, Sophie's eyes lock with Erigan's for only a brief second.

"They seem like nice people," Erigan says. The two go back to the office.

"I hoped you'd like them," Peggy says. She giggles her trademark giggle. "You're going to be their next door neighbor. Isn't that special?"

"That sounds so fortuitous," he says.

Peggy hands him a clipboard of paperwork. "I'll just need you to fill out all of this and hand me a your ID. You know, for security purposes."

"And what kind of ID are you looking for?"

Peggy shrugs. The question must not come up very often. "Driver's license or passport, I guess."

"Well I'm from out of town. I don't really have those things."

Peggy's blank look confuses Erigan for a moment. Was he in trouble? Was she thinking? Did her brain freeze up?

He looks at the clipboard. The first line, Name, seems pretty easy. He scribbles in his best handwriting "Hermes Erigan" in the English alphabet.

The next line says address.

Erigan snaps his fingers in front of her face. "Peggy?"

Peggy comes to, blinking heavily and then focusing her attention to Erigan. "Yes?"

"Do I need to fill out the part here, where it says address? I'm applying for an address." Erigan smiles. It seems like an obvious question, but Peggy smiles and nods. Blank expression.

"Just put your past residence."

Greece, he scribbles.

Next.

Social security number.

"Um, Peggy," he says again. Erigan taps the pen against the laminate countertop of her desk. "I don't have a social security number."

"You don't have a number?" The woman's southern accent makes it sound more like "numba" to Erigan's ears. The accents in Earth strike Erigan as comical nonsense sounds: *Bar-bar-bar.*

Erigan nods, grins, then winks.

"You know what?" she says. Peggy reaches across the desk and takes the clipboard from Erigan's tight grip. "You know what, how about I worry about this little— inconvenience." She eyes the paper then looks up and says "Do you have a job?"

Erigan thinks. Does he tell the truth or lie his horned ass off?

"I used to," he says. "I think I just got let go."

"Fired?" she says. Peggy's mouth turns upside down, then crinkles into a shriveled pink prune. "Listen, Mr, uh," she checks the form again. "Senior Eric-gan, but I don't know how much more I can help you." While keeping eye-contact with Erigan, she holds the clipboard over the trashcan and pulls the clip open. The paper slides off the particleboard backing like a theme park ride, landing in the brown plastic trash pail. "I'm sorry."

"It's, um, Erigan. Hermes Erigan," he says. "But what if I came back with some money?"

"I'd need first and last month's rent," she says.

Erigan flashes his blue eyes, flashes them hazel for only a brief moment, then back to blue. He tests the waters with her reactions. Whatever color will get him the most mileage.

"Well," she says. "Maybe first month's. We'll talk about the rest. And get some ID. You know, for security."

"So if I come back, you'll hold that apartment for me?" He blinks again. "It just, you know, spoke to me."

"Well, if you come back soon," she says.

Erigan feels blood rush to his face. "Do you not know who the Hell I am?" says Erigan.

He stands up and rests both of his hands on the desk. He blinks his eyes. For a moment, the flash red then back to their bluish gray.

"I could turn you into a fucking frog and squash you and take the damned apartment myself."

The door bursts open and just by the smell of body odor and arrogance, Erigan already know who's arrive.

"Erigan!" says the burly voice. Strong arms grab Erigan from his seat and lift him up into the air with a giant bear hug. "There you are! You said you would wait outside."

Erigan coughs, trying to catch his breath.

Behemoth drops the poor ex-godling and offers his massive hand to Peggy for a handshake. Peggy's hand disappears in Behemoth's oversized knuckles. "Who is this might man?"

Everything about Behemoth appears oversized in this tiny office. Behemoth's chosen disguise appears to be a charcoal gray suit. Red tie. Light brown pinstriped pants. The only part that screams typical Behemoth is the lion hat. This time, it's in the shape of a hat with a wide brim in the front. Two white, triangle-shaped fabric teeth hang from the tip of the hat's brim.

Peggy winks at Erigan. "Is this your, you know. Friend?"

Erigan feels the immediate need to explain when she sees the disappointed twinkle in her eye. "This is not who, um, it might look like."

"Name's Herc, ma'am." Behemoth pulls out the other chair next to Erigan's and sits down. His massive legs and knees nearly dwarf the desk they sit at. "I'm a friend of Erigan's. Showing him around town."

"So you're from here?" she says. "That's great." She turns to look at Erigan and winks. "I see."

"So whatever you need, you know, you can just let me handle it." Behemoth nods toward his friend.

Erigan immediately sees what this is—Behemoth wants to take over the transaction. Help him out.

"You see, he's a little off the handle sometimes. Not dangerous, really, but, you know. His bark is worse than his bite." He gives Erigan a smirk and pats his knee. "I'm just here for support. First time our buddy's on his own."

Erigan grits his teeth. If they weren't cracked already, they were on their way.

"Don't enjoy this too much," says Erigan. He picks up a pen like he's already in the middle of something. He slouches over the desk and looks for something to write on.

"How do we make this official?" Behemoth says.

"Well, you see," says Peggy—directly to Behemoth, not Erigan, "I need some kind of money, payment. And verification of a job. You know, for security."

Erigan smiles. "Sounds great there, Peggy."

Behemoth—or Herc—takes out a wad of thin green paper strips and begins counting them, licking his fingers every few numbers. "How much, exactly."

Erigan rolls his eyes and turns away. He continues to hear his friend flapping through the money and slamming a few of the bills on the desk. "Will that be enough much?"

Peggy is quiet for a moment. Eyeing, but not touching, the money. "You do know those are hundred dollar bills?" she says and points.

Behemoth throws down a few more. "I'm sorry," he says. "Will that do?"

Peggy snatches up the money and folds it into her pocket. "Yes, that will do." She takes the money out of her pocket and counts it one more time. Half of the pile goes into one pocket, the rest goes in the other. "I think that'll do great. There is still the business of having a job," she says. Her eyes are huge, delirium. "You know, for security."

Behemoth stands up and drags Erigan to his feet. "Not a problem, ma'am, we'll be job hunting today." He smiles his prize-winning smile and makes each one of his pecs bounce. "Unless you know about any good job leads."

Peggy doesn't hesitate to shake her head "Um," she says.

Erigan stretches his hands, takes both of hers in his hands and shakes. "It's okay, we don't really have the time for this."

Peggy reaches over into her cabinet and fingers through a file. "Here we are." She holds out a metal ring with two keys that clang against each other like wind chimes. "For you and your, um, friend."

"Just friend," says Erigan. "Thanks."

"Oh don't be shy now." Behemoth takes the key ring

and effortlessly distorts the ring to take his own key off. "We're not *just* friends."

Peggy giggles.

Erigan rolls his eyes. Grabbing the key tight in his fingers is all he can do to keep from slapping Behemoth.

"Oh," she says before he can pull on the door. "I'll also need you to sign this."

At the bottom of the form he signs Ερμης and hands Peggy back the pencil.

Peggy holds the clipboard away form her face, then closer as if the words will magically get bigger.

Erigan knows he could make that happen if he wanted to. He just chooses not to.

"That's an interesting signature," she says. "Is that Mexican?"

Chapter Twenty-Two

The humming fluorescent lights nearly bleach the white walls of the apartment's hallway just outside the office. The walls smell like paint. Fresh, wet paint, though the dark splotches—stains, really—indicate that the walls may not have been repainted in years. The wet smell Erigan attributes to the hair-curling humidity outside.

Erigan and Behemoth square off just beyond the reach of Peggy's hearing. At least Erigan hopes. As the conversation continues, he takes gradual steps away from the office door just in case.

"Just what in the ninth level of Hell was that?"

Behemoth's laugh rumbles the walls like a herd of running bulls. "You needed my help, little man."

Erigan shoves off Behemoth's large paw of a hand from his shoulder. "Don't call me little," he says. "And I didn't need your help."

"You were already threatening to turn her into a toad."

"Frog."

"Trust me, bro, you needed my help." Behemoth looks around the hallways, then looks up the staircase. "Are you sure you want to live here?"

Erigan nods and lowers his voice to a whisper. "I have to. I was just. I don't know. Pulled here."

"Pulled here?"

Erigan nods. "Sounds crazy, right?"

"It appears the Fates are twisting you around again," says Behemoth.

"Well, they would be if they weren't busy working for the Light Bringer."

Behemoth laughs. "Prometheus?"

"Lucifer, you halfwit."

Any minute now, Erigan suspects someone will come out of their apartment and tell them to shut up.

"Your paranoia is not entirely unfounded," Behemoth says. He grabs Erigan by the shoulder and turns him toward the first set of glass doors of the foyer.

The sun's blinding rays outside pale in comparison to the bright, unnatural intensity of the lights on the inside. "You know, Apollo was never this bright."

Behemoth squeezes Erigan's shoulders. "You have a lot to learn about humans."

"What do you know about humans?"

Behemoth stops. "Did you forget already? I was once one of them."

"You were a demigod. Not the same thing, my oversized friend."

Erigan begins walking toward town.

"Where are you going? We have to get you a job!" shouts Behemoth. His voice rattles the metal handles of the stairwell.

"I'm going into town, halfwit. I need to find something like a job."

Behemoth follows him outside and onto the streets. The small roads only allow maybe two cars to pass by each other in opposite directions, if they were both to ride the curb of the sidewalks.

It only becomes apparent just how small the roads are when Behemoth decides to walk down the middle of the road. Straddling the yellow dotted line, He takes long, staccato strides to match up with Erigan's pace.

"Do you know what you're going to do?" Behemoth asks.

Erigan shakes his head. "Haven't a clue. But I need that apartment."

"You don't really need the apartment. You just really want it."

"I'm telling you, someone wants me to have that apartment."

"Who? Behemoth laughs. "Zeus? He's gone. M.I.A. The gods?" His chuckles roar through the thin alleys between the houses. "The Gods don't exist anymore. We're just child's play, fodder for the wars between Jehovah and Lucifer. The only reason we got cast down into Hell is because He—the big H—is afraid of anyone worshipping anyone else."

Erigan grits his teeth to keep from saying anything he may not regret.

"Say what you want, Erigan, you know that it's true."

"It doesn't mean I don't have to like it."

"Like it or hate it, my little friend. You do have to accept it."

"You mean to tell me that you're perfectly fine being cast down into that pit? You're perfectly okay that your dad just disappeared?"

"Some dad, wasn't he?" Behemoth chuckles. "Never saw the man and barely allows me on Olympus after I'm done with my twelve penances? Ya, fuck him. I hope Kerberos ate him."

"No you don't," says Erigan. He tries to smile to lighten the mood. But Behemoth's eyes, the sudden intensity—Erigan had seen that look before, that same look came before he murdered his family by Hera's manipulations.

And the conversation went silent. They walked on down the roads. After some convincing and three honking cars, Behemoth decided to take up to the sidewalk, trailing behind Erigan. This also had the added effect of keeping the Erigan out the sun's annoying rays.

"You have no idea where you're going, do you?"

Erigan shook his head. "Not a damned clue."

"Then off to the tavern," says Behemoth. He lifts

Erigan up into the air and then tosses him onto his shoulder.

"Put me down, you oaf!" Erigan slams his hands against the strong, muscled back. He stops when he began to feel the beginnings of tingling pain in his fists.

"Not a chance," says Behemoth. "We need to loosen you up. Then we'll get you a job."

Chapter Twenty-Three

"Oh for fuck's sakes! You again?"

Erigan smiles. He knows that chaos could definitely ensue if he opens his mouth. He considers it for only a second when he's distracted by Behemoth's mournful cries.

"Why's it so damned dark in here?" he says. Dark wood surrounds them, the smell of vomit and some lemon-based cleaner welcome Erigan back to finish his first drink.

"Because I likes it that way!" says Barry. "Now get the Hell out!" The bartender's old hands reach for something under the bar, but come up somewhat empty handed.

The five other people at the bar dam near drop their beers when they get a focused look on Behemoth's prideful stature.

"Damn yous a big 'un," says one man. He downs his beer and offers the glass unsuccessfully to Barry the bartender. "What you been putting in these? I can't decide if I want none or not."

Erigan snaps his fingers and steps up to the bar.

Behemoth smiles. He knows what's about to ensue. "We need two please." Behemoth pulls out a stool but finds that it's too small for his muscular ass.

"Two of what?" says the bartender. He resigns himself to helping the two. His tone of voice becomes a dull southern drawl, drags along the bar. Lazy. Resistant. "You gotta tell me what kind of drink you want."

"Mead?" says Behemoth.

Erigan nudges his friend and shakes his head. "Tried that. Ain't got it."

"Ain't got mead? That was the best thing to come out of the middle ages!" he says. "What about honey wine?"

"That's what mead is, halfwit." Erigan offers the reluctant bartender a smile and pulls himself up onto the bar. "Two of the big green stuff," he says. He points to the bottle with a white label and fancy letters in a language Erigan hasn't bothered to study. "That stuff, ya."

The bartender reaches over and looks at it. "You liked it that much, eh?" he says.

Erigan nods and then nudges Behemoth. "You're gonna love this stuff."

The bartender lets two shot glasses slide next to

each other, landing in front of the two would-be drunks. Erigan catches a whiff of the strong liquorice scent, strong enough to punch Behemoth in the back of the throat.

As it does Behemoth coughs. "This smells amazing," he says.

"Oh it is, brother. It is."

The bartender eyes the two and shrugs. "Whatever fellas. Ten bucks."

Behemoth shuffles through his pockets and tosses out another long green strip of paper. "This enough?" he says.

The bartender holds the bill up to the fluorescent light and winces. "How many drinks you want?" he says. "I ain't got change."

Erigan smirks. "How many will that get us?"

"Five each, I s'pose."

Behemoth smashes his fists on the bar. Erigan swears he hears a crack from the wood.

Judging from the bartender's concern, he did too.

"We'll take it, Barry," says Behemoth. "I'm Herc. Nice to meet you."

The bartender considers offering his hands but retracts when he sees just how large Behemoth's fists are. "Please," he says. "Holler if you need anything."

Barry leaves the bottle with the boys and goes to lean on the opposite direction of the bar.

Behemoth holds the shot glass of green liquid under his nose. "This looks like it glows. Like that moss on the southern walls of Dis."

"But it doesn't taste like it. Believe you me."

The two hold their glasses, careful not to spill any of it. The shot glass looks no larger than a marble in Behemoth's oversized hands. "What shall we drink to?" says Behemoth.

"What about to friendship?"

Behemoth smiles. "How about a new job?"

"I don't have a new job yet, buddy. That's not how this thing quite works."

"Hey buddy!" shouts Behemoth.

Everyone in the bar jumps where they sit or stand. At once, he has everyone's attention.

"Can you get my friend here a job?" Behemoth's violent gestures on Erigan's shoulder nearly spill the shot.

"I don't have any room for new hires," says Barry. "Try somewhere else in town."

Behemoth offers the man another bill. "Are you sure you can't help us out?"

"You got all the money," says Barry. "Why you don't just give it to him?" Barry wipes his bald brow. The top of his head only shines when he stands next to the buzzing red and blue Budweiser sign.

"Ya, why don't you just give me money?"

"Because if you want to be human, you have to have a job," says Behemoth. "Ain't that right, friend?"

Barry bites his lips. Lost in confusion. Erigan reads from Barry's face that he's probably putting some pieces of the puzzle, but doesn't know what the final picture is supposed to look like.

"We're not aliens, or nothing," says Behemoth.

"Listen, I don't care," says Barry. "Keep on bringing in Benjamins, and you can be the goddamn Queen of England for all I care."

Behemoth begins to stand when Erigan's hands gently push him back down. "Don't bother," he says. Erigan holds up the drink in celebration. "Cheers!" he says. "To being human."

The shot glasses clink together and they down the liquid in one gulp each.

"How's it, buddy?"

Behemoth smacks his lips together and then wipes his beard with a giant bear-paw of his. "Tasty," he says. "Another?"

Erigan offers his glass. "You know that's right."

Chapter Twenty-Four

No matter how Erigan holds his hands up in front of his face, he can't seem to block out the unforgiving and accusatory rays of the sun.

The bar's door creaks shut behind Erigan and Behemoth as they step out into the sidewalk along Main Street. The thick tar smell of car emissions meets them both at first breath. Heat radiates from the sidewalks and brick walls of buildings like walking in an oven as big as a city block.

"Has Apollo's chariot always been this bright?" says Erigan.

Behemoth wipes a bit of sweat off his brow. "This is no doing of Phoebus Apollo, friend," he says.

Erigan immediately begins to feel his own skin get damp. His shirt sticks to this thin shoulders and his concave chest. "The good ol' days, eh, buddy?"

"They're gone now, Erigan. You know that." He extends his hand to slap Erigan on the back.

Erigan stops, freezes, and braces for impact.

Behemoth's chuckles turn into a dull roar. "You're funny, little man."

"I need to get home. Find a job."

Behemoth coughs.

Erigan rolls his eyes. "Or *another* job." He looks over at Behemoth and punches him in the forearm. "Any sign of who might have locked me out, buddy?"

Erigan tries to smile but finds it's mostly a reflex from the overly bright sun.

"Still looking into it," says Behemoth.

He reaches into his pocket and pulls out a stack of green slips of paper. Cash money. And lots of it. "This should tie you over until we can figure it out."

"Do me a favor and not hurry." Erigan grins to himself, tries to hide it from Behemoth. "I might need a little vacation after all."

"So you're going to take my advice?"

They cross the street in front of the library and Behemoth suddenly stops. Erigan takes a few steps before he notices that he isn't being followed.

"I gotta go," says Behemoth. He points downward into the ground. "I don't want anyone finding you just yet."

"Ya, well," Erigan kicks the rocks at the edge of the sidewalk. He misses each and every one. "I'll see you soon."

Behemoth shrugs and smiles.

When Erigan shields his eyes from the sun with his palm, he realizes that his friend is already gone.

As the Fates would have it, Erigan's neighbors were leaving their apartment at the same exact time he was going into his own.

"Good afternoon," he says.

Sophie smiles with only half of her mouth and nods. Her golden hair falls down her temples and cheeks, obstructing the classic Roman nose that sits properly on her face.

Erigan turns around and leans against his door. "How are you today?"

He remembers to smile. Cross his arms as if he's relaxed. Make nice.

The boy smiles at him and waves. When Sophie sees, she slaps his hands away and steps forward like a lioness protecting her cub.

"We're great," she says. She only pretends to drop her apartment key into her leather jacket pocket. Erigan can see from the rounded protrusion that she's holding it still, pointed end out. Protecting herself.

"That's wonderful," he says. "Just great."

The conversation trails off. Awkward. Erigan nods.

Sophie nods.

Brad begins to wave again. Sophie smacks his hands down again.

"Well, we have to get going," she says.

"Oh?" he says. "Where?"

Sophie's face freezes in a twisted smile. He's crossed a line, he can tell. He just doesn't know which one.

"I mean, I'm just going to go inside now," he says.

Sophie nods and nudges her son to the stairs. "Right."

"Nice seeing you, Mr. Harrigan."

Erigan winces. "That's Erigan. No H." He sticks his key into the lock and turns it with a click. "You know what? Just call me Hermes."

Brad laughs. "Hermes?"

Sophie smacks Brad upside his head, leaving a lock of blond hair sticking straight up.

Without any prompting from his mother, Brad looks at her and puts his head down. "Sorry, Mr. Hermes." He cracks a smile but it disappears quickly.

"That's quite all right," Erigan says. "It's Greek. Sounds funny to you English speakers."

Sophie says, "You don't sound like you have an accent. How long have you been living here?"

"About an hour or so?" he says.

Not technically incorrect.

Sophie smirks. "I meant here in America."

Erigan shrugs. "About an hour or so." He nods confidently.

Sophie's eyes narrow. She winces the way humans do when they have a headache.

Erigan wonders for a brief moment, did he stop speaking English?

Did he go back into Latin? Maybe Greek? He has

only been human for a few hours now.

"I'm sorry, did I say something funny?"

Brad laughs and Sophie shakes her head. "No. No. We're going to be late. Have a nice afternoon, Mr. Erigan."

Erigan watches them both go down into the stairwell. When the door opens, Brad thinks he's whispering when he says, "I like him, mom. He's funny."

They leave into the foyer.

He taps his foot on the ground, counting to ten.

When he's just about to say the word eleven, he walks over to his neighbors in 1C and walks through the solid wooden paneling of their front door.

He may have been locked out of Hell, but he sure didn't lose his abilities. Erigan would feel thankful if only he knew who to thank.

He takes a moment to survey the walk-in area and take in the environment. His first time seeing this all as a human being, with human eyes and a human nose, his brain feels confused. Attacked.

It smells like outside, but sweeter. Like wetness. Rain, he thinks. If he could remember way back long ago. At his feet is a pile of shoes. Little ones for the boy and tall heeled shoes with straps.

Erigan kicks one over with his own foot, measures his foot size with hers. It comes nearly even. Does that make him big? Small?

Trying them on will have to wait for another time.

He walks into the living room and peers around the

room. A mirror sits just above the television on the far end of the room. It's a flat screen. Big, but the one left to him at his apartment is much, much bigger.

Colorful towers of plates and bowls flood the kitchen sink. He counts the silverware to himself and always comes up with an even number. No one else lives here with them.

This could be easier than he thought.

If only he knew what he was supposed to do with this brat.

He leaves the kitchen and walks the fifteen feet down the carpeted hallway to the boy's bedroom. The word BRAD hangs on the door in blue foam letters.

The color blue covers nearly everything in the bedroom. From floor to ceiling. A scene was painted on the walls a short time ago. Clouds, blue skies. A sun in the upper corner near the closet door.

A mountain rises from behind the bed's headboard, up into the wispy painted clouds.

Erigan's heartbeats feel heavy in his chest.

He spots a peak near the base of the mountain to the right. The peak juts out away from the base, not enough to draw attention to it.

He takes a pencil from the boy's desk and kneels down by the wall. He sketches out a triangular roof, held up by two columns. He draws a table. A chair. And a bassinet.

Erigan sits back on his heels and traces the pencil lines with his fingers. His fingertips feel the rough painted surface of the wall. The texture feels natural and seems to fit his imaginations and memories of the rocky surface of Olympus.

He notices the gray lines smudging under his touch. Without much thought, he smudges the left side of each shape, drawing it out into a shadow. The dark side on the left, the thin light side on the right.

Rudimentary and basic, but the shapes remind Erigan of a home he left so, so long ago.

Staring at the entirety of the painting with his addition, he hears the heavy knocking of boots on wooden floorboards behind him.

"I understand you're not from around here," says a voice. It sounds heavy. Official.

Erigan tries to look over his shoulder, but he's pulled upwards to his feet by a heavy, white hand.

"If you'd just come with us to your place, we'd like to have a talk with you."

Chapter Twenty-Five

Erigan's head disappears inside cupboards in his own kitchen. The soft wooden slam of those same cupboards closing breaks the silence in the room.

"You know, guys, I'd love to offer you some coffee or tea if I knew where that shit was."

The first of the two men stands up and crosses his arms across his fairly muscular chest. Erigan measures up the man and figures that Behemoth would still kick this dude's ass.

"It's fine," the first man says. His white button down dress shirt looks pressed. His gray slacks perfectly fitted. His hair burns a bright red in the bits of sunlight that slice through the vertical blinds. "We will not be staying long, will we, brother?"

The other man stands up as well. He towers over the wooden kitchen table, the small dark wood almost disappearing completely in the man's shadow.

He nods.

"We just need to make sure that you are not going to pose any problems for us."

Erigan's hands clench into tight fists. He's not much of a scrapper, he knows. "And just who the hell are you?"

"We're from the other side." The first one extends a hand. Golden rings catch Erigan's eyes. A full white metal bracelet hangs delicately around his wrist. "I'm Jason. Nice to finally meet you, Erigan."

"Finally?"

The second man steps forward and also offers his hand. He wears a suit, jacket and tie, that fits tight around his shoulders and waist. With each second Erigan changes his opinion of the suit from fashionable to ill-fitting and back again.

"We just need to make sure you understand your role," he says.

Jason uncrosses his arms and leans on the counter. He tries to look relaxed but Erigan isn't fooled. If he's an interrogator, he's not very good at it.

"What my friend means to say here is that we have a job to do, and your sudden presence might not bode well for our job." Jason's eyes raise. "*Me katalavenis?*"

Erigan nods. "*Neh.*"

"Good," says the other man. He moves in front of Erigan and rests both of his hands on Erigan's shoulders. "The faster you understand that, the better."

"For the record, I never said I was going to do anything."

"You also never said you weren't going to do anything," says Jason. He raises an eyebrow and points a finger at Erigan like a gun.

"Up until three minutes ago, I never even knew you Argonauts were up here." Erigan tries to walk to the kitchen but the other bigger guy refuses to move out of his way. "How can I even get in your way?"

Jason waves for the other man to follow him to the front door. Their steps are heavy. The thick black boots definitely don't make them any stealthy. "We're keeping an eye on you."

"Keeping an eye on me for what?" says Erigan.

He sidesteps the nameless man and approaches Jason.

Moving quickly with his winged sandals, he's already in front of the door before both of them can turn the corner.

"What did I do? What do you think I'm going to do? Just who the hell do you think you are?" Erigan tries to study the men's eyes, but they reveal nothing.

Their pupils don't dilate. No twitching muscles.

Erigan stretches his hands across the hallway and grips each wall tightly. He relaxes his muscles for only a moment and feels his shape changing. He grows slightly taller, his hair recedes and the sudden weighty poke of a single horn protrudes from the left side of his forehead.

"Don't make me get angry," he says.

Jason flicks Erigan's horn and checks it closer. "Nice horn," he says. "I have a few dozen of these things at home." Jason's light brown eyes blink. "Are we done showing off now?"

"Not until you tell me who you work for."

"I told you," he says. "We work for the other side. Now if you'll excuse me."

Jason taps Erigan's bare side just beneath his exposed armpit. He feels his muscles pull tight on one side in response to the tickle.

"Thank you," says Jason. His hand grips the doorknob despite Erigan's strong presence and he pulls on the door.

Erigan's feet shuffle forward, inch by sluggish inch.

"A little faster, please," says Jason. "We really do not have time for this."

Erigan presses himself up against the hinged side of the door and watches as Jason steps into the brightly-lit hallway.

Jason taps his foot. "Come on, now, Bell."

The other man nods, grim-faced, at Erigan. They both wander out into the foyer and then disappear behind the glass doors.

Erigan closes his apartment door and sits down on his dark leather couch. His ass bounces on the springs, a feeling he considers fun at first then just annoying.

"Herc!" he says. He waits for an answer but sees, smells, or hears nothing. "Herc! Get your ass up here! What's going on here?"

Erigan waits again. He taps his sandaled foot against the dark leather padded cube that was somehow intended to be a coffee table. At least that's what Erigan figures.

His attention turns toward the coffee table. He sees lines, crevices really, that trace around the entirety of the table. A separation of the top from the bottom. A lid.

He tries delicately but is unable to force it open with his shoed feet.

He kicks his sandals off across the room. They land somewhere behind him into the kitchen. It doesn't matter where for now. Nothing crashes or breaks.

"What are you?" he says. His toes tap-tap along the edges.

Erigan tries to listen for any signs of echoes or hollow sides, but it's pointless. The whole thing seems to be one big mindfuck. Padded so heavily on the outside that he sounds become absorbed into the fabric.

Erigan curses as he pulls his shoulders forward and clutches an edge of the table. He pulls up.

The leather padding squeaks against his fingertips. It's a tight fit, he feels, but it does give.

Excited, he pulls again.

He lifts the lid off completely and peeks inside. The interior appears padded as well, softened with a leather hide that Erigan recognizes better than he'd like to admit.

This hide. He's seen the rough patches, dried and scraped from battle.

This is a minotaur hide. Erigan rubs his human fingers along the sides of it. Each crack in the dried skin tells a story of victories on the battlefield. Some cracks feel smooth along the edges. Evidence a sharpened blade.

Professional cuts. Not just a little human warrior, but a demigod. Maybe even an angel.

"You're fucking kidding me," he says.

His hands pull up a bundle of wrapped cloth. Black with golden designs. Angular spirals that twirl from one corner to the others. In the center, a snake and a bull.

Erigan looks around. This can't be something just left here. It was left here for him.

His hands unfold the wrappings. He nearly falls backwards, catching himself against the couch.

"What the fuck is this?"

The black cloth falls away to the floor, leaving a small figurine: a ram carved from marble.

Erigan smiles to himself. He remembered the story well.

To help the city of Tanagra avoid a disastrous plague, he carried a ram around the city walls. It even landed him a nickname, an epithet. Kriophoros Hermes.

Erigan smiles and sets the ram next to his feet.

This tricky coffee table holds nothing more, so Erigan sets the lid back on and taps each of the corners to seal it tight.

He rests the ram figuring on the table and stares at it. He leans over the table, holding his head in his hands.

"Who knows I'm here?" he says.

Chapter Twenty-Six

Not wanting to miss his mark, Erigan quietly watches Brad sleep alone in his big boy bed. The light from the moon and stars outside cast a subtle illumination along the edges of the wooden frame.

It's not that Erigan needs the light to see, but he's grown to like the drama lights bring to the scene. The struggles between light and dark. The visible and the unseen. Perfect for a trickster like him.

However at the moment, he finds himself distracted by the shinies around him. The brightly colored toys and metal pieces that reflect light back into Erigan's red, sensitive eyes.

He's in his demon form, a relaxed form that allows him to blend in with the shadows in case Sophie rears her attractively blond head.

And the boy, well, he's been too still to notice.

"Who are you?" Erigan says. He steps out of the shadow and kicks a plastic box. The casing gives way under his strong kick, but it catches Erigan off guard.

Grumbling, he kicks it to the side so as not to make noise. Then, he opts for the safer option: flight.

His ankle wings flutter silent as sparrows in the night. He floats just above the ground, above the messy plastic and metal toys that litter that damn boy's bedroom.

He flutters to the edge of the bed and lets his toes just barely touch the red and green bedsheets.

He looks up, his eyes catching the peak of the painted Mount Olympus. Its base rests, hidden away, behind Brad's headboard.

"Where are you from?" Erigan says.

The boy begins to twitch. Erigan reacts, pulling back. His skin turns black, fuzzy and faded like a shadow.

He nearly holds his breath, watching the boy's eyes not show any sign of wanting to open.

False alarm.

His wings begin to flutter faster and they carry him toward the boy's head.

He peers downward at Brad's blond hair. Long hair that curls around his ears and the back of his neck. The boy looks peaceful, harmless even, as he sleeps.

Erigan regrets that he's gotta do what he's gotta do. If only a second.

Erigan's body tilts forward and soon he's parallel to the bed, falling downward.

Erigan lets his demonic tail flicker about behind him. With the tip, he feels the rough popcorn ceiling. The tail gently wraps around him and pokes at the boy's bed. It traces along his legs, up his side and eventually to the boy's armpit.

The boy giggles.

Erigan freezes cold, motionless.

"How long?" he says.

Brad's eyes squint tight.

"I know you're awake," Erigan mutters. "How long have you been awake?"

"Long enough to see you do that cool thing with your tail."

Erigan sighs. He's losing his touch.

With a thought, he flutters to the side of the bed and rests his toes on the carpet.

Brad's lightning blue eyes open and meet with Erigan's yellow ones.

"Are you going to eat me?"

"Not this time," Erigan says. He grins, allows the moon's light to glimmer off the tip of a jagged tooth. "I'm full for the moment."

"Are you going to kill me?"

Erigan looks upwards, stares at the ceiling as if in thought. Then, folding his legs and sitting Indian style in the air, he says, "Not yet. No." He smiles again. This time, friendly.

"Then why are you here?" Brad says. He lifts his little body so he sits up completely. His pajamas become more apparent. He wears a Thor superhero shirt.

"That's what I would like to know myself," Erigan responds.

Brad cocks his head to the side. Then, dismissing that thought and running on to his next he says, "Can you teach me to do that?"

"I could, but then I'd have to kill you."

Brad at first cringes in horror, but apparently relaxes fast. "I bet it'd be worth it."

"You're a strange little boy," Erigan says. He floats forward, almost touching the bed with his tail and knees. "Who are you?"

"I'm Brad." He smiles as if to say "Pleased to meet you."

"I know you're Brad," says Erigan. "Don't be stupid."

"You shouldn't call other people stupid."

Erigan's jagged teeth bite his lip. "I could kill you, you know."

"I know."

"Then shut the hell up."

"You swore."

Erigan raises his eyebrows and Brad pulls away from the headboard. He shifts his weight to the other side of the bed.

"What are you doing?" Erigan asks.

Brad freezes. "I'm getting up."

"Why?"

"Thirsty," he says.

Erigan sighs. "Stay here, I'm not done with you yet."

Brad looks disappointed. His lower lip sticks out, but just a bit to not be too obvious. Erigan doubts that Brad even knows that he's doing it.

"You can get water when I'm done with you," Erigan says.

Brad nods and pulls himself back into bed.

"You're kinda cool," Brad says. "I like your horn."

Erigan scowls. "I should really just kill you."

"How'd you lose it? What happened to it?"

"I lost it," Erigan says. "A long time ago."

"Did you look under your bed?" Brad asks. He's completely serious, much to Erigan's delight. "That's where I lost my tooth once. Tooth fairy missed it."

"There is no tooth fairy, Brad."

Brad grins. "I know. I'm not a little kid."

Erigan shakes the smile from his face. "So you don't know where you're from, kid?"

Brad raises an eyebrow.

"I'll take that as a no."

Brad's facial reactions freeze still. His eyes move slowly toward the door.

The door handle rustles.

"You should be careful," he says. "My mom is coming."

But when Brad tries to look for Erigan, he thinks that his new funny-looking friend is already gone.

"Where'd you go?" Brad says.

Erigan sits in the shadows of the room at the end. Wedged between a box full of toys and a rocking chair currently occupied by a stuffed bear sitting upright.

Sophie pops her head in between the door and the wall. The hallway light creeps in through the doorway's cracks. Sophie's hair appears pulled up behind her, not in a ponytail but just bunched together to be out of her face.

Erigan likes the look as he imagines it on the dead white and black-streaks color of Lilith's hair.

Brad tries his best not to show his mother that he knows something she doesn't. His grins would certainly give it away if Erigan had to guess, but he sees from the bags underneath Sophie's eyes that she's not in the mood to care, let alone notice.

"Who are you talking to?" she says.

"My friend."

"Again?" she says.

"He's not imaginary, mom. I promise."

Erigan grins, holds still.

"Well maybe I'll meet him someday," she says and then before losing the door she says gentle but firm: "Lights out, buddy."

"My light is out."

The door opens again and without a single word from his mother, Brad looks downward at the floor and mutters, "Sorry."

Erigan waits for the sound of the door being shut completely, but it never comes. It remains cracked just slightly. Enough that she could not see him walk about the room, but enough that she could easily hear the conversation.

Erigan walks from the shadowy corner of the bedroom and puts his index finger to his lips.

Brad nods and pretends to lock up mouth and throw away the key.

"I have to go," Erigan mouths. His breath and voice just loud enough for Brad to recognize the words. "But I'll be back."

Brad nods and pretends to lay down again.

His eyes, however, remain open.

"Go to sleep, Brad," says Erigan in a whisper. "I can't do this while you're watching."

Brad closes his eyes and then brings his hands over his eyes with such force that he slaps himself.

Erigan shrugs and darkens himself. In this form, he gets to play with drama. With emotions.

More importantly, he gets to have fun. And fun he has. Erigan twirls his tail around his waist and allows for his body to walk the lines between realities.

At the moment he exists somewhere between the air molecules and the light. He sees everything but knows that simple human eyes cannot and will not sense him.

He walks through the wall and into the next room of their apartment.

As he leaves, however, he catches the faintest whisper. The sound of Brad mumbling or whispering—he can't tell which—the words, "Goodnight, friend."

Chapter Twenty-Seven

Since demons and ex-gods do not have to sleep, Erigan waits patiently for Sophie to come to bed. He sits only at the edge of the bed, nigh invisible except for the subtle weight and pressure he exerts onto the bed sheets.

Erigan doesn't want Sophie to see him, only to sense him.

The woman, he figures, might be the answer. Or an answer. He doesn't care which, as long as something happens.

When the lights in the apartment flick off Erigan sits upright and lets his ears do all the work. He listens to the lazy scratches of Sophie's padded house flippers slap along the wooden floor. When they reach the bedroom, she doesn't turn on the lights.

Two thousand five hundred years ago, he'd take

advantage of this situation. Hell, he and the other gods would have running bets who could bed her first.

Zeus almost nearly always won. He was the King of the Olympians. They sort of had to let him. He was a proud and vengeful king.

But here and now, nothing would stop him from getting into her bed, turning them both into animals—maybe swans—and having his way with her. With no water, he'd need something domestic. Maybe dogs. That was a thing, wasn't it?

Sophie undoes her pants and lets them drop to the floor. She leaves her shirt on, an oversized white shirt with red sleeves. On it, a black and white mouse looks like he's presenting himself in front of an audience.

It was cute, but Erigan never understood the appeal of a cartoon mouse.

What he cared about was what was underneath that shirt.

Sophie moves like she's half-asleep to the left side of the bed. She plops down and almost immediately closes her eyes and begins to doze off.

It's as if he can feel the air begin to vibrate, signs that she may begin to snore at any moment.

Nothing irritated him more.

Well, that and arrogance. Humans should leave the arrogance to those that have actually earned it.

Sophie turns her body to face her bedroom window. The shades are slightly drawn open, allowing for her to see a great view of the town's downtown area. Even from his vantage point, Erigan can see almost down the Main Street area and into the parks at the other end of the bars. The street lights cast an eerie yellow-white glow along the streets in small circles that provide little places to hide.

Lots of shadows, however, for those who are looking for them.

When Sophie's body remains calm for a few seconds, Erigan turns around and still on the bed. He allows himself to gain more mass, becoming material enough for her to feel his weight shift on the bed.

Sophie turns around.

Erigan, still invisible, thinks of grabbing a quick kiss, but lets her eyes tell the story. She's panicked, but too brave to show it.

He's seen this look in humans' eyes before. And each and every time, he's loved it.

He allows his fingers to glide gently down her arm, barely touching the thin, light hairs along her bicep and forearm.

Sophie shivers at first and then scratches along her right arm.

Erigan shivers himself. But his comes more from delight than fear.

He allows his fingers to pull lightly against her hair. He looks for a place, an empty plot of skin, for him to cause her to get more chills—the fun kind of chills.

Erigan spots a small, blank spot on her shoulders, just below her neck. In the light, it looks almost blue.

Cold. Soft.

The color almost reminds him of the blue skies of home Olympus.

Hell could never be considered his home.

Leaning in, his nose meets with the fading scent of roses and another scent he cannot recognize. Sweet, but not.

This close, he also senses bits of the alcohol from the perfume. The drying agent that keeps it on the skin.

Erigan's nose is so close he feels the fine hairs of her back against the tip of his nose.

Sophie squirms, her shoulders moving in a wave motion.

She feels it, too, it seems.

Erigan smirks. He opens his mouth just wide enough to blow a light gust of his musty breath across her skin.

Sophie shivers again, her shoulders reacting with goosebumps up to her ears.

Time to go one step closer to the edge.

With his mouth still open, he lets his tongue come out of his mouth and lick against her back. He tastes the salt, the flowers, the cream—all of it mixed up into a harsh combination that almost burns his taste buds.

"What the fuck," Sophie says quickly. She moves to get out of the bed but misses something in her haste. Her hands slap against the floor and her knees thump.

Erigan bites his cheeks to keep from laughing.

Sophie, however, panics. Loud, deep breathes. Her shoulders heave forward, then back. Opposite of her chest.

She peeks above the bed but sees nothing.

No, not nothing. Something.

She sees him.

Erigan rolls backwards just slightly. He watches with great interest, a smile along his face and excitement driving down his muscles like race cars.

Sophie's hand slaps the bed, feeling for where the dent used to be—the spot just in front of where Erigan deliciously taunts her.

He smirks and snorts.

Sophie sits up. Her eyes wide. Her back straightens out and before she seems to even know it, she's exposed her entire body to anyone who might want to attack.

It's then that she freaks out. And climbs back into bed.

Erigan can see the confusion in her face.

She doesn't risk being exposed in the darkness. But she knows that the trespasser might be in her bed.

Which was the safer option? She wonders.

Erigan has seen this before. He loves every steps of it. Could right a book about it if he had ever bothered to read.

He was a God. Never needed those types of things. And English hadn't been invented for a few thousand years after his newborn feet ever touched the earth.

"Who are you?" he whispers.

Sophie shivers. "Hello?" She grasps a tight hold onto the sheets and pulls it up around her neck, to her chin.

"Who's there?"

Erigan sees that she didn't answer the question. Means she didn't hear it. Sensed it, but didn't hear it.

It was just as well.

Erigan climbs out of the bed. He recognizes the sudden sense of relaxation in Sophie's body. Her shoulders drop, her body loosens up under the covers.

She knows—somehow—that she's out of danger.

Erigan watches for a moment as she tucks herself back into her bed. She feels more confident, he can tell. Her breathing slows and soon her chest moves up and down rhythmically to the patterns of a deep sleep.

"Why are you important?" he says before fading into the shadows.

Chapter Twenty-Eight

Erigan had spent that morning watching the television. He had discovered something that both entertained him and made him feel like his old self again.

Reality television. At least that's what a news reporter calls it on another channel.

On the show, a bunch of young men and women yell and throw things at each other. The word "bitch" is thrown around like a common epithet.

But whereas an epithet is a title of honor, a story-within-a-word, these women get angry when called a bitch.

Erigan takes note. No calling anyone a bitch. Unless you want someone to throw a high-heeled shoe at you.

Watching closely, Erigan takes note that the two women want to fight. A coliseum battle without the coliseum.

The concept interests him. Back on Olympus, he and the other gods had spent many hours of their lives trying to wager bets. Observing the silly, arrogant humans down below was more of a sport than a hobby.

Aphrodite used to even call it her job.

Whatever happened to her? He wonders.

Watching all morning, he feels something nag at him. He can be a human and walk around in human skin all his unnatural life, but he still needs a job to make it official. To fit in.

The teenagers on the shows, they didn't seem to have jobs. Just lots of money. And this thing called a computer. And a cell phone.

To fit in, he needs one of those.

Behemoth would be useless in this endeavor. To acquire these cell phones, he needs someone more knowledgeable. More human.

And with that, he changes his clothes with a snap of his fingers to something he saw on the television: dark blue jeans, sandals (those weren't going anywhere), and a pink and white striped shirt with the collar popped up.

It looks to be popular all over the television. The shows change, but the style always remained the same. Pink. Stripes. Jeans or sorts.

Erigan, being the logical little god that he was, sees that this must be the acceptable form of dress. Maybe even attractive.

He hopes—without knowing why he gave a fuck—that his next door neighbors will like it, too.

Erigan locks up behind him and walks the ten feet to Sophie's apartment door.

There's some clicking on the other end. Chains sliding and pieces of metal banging against wood. It reminds him of the torture machines the humans got creative with in the medieval ages.

Finally, the door creeks open and remains cracked enough for an eye to peer through.

"Hello?" says Sophie's eye.

Erigan smiles and puts his best face forward. "Hello, Sophie," he says. "Good morning."

"How do you know my name?" she says.

Erigan is not prepared for that question. He looks behind him, at the office and then turns to face his would-be accuser. "I was told it," he says. "By her. You know. That lady."

"Peggy?" says Sophie. "Ya, figures. She's got a big mouth." The door tries to open again, but meets resistance. "Wait one second," she says.

The door closes and one more chain scrapes against wooden. Finally, the door pops open and Sophie stands there in a red shirt and black shorts.

"What can I do for you, sir?"

"I need a phone."

Sophie shrugs. "I can't help you with that," she says. "I'm fresh out of minutes." She begins to close the door.

"But you do know how to get one, right?" Erigan's rather small hand grips the handle on the outside. All of his muscle power goes into keeping from slamming into his face.

"Sure, you go into the store and ask for a cell phone."

Erigan pushes the door open and, seeing the look of fear on Sophie's face, he continues to push even harder. He even rests a sandaled foot in the doorway.

"Listen, if I'm going to do this, I need someone who can help me out. You're my neighbor, so I was hoping you could help me out." Erigan raises his eyebrows, puts out his lower lip the way he had seen Brad do only earlier. "Please?"

Sophie's face relaxes. Almost a smile. "Why the hell not," she says, "I don't have much else going on right now."

She opens the door and Erigan steps in. He looks around.

"Where's Brad?"

"My son?" she says. "At school. We have to be back by three-thirty or he'll freak out."

Erigan nods and rubs his hands together. Even he could not see this going any better. "Cool," he says.

Sophie pauses. "Say that again?"

"Cool?" Erigan holds his smile.

Sophie shakes her head. "That sounds so strange coming from you. I don't know why." She throws her purse over her shoulder and grabs keys from a hook on the wall. "Where did you say you were from?"

Erigan thinks back. Did he say he was from somewhere?

"Um, Greece?" he mutters.

Sophie nods. "That explains the shirt."

Between the alternating white and pink walls of the store and the bright flashy lights of the cell phones, Erigan's eyes wander every half second. He tries to concentrate from one phone to the next, even pressing buttons and listening to the different tones.

"Why do the numbers make music?" he says.

Sophie shrugs. "I don't think anyone has ever asked that question before. I don't know."

"What can I help you with?" says a young man, glasses and quite rotund. The man's brown hair seems to be falling out, almost balding. He introduces himself as Raymond. "You know, everybody loves me."

Sophie grins and turns around to hide her laughter.

Erigan shrugs and nods. "I don't sense the touch of Cupid upon you."

Sophie stifles a bit of laughter.

Raymond's face turns flushed. His nose and cheeks turns a bright red. "So you're looking at this one?" says Raymond. "Nice choice. It has an amazing screen and an eight megapixel camera."

Erigan shakes his head and shrugs. "I have no idea what you're talking about."

Raymond's eyes narrow. Erigan can sense that the man is just as confused as he is. Two different topics, but just as confused.

"A megapixel is a way of measuring the dots in a picture."

"Dots in a picture. Got it." Erigan nods and holds the phone next to Raymond's in the same manner. "Like this?"

Raymond shrugs. "I'm sorry?"

"Does this have eight mega dots?"

Raymond tries not to smile. "No, sir. It does not." He doesn't attempt to correct Erigan.

A mistake, Erigan thinks.

"Why do I want lots of mega dots in my pictures?"

Sophie chimes in, leaning over the counter. "In case you want to take a lot of pictures, it helps with the quality. The higher the number, the better the picture."

Raymond nods with approval.

Erigan shrugs. "No, not that one."

Raymond rests the phone back on the counter. "What do you intend to use your phone for?"

"To get a job."

There's a stunned silence. Raymond looks to Sophie as a measure of his response.

Sophie nods and turns around to view the rest of the store.

"So you don't have a job?"

"Not here," says Erigan. "I do back in Hell."

The two humans both blinked. Frozen in confusion.

"Hellas," Erigan corrected. "In Hellas." The humans' confusion continued. "In Greek we call Greece Hellas. Sorry."

Raymond moves slowly, trying to adjust and examine what just happened here. "Ri-i-i-ght."

"So what did you want to do with your phone?" says Sophie. "Record stuff? Take pictures? Call people? Get on the internet."

The last word catches Erigan's ears and he smiles. "That one. The internet one."

"Good," says Raymond. "I have this one here. Made by Samorola." He eyes Erigan and takes a long breath. "It's easy to use—"

Sophie snorts back some laughter.

"—and not too expensive."

Erigan takes the phone into his hands, holding just as he saw Raymond grip it. "And how much?"

"Only three ninety-nine."

Erigan offers a blank look.

Raymond nods. "Right. From Greece. Dollars. Here in America we deal with dollars."

"I don't have dollars."

"Drachma?" says Raymond with a sarcastic smile.

"That is not really comparable to dollars," says Erigan. "Don't be silly."

"I'm being silly?" says Raymond. First a question, then a statement. "I'm being silly. Sorry about that."

Erigan nods. "And what I don't have money?"

Chapter Twenty-Nine

"No job, no money, no bank account," says Raymond. He rips the half-completed credit application. "I can't really take you seriously if you're not prepared for this."

"But I demand that I have the phone, you retarded mortal."

Sophie bites her lip, but manages to hold back the laughter. She pulls back on Erigan's shoulder and looks him in the eyes.

"Listen, we can maybe get you some cash somewhere else, okay? Then you can get the phone."

Erigan measures the honesty in Sophie's eyes. Each of them look to be green, though it depends on the angle at which he looks at her. The one constant, he does notice, is the fact that each are speckled with brown flecks along the lower half.

"You have beautiful, unique eyes," he says.

Sophie takes a step back and fixes her hair.

Raymond tosses the pieces of application into the trash bin and folds his hands on the desk. "If there's anything I can help you with, please feel free to let me know. You know, if you happen upon some money or something."

Erigan's fist clench tightly at his sides. If he wasn't so worried about making a show right about now...

"Thank you," says Sophie. She releases her grip on Erigan completely. With her hands on the door and just talking to no one in particular, she shouts out. "Have a nice day!"

Erigan waves goodbye to Raymond, who's not paying attention, but lost in the screen of his computer.

"Where are you going? You said you'd help me find a phone."

Sophie stops at her white two-door vehicle, putting her foot inside the driver's side. "I'm going home."

"So you're not going to help me get a phone?"

"You don't have any money, Erigan!" Sophie's voice echoes across the parking lot and off the strip mall behind them. "Did you just expect me to pay for them?"

"That was an option?" says Erigan. "Then why didn't you?"

Sophie doesn't give that a response. She blows air upwards, moving her bangs temporarily out of her eyes. "Good bye."

"Stop!" he says.

She doesn't.

Erigan runs to the front of the car. He's there in a blink of an eye.

Sophie is too distracted from her attempts to get the car started to notice. "Get off my fucking car!" she screams.

"I'm not on your fucking car," says Erigan.

"Your hand?"

Erigan looks down. "You will not leave me here. Alone."

"Who the hell do you think you are to give me orders!" says Sophie. "You're lucky I thought you were cute enough to go shopping, but sir, you clearly have no idea what the hell you're doing."

It was even evident to her.

"You think I'm attractive?" he says.

"Notice? What? Why?"

"Never mind that." Erigan walks to the passenger side of the car and rests his hand on the door's black plastic handle. "Where else can we go get a phone?"

"With no money? It's not happening."

"Things were so much easier back in the good old days."

Sophie slaps the steering wheel. "Tell me about it."

Erigan opens the door and sits next to Sophie. The interior of the car is all gray, soft and cushions. The dashboard appears to be pulling away from the harder plastic pieces underneath. The dark gaps—tiny and more like crevices than real gaps—reminded him of the crags of rocks in Hell.

"So?"

Sophie shrugs. "So what?"

"You think I am cute," says Erigan. He smiles with one side of his mouth. Winks at her. Wiggles his nose.

Sophie beings to laugh. An uncomfortable laughter.

Erigan pretends to laugh as well. He likes her disarmed like this, uncomfortable. It makes her easier to pick off later.

"You're cute. Ish. I guess," she says. Her eyes drift away suddenly from Erigan's green eyes to brown stucco outside of the strip mall building in front of them.

"You are not too bad yourself," he says.

"You don't say." She smiles. Pushes her hair behind her ears. Finally she gives in. "Fine," she says in an exasperated huff. "If you want to get a phone, we can go over there. Wally's World. You'll find damn near everything over there. You won't have a great plan, but you'll have a phone."

The drive is a short one to the store building across the parking lot. As they move, however, Erigan catches Sophie giving him a look twice.

"What are you looking for?" he says.

"What was Greece like?" she says. "Before you moved here?"

"Hellas was a great place. Green. Lots of farms. Lots of people in smaller villages. Animals all over." Erigan feels as if his heart is being crushed under his chest. Yet, it's not an unpleasant feeling. "I miss that time so much."

"Why leave? I mean, if you liked it so much."

Erigan nods. "I came here for a job, but I got let go as soon as I got to Saraday."

Sophie's face curls to one side of her face. "That sucks, man. I'm sorry."

"You were not responsible," he says. Erigan watches her face for a reaction, to test if she was responsible.

No traces of twitching. No smiles.

She's either that good or she's as fucking clueless as he is.

"So I came here, got let go, and now I'm stuck with no money and no phone."

"And no job," she adds.

Erigan nods. "Right. No job."

Erigan and Sophie walk in silence to the end of the store. A large blue and white sign—Electronics— hangs from the ceiling with thin chains. Erigan grows enamored with the bright colors and intensity of the lighting.

"This place is a circus," he says. "How does one shop here without getting distracted?"

He taps on the glass that separates him from a few dozen reflective plastic electronic pads.

"What are these?"

"These are tablets. And out of your price range."

"I have no money," he says. "How does one have a price range without money?"

"Didn't you have money in Greece? You know,

Drachmas or something?"

"We had money, sure, but we still bartered." Erigan taps on the glass again. "That one is pretty. And basically anything we needed, my father made sure I had. There was little I was left wanting."

Sophie is half-paying attention as she fingers through a big basket of thin plastic rectangles with colorful pictures of people on them.

"Your father gave you everything?" she said. She holds something up and reads the back of it. The front of it reads Spartacus in bold red letters. "Is your father like a millionaire?"

Erigan nods like he knows what she meant by millionaire. "He was the master of all he saw. People trembled at his feet. He could take anyone he wanted, when he wanted. As long as his wife wasn't watching."

"So he was like some mob boss or something?"

"More like a big family," he says.

"So like the Mafia?" Sophie drops the box in the basket. "That's pretty cool. Never knew a mob boss before."

She looks up when she realizes that the small glass display cases were being opened. "Oh good, you found. Wait, what the fuck are you doing?"

Sophie throws her hands onto Erigan's and tries to pull them out of the display case.

"I wanted to see these," he says. "To see if they are any good."

"You can't just take them."

Erigan raises an eye.

"That's why there is glass in front of them," she says. "To keep people like you out of there."

"People like me? Strong, handsome gods?"

Sophie holds out her hand and waits for Erigan to hand over the white phone. "You might be adorable, but you're poor and naïve. That will get you nowhere with any girl."

"What about you?" he says. Winks.

"I said any girl, right?" She closes the door just as they both hear footsteps coming in their direction.

"Is there something I can help you find?" says the voice those footsteps belong to.

The voice reveals itself to belong to an elderly lady wearing a red vest and a shirt with purple and blue flowers all along, well, everywhere. Her white hair is short and curly, looser curls than Erigan's, but not too different.

Erigan pats his own hair down as he peeks a glance at hers.

Erigan points to the glass. "I'd like that, please."

Sophie kicks Erigan in the shin. "You don't have any money, you dolt."

"Would you like to apply for a Wally's credit card?" The clerk's name badge reads "Madge." Her speech slows as she tries to repeat the hard c sound over again.

"Do I need a job or money to apply for this plastic money?"

The clerk looks confused. "I don't think so. Why

would you?" she says. "Let me go check the form." She wanders away toward the center of the department.

Erigan reaches back into the case and takes the phone out.

"Put it back," Sophie whispers. "You'll get yourself arrested."

Erigan shrugs. "They wouldn't dare." Erigan spots a smirk in Sophie's lips. "Come on."

Erigan twists around on his heels and walks toward the front of the store.

Sophie says nothing as she trails behind him. A safe distance, Erigan realizes, but not too far either. He senses her fear.

Sniffing out fear was his specialty in Hell.

"If you want to do this right," he shouts back to her, "you will need to be up here with me, beautiful."

They leave the front of the store and out into the bright, humid outside air.

Erigan stops about five steps away from the front door.

"That electronic thing," she says. "Those sensors didn't go off." She points to Erigan. "You're lucky."

"Bah," says Erigan. He smiles and blushes. "It wasn't anything special."

"But you do know that if you don't sign up for service you won't get that thing to work."

"Sign up? Service?"

Ten seconds later, the two are back in the electronics

department.

"Where did you go?" says Madge the clerk. "I've been looking around for you." She holds out the paper. "It doesn't say anything here about having a job or money."

She flips the form front and back. She only pretends to read the small print on the bottom of the form.

Erigan watches her eyes not move as she pretends to read.

Madge smiles. "So if you'd like to help me out, you can fill this out right here."

Chapter Thirty

"Can't you wait until we get home to open this box? You're like a kid at Christmas."

Sophie rolls the windows down to take care of the rattling sound that can only be described as excessive. And maybe to cool down the hot car in the ninety-five degree sun.

"If this is what Christmas feels like, sign me up," says Erigan. He takes out a plastic sheet of something. Something pink and full of air bubbles. He squeezes the bubbles and one of them explodes in his hands.

Sophie jumps in her seat and grabs her chest. "Don't do that, okay? You nearly gave me a heart attack."

Erigan pops two more before tossing it out of the window.

"You shouldn't really do that," Sophie says. She pulls over into the far right lane. "I should stop and make you pick that up," she says. She pauses, the realization of what she did washes over her. "But you're an adult and that would be weird. "

Erigan looks out the window and shrugs. She starts the car again.

Sophie continues, "Here in America, we have a no littering policy. Are you serious? You never had Christmas before? Are you Jewish or something?"

Erigan had only met Jesus once before wandering a desert. However, he had no understanding what Jews actually were at the time.

Erigan just knew that the Jews didn't particularly like Erigan or anyone who worshipped him.

"Evil worshippers," they called his followers.

"No, I'm not Jewish," said Erigan. He flips through a thick white book about the size of his palm. Full of dull black words, he tosses it off to the side. "I know full well about Christmas, though."

Erigan's eyes don't leave the package on his lap. Instead, he sniffs the fresh humid air and melting asphalt as the trucks in front of them attempt to repave the road amongst daytime traffic.

"Could they possibly make this any more inconvenient," Sophie screams out the window.

The men, they don't pay her any attention. They probably heard that same scream about ten times just this morning.

"If you have to ask, the answer is probably yes."

"Why are they doing this now? Why in this heat? Are

they fucking crazy? Proof," she says, pointing at the men and then slapping the steering wheel, "that there is no God," says Sophie.

"Oh there's a God alright." Erigan shrugs. "Lots of them if you want to get technical."

"So you're like what? Hindu or something?"

Erigan shrugs. "No, I think cows are too tasty to give up." Erigan looks to Sophie's exasperated stare into the traffic cones in front of her. "You wouldn't believe me if I told you."

"Try me," says Sophie. She smirks and winks. A girl who likes challenges.

"Fine," says Erigan. He starts to say something, but nothing comes out of his mouth. His words decide that it's bad idea before they cross the crooks of his jagged white teeth.

So backtracking, he says, "I'm a firm believer that there is plenty of stuff you don't know about the world. For instance..." he begins, but there's a tap on his window.

Erigan looks over. He immediately rolls his eyes and then rolls down the window.

The big brute with his bright orange vest blocks all of Erigan's view. If the vest were any louder, he'd be able to hear it.

"Excuse me, sir? You're free to go, you know," the brute says. The giant paw waves them forward.

"What are you doing here?" Erigan says.

"I'm sorry, you must have me pegged for someone

else, sir."

"Bullshit," Erigan says.

Sophie taps Erigan on the shoulder. "You know this guy?"

"Yes, yes, I do." He smiles, but the man waves his hands.

"No he does not, ma'am. Now if you'd kindly like to go around our truck, you can move along now. We're almost done."

"Behe—um, Herc, what are you doing here?"

The brute zips across his mouth and then gently and quickly moves his index finger across his throat.

Erigan nods. He's not sure what he's done, but he knows it will be a topic of discussion when he sees his giant friend next.

"Let's just go, then, Sophie, shall we? Thanks, sir I've never met before!"

Sophie won't stop leaning over Erigan's lap. "Hey, who are you? Have I seen you before?"

Erigan taps the back of the woman's head and points forward. "They're letting you go, you know."

"But you said you knew that man?"

When Sophie looks up and then back out the passenger side window, she notices that she's looking at buildings and sidewalk, not a large seven-foot brute.

"Where'd he go?" she says.

"Are you going to go or not?" Erigan waves his hand forward and someone honks behind them. "See? Go."

Sophie keeps peering through the corner of her eyes,

looking for strange tall men that might be standing at the edge of the road.

"Stop it," says Erigan. He scolds her without looking up at the road or back at her. Pieces of white scraps of paper and cords fall to the floor of the car. "He's not there. And I never said knew him."

"But you just said—shit!"

Erigan looks up, half expecting an accident.

"Do you mind if we make a quick stop and pick up Brad?"

Chapter Thirty-One

Though he had no right to say it now, and he knew it, Erigan would have liked to straight up refuse to go pick up Brad from his elementary school.

But there he is. Windows rolled down in the white two door coupe that Sophie called a Forks-wagon.

Erigan's elbow rest out the window as his eyes and fingers fiddles with his new cell phone.

The thing is a black and shiny marvel of human technology. Pressing this thick button on the side, the screen lights up with black and green bits flying in every direction, finally welcoming him with warm pink lettering.

Erigan turns it off again and then on.

"You know, if you keep doing that, you're going to wear out the battery." Sophie stands on the side of the road, her ass resting along the side of the car. Her arms lie crossed across her chest. She looks happy, but impatient.

Erigan smiles as the pink words welcome him back to the phone.

"When is your child supposed to be free?"

"Be free?" Sophie says. He can hear her repeating the words to herself. "Why do you have to say it like that?"

"He's being released, is he not?"

Sophie shrugs.

"Then your child is going to be free. Being released implies that he's being held prisoner." He looks out the window and is greeted with the side view of Sophie's round ass. "I should know."

Sophie pauses. "You were in jail?"

Hostility in her voice.

"No, I was not in jail, but I had a place—an old job—that I just couldn't wait to get away from." He pauses and sticks his head out again. His eyes nearly water from the bright sun. "To be released, if you will."

Sophie shrugs. "Cubicle office job?"

"How did you know?"

"I know the feeling. Couldn't wait to get the fuck out of there. All day making copies, taking phone calls. Telling people to hold on because whoever they wanted wasn't there."

"Whomever."

Sophie waves him off.

"Is he here yet?"

"No."

"Is he here now?"

"No."

"What about now?"

"Listen, if you don't have to wait, you're free to leave."

Erigan considers it for a second, then looks back down at his phone. "How does this help me get a job?"

"Brad!" Sophie shouts. She opens her arms and hugs her little boy. By Erigan's account, the boy looks tired. His blond hair a mess and eyes almost shut closed.

"You're here!" says Brad.

Erigan adjusts his shirt and looks up to Sophie. "I can explain," he says.

"The man we met in the hallway, right? Our new neighbor!" Brad extends his hand out to Erigan to shake it.

Erigan does so, but with his eyes fixed on Sophie. Waiting for a reaction. To know that this isn't as bad as it seems.

"Brad," says Sophie. "Erigan. Erigan, Brad."

Brad's eyebrows arch. "Erigan?"

Erigan smiles, nods. "Strange name, I know." He taps the phone to his lap. It would only take a few seconds to kill them both if he had to.

But only if his cover was blown.

He looks at Sophie's perfectly contented face. She sits in the car seat and watches the rear view mirror until she hears a click from the backseat.

"Thank you," she says with a wink.

Okay, it would probably take about ten seconds if she decided to run. Maybe he'd have to kill her first. The boy is—apparently to someone—more valuable.

"Wow! You got a new phone!" says Brad. He reaches out in front of him. "Can I see it?"

Erigan hands it over without much thought, but Sophie's eyes dart from the rear view mirror to Erigan to the phone in the backseat.

"Brad," she says, "please give that back to Mr. Erigan."

Brad offers the phone for brief second, then snaps his hand back to his chest. "I know someone named Erigan," he says.

"You do?" says Erigan.

Sophie's ignorant eyes have left the road completely, just concentrating on the rear view mirror. "You did, honey? Where?"

"You don't like him, Mom. Remember?"

Erigan grins. "You don't?"

"He has this imaginary friend that visits him. He's a little too old for imaginary friends," she says. Her voice puts extra emphasis on the too old part.

"Is that so?"

"Did you have any imaginary friends, Mr. Erigan?"

Erigan thinks for a moment. Can an imaginary friend have an imaginary friend? "No, Brad. I never did. Sadly."

He smiles and turns around. "Can I have this back?" Erigan says.

Brad's tongue sticks out the side of his mouth as he

taps a few more buttons on the screen. "Just a second," he says. He makes one final tap with a wild flourish of his fingers. "There you go."

He offers the phone back to Erigan and crosses his arms across his chest like his mother.

"What did you do?" Erigan says. He flips the phone over twice to check for signs.

"I just cleaned it up," Brad says. "Got rid of some stuff for you."

"Oh, thank you, Brad. I wish I had an assistant like you at my old job."

The car pulls up to the apartment building and everyone gets out of the car.

"Can Mr. Erigan come over for dinner tonight, mom?"

Sophie pauses, put on the spot. She shrugs. "No, hun, not tonight. Maybe some other time."

Erigan's lower lip slips out again.

"Okay then," says Brad. He hauls his backpack over his shoulder and holds the door open for the other adults. "Next time then. Good bye, Mr. Erigan."

Brad waves at Erigan and then goes inside his apartment.

Erigan, however, sits outside on the steps, entranced by his new device. Try as he might, he finds the letters a bit difficult to make out on the small screen.

"Why do we not have these in Hell?" he says.

"You know how Hell is," says Behemoth. His body finishes fading into Earth's reality and he sits down. His chosen dress for this occasion is a fancy set of black pants and a black wife beater that simply makes his shoulders seem as large as his head. "We can't get any good technology down there. Just Commodore 64s and the original iPhone. That's part of why it's Hell."

"Did you find out anything about me being stranted here?" Erigan says.

"No answers," says Behemoth. He sits down next to Erigan. It's not Behemoth's butt, but the broadness of his shoulders that forces Erigan to scoot over no less than three times.

"I need a job to fit in. Living up here is expensive."

"I can give you the cash you need," he says. Behemoth pulls the money out of his pocket.

"How do you get all of that?" Erigan says.

"You know how they say you can't take it with you?" says Behemoth.

Erigan nods.

"Well, it's true."

"So you just used magic?" says Erigan.

Behemoth hands over another stack of hundred dollar bills. "You're no fun up here."

"I'm trying to figure this whole thing out," he says. "Last night, I found a statue of a baby ram hidden in this giant leather box."

"A ram? So what?"

"I'm Hermes Kriophoros. Now tell me who the hell knows about that up here, amidst these Christians and atheists?"

"I think you're just reading into things," Behemoth says. He lightly taps Erigan on the back.

"I can't enjoy this vacation while I feel like I'm being watched."

"And now the tables are turned?" says Behemoth. He smirks.

"And now the tables are turned." Erigan looks at his bestial friend and says, "I'm not liking this. Not one bit."

"It's just a ram's statue," says Behemoth. He stands up and adjusts his pants. "You're reading into things," he says.

Behemoth reaches into his pants and pulls out a leather wallet. "Here, for you."

"What is this?"

"Enchanted. A wallet. Every time you open it, you get money. Stole it from Mephistopheles."

"I cannot use this. We all know what happened to Midas," says Erigan. "Are you sure this is okay?"

"The Olympians aren't watching you, so it's okay to take it. Besides, you were Zeus' favorite."

"No, that was Athene."

Behemoth shrugs. "Potato, potahto."

Behemoth disappears just as fast as Erigan can blink and open his eyes.

He opens the wallet once and a handful of bills pops out of the opening. He closes it and opens it again.

More money, almost twice as much, explodes out of the wallet.

He takes out a wad of bills and stuffs it into his pants.

Chapter Thirty-Two

Sophie's eyes are greeted with green bills, fanned out in front of her face.

"Dinner is my treat," says Erigan. He smiles proudly, like a lion who just caught a gazelle.

"We can't, really," she says.

The door slides open and bounces off the wall inside. Brad's head sticks out beside Sophie's waist.

"Cool! Where'd you get the money!"

Sophie's eyes open wide. "Ya, where'd you get the money?"

Erigan hands the fanned out bills to Sophie's shaking, reluctant hands. "Please, take this. For the phone."

Sophie goes through the bills, counting while her lips move. "This is a little bit too much," she says. "Here, take it back."

She thrusts the money back at Erigan but he gently

presses her hands away. "No, it's yours. I promise, I'll be fine."

"Where did you get the money?" she says again.

"It doesn't matter," he says. "So, dinner or no?"

"Can we go to Peter Piper?" says Brad. He tugs on his mother's leg. When that doesn't work, he stands between her and Erigan. "C'mon? Pizza?"

Sophie sighs. Her shoulders collapse. "Fine," she says. "Pizza."

"Yes!" Brad says. He thrusts his arms downward and then shoots upward. "Pizza!" He runs into the apartment and comes back only seconds later with his shoes half on.

He pauses. Checks the looks on both Erigan's and Sophie's faces.

"Wait. Are we not going now?"

The three take a table nearest to the video games. The music blares something that Erigan finds himself tapping his foot to. There are balloons at each and every table. Bright ones that all say Happy Birthday on them.

The tables—red, purple, and yellow—are currently vacant, but with the table settings and balloons, they already look busy.

"Are you sure if we sit here?"

Erigan nods. "Yes, I am sure we'll be fine. No one will dare move us."

"You've never even been to this country before," says Sophie with a smile. She slaps the red table. "How would you know?"

"I guess you do not," says Erigan. "But you can trust me."

"Is that so?" she says. She takes the money out of her pocket and lays it on the table. "Listen, you aren't going to buy me, you know."

"Buy you? For what? Slavery is allowed again?"

"Buy my affections. You *are* trying to date me, right?"

"If I had wanted you, I would just take you," says Erigan.

It was true. He remembered the Gods taking whomever they so desired. At night, raping them in their sleep, as animals. It didn't matter. As long as they got their rocks off, all was good.

The women—and the occasional man—knew better than to fight.

But this one. She was feisty. Aggressive. Protective over her spawn.

There was something about it that Erigan had not seen in nearly a thousand years.

"You love your son very much. I get it," says Erigan. His voice is low, calm, seductive. "But—and I know this is a stretch—but I am not interested in you."

It was only completely a half lie.

Sophie sits back. "So you're saying I'm ugly or something?"

Erigan wipes his face with his bare hands. "No, I'm not saying that you're ugly. Quite the opposite. But I'm not interested in anyone at the moment."

Correction. Only interested in you and your son.

But saying that out loud, in this restaurant, is likely to cause more trouble than it's worth.

"I'm simply saying that I just got here and I am trying to figure things out."

To his surprise, all of that was truth.

"Right," she says. She sits back even further, even slumps in the seat. "So you're being nice to be nice?"

"Is that so unheard of?"

Sophie raises her eyebrows and widens her eyes. "It surprisingly is. Let's order some pizza." Her mouth flattens out and Erigan notices that she's angry.

At him? Maybe. He doesn't know what he did wrong.

He stands up anyway and follows at a safe distance.

Off in the distance, Brad plays around with a game with bright flashing lights moving around in a circle. Surrounding the circle are bright white numbers.

"Come on," cries Brad. "You cheated!" He looks over at Erigan and his mother walking toward the counter. "We getting pizza finally? Don't forget the ranch."

His hands don't budge from the controls, but hover just over a small button that flashes red in rhythm with the musical sounds coming from the music.

So many flashing lights and pitchers of beer, Dionysus would have been proud to call this place home.

"Two pizzas, please," says Sophie. "Pepperoni and sausage. No vegetables. At all."

The boy behind the counter takes the order and tells them fifteen minutes. He places a small white piece of paper on a metal rack behind them and then disappears behind what looks like a giant metal oven.

"Do we wait here?" says Erigan.

"Unless you want to go play video games," she says. She shrugs and hands him a dollar. "Here. Go play. Have fun."

Erigan takes the money and folds it in his hand. He takes a single step toward the gaming area and then stops.

Where to go first?

He had faced the great witch Calypso and the anger of Hera herself, yet this mass hysteria of lights and music being thrown at you from every direction confused and intimidated him.

Hell certainly had nothing like this.

Well, not for fun, anyway.

"What's the point of this game?" Erigan says.

Brad nods toward the flashing lights. "See those lights? You're supposed to press this button on the highest number up there. Then you get that many tickets."

"You do this for tickets? Not money or something?"

Brad points over at a machine in the center of the room. "That one over there gives you coins if you win. But you don't get no money."

Erigan takes a step toward the game and looks at the golden tokens. Each one has words etched on the sides, though the flashing lights inside the machine keep the words from being easily read.

Erigan taps the machine and a few coins come out.

"Wow, do that again!" says Brad. He runs over toward Erigan and stretches out his hands. "Can I see?"

Erigan hands over one coin and keeps the other to himself. When he holds the coin up into the air to get a better view, he spots a familiar face in the background. Bearded, with a lion's cap.

"Dammit to hell anyway."

Chapter Thirty-Three

Erigan keeps a close eye on the beast-slash-best friend behind the counter. He works slowly, tossing up dough in thin discs into the air and then catching them with his volleyball-sized forearms.

"Can you hit it again?" says Brad. He tugs on Erigan's shirt. "C'mon, just one more time?"

Erigan bangs against the machine with the back of his fist. Coins come out in small trickles.

Still keeping an eye on Behemoth behind the counter, he slams his fist into the machine one more time, leaving a small dented mark.

The coins fly out in droves.

Brad drops to his knees and shoves the coins into his shirt.

"Excuse me, sir," says Behemoth. Once again he does not look at Erigan, but through him. "Could you please not beat on the machines?"

The boy who had originally taken the order moves around Behemoth, not paying any attention to him whatsoever.

Is he really here? Just messing with Erigan?

"Come over here and make me," Erigan says.

Behemoth smiles. His beard stretches clear across his face and his giant hands adjust the table. He slides over the counter and damn near hits his head against the metal clips that hang overhead.

The massive man steps up to Erigan, coming just close enough for Erigan's nose to massage the Behemoth's belly button. "I'm sorry, sir," he says slowly. "But I need for you to stop hitting the machines," he says through his teeth.

"Why are you here?"

"Why are *you* here?" says Behemoth.

"I am still trying to figure that out."

"You're supposed to be in hiding," says Behemoth. "Don't you realize who you pissed off?"

Erigan shrugs. "They will find me if they want to," he says. "Hell, they probably already did."

Behemoth smirks. "Especially if you're going to keep going on like this. I gave you that wallet to keep you still, but you're being a dick about this."

Brad looks up at the word "dick." His mouth makes a big, gaping "o" shape.

"Keep picking up those coins," says Erigan.

Brad shovels he last pile of coins into his shirt and

he walks slowly, legs bent like he's carrying a heavy goat in his arms, toward the table. "Mom! Look what I got! How many games you think this is?"

"You're cavorting with humans," says Behemoth. "And not in the fun way."

"I'm just getting to know the neighbors. You know. Being human."

"You gonna tap that?" he says. He looks over at Sophie, just collecting her pizzas and going to the table. "Cuz if you're not, I'm just gonna go for it, man. I know you saw her first so I'm giving you the benefit of being the first one in."

"I am not going to tap that," he says. "But you're not either. You will get our—correction—*my* cover blown."

"That won't be the only thing blown." Behemoth winks, smiles, and nudges Erigan's shoulders.

Over by the table, Sophie sits up like a groundhog. She stares in Erigan's direction. She looks confused.

"She already thinks she's seen you before," says Erigan. "You're going to ruin this for me."

Behemoth turns around and waves at Sophie. "Hello, miss!" he shouts.

"You're such an ass," Erigan says.

Behemoth goes over to the table and holds his hands behind his back. As he does this, his massive chest nearly rips the red polo shirt in half. He knows this and, once he realizes he has everyone's attention at the table, proceeds to make his pecs dance up and down.

Sophie's eyes widen, a slight smile, as she watches

the show.

"How is everything here tonight?" says Behemoth.

Erigan rolls his eyes and waves for Behemoth to leave.

"It's good, I guess." Sophie searches Erigan for answers.

He has none.

"Great. That's great." Behemoth wraps his arm around her shoulder and walks her back to the yellow counter. "How about we get your son there—he is your son right? He's cute—get you some free cinnamon bread. You know, on the house."

Sophie smiles and shrugs. "Thanks?"

"Not a problem," says Behemoth. He motions over to the man-boy behind the counter and just screams, "Cinnamon bread. Now!" He looks back over to Sophie and smiles. "It'll be right up."

"Thanks," says Sophie. She peers over at Erigan, who peeks through his fingers.

Sophie breaks away, but not before Behemoth whispers something into her ear. She blushes, shivers, and then walks away with more pep in her step.

"What did he just tell you?" he says.

"Nothing," says Sophie. She winks at him and giggles. She sits down and grabs a paper plate in front of her.

Erigan stands with his hands on his hips.

"What?" she says. "He said nothing. I promise."

"That was not nothing," says Erigan. "Whatever he told you, it's a lie, okay?"

"He looks familiar," she says. She pulls a piece of pizza off the hot metal pan. The cheese stretches for what seems like a whole three feet before finally cutting the piece free. "Did we meet him somewhere?"

"We?" says Erigan. Erigan smiles. This bodes good well for the little ex-god.

"I don't know," he says. "He looks like a lot of people."

"The man is built like a Greek god," she says. "Trust me, not a lot of men look like that hunk of man." She takes a bite of the pizza and cuts the stringy cheese with her hands. "Believe me. I looked."

Suddenly her chewing of the crust annoys Erigan. He grinds his own teeth and thinks he could wave his hand and let the bitch choke on the pieces of sharp burnt crust.

But that would leave him nowhere. No answers. And whoever she is supposed to be, she's obviously important.

He had been sensing it. But still cannot tell just how.

"Are you jealous?" she says.

Erigan rolls his eyes. "Yup. Sure. Jealous. That's what it is." He stands up from the table, walks to the gaming room. "Brad, your pizza is done."

Brad waves him off. He stands with hands on a glass counter. His fingers spread out on each hand, his eyes about to pop out of his head and go into the damned glass.

"What are you doing?"

"Shopping," says Brad. "Should I get the ring over there or the necklace?"

Erigan shrugs. "For you?"

"No," says Brad. He taps Erigan's foot and suddenly realizes his wearing sandals. Brad smells his hand and then rests it back on the glass counter. "For Mom."

Erigan nods. "Go for the ring." He brings out his wad of cash and takes out a few bucks. "How much for it?"

Brad pushes the money away. "No, dummy. They take tokens here."

Erigan shrugs.

"These." Brad dumps his pile of tokens on the counter. They ring out like a cacophony of a dull metal waterfall. "They take these."

Erigan shoves the cash back into his pocket. "Oh."

"So the blue one or the pink one?" Brad gasps. "Or the purple one there. She likes purple."

"If she like purple, then get the purple one." Erigan looks up from the counter to check on Sophie.

Erigan's slams his head onto the counter and groans. His view of Sophie is blocked—by his best friend's ever-impressive muscles.

"Sir, could you get your head off the glass?"

The boy from behind the kitchen counter comes out and taps on the top glass counter. Erigan feels the vibrations for his forehead. He likes the feeling, how it numbs his eyebrows.

"Sir?"

Erigan raises his head and nods. "Fine, fine."

Brad chuckles.

"Just get your mother the rings. I'll be right back."

Brad nods and points to the glass counter. "Can I get two of those?" he says.

Chapter Thirty-Four

"Get your fucking hands off of her," Erigan says. He stays behind the wall that separates the seating from the play area.

Behemoth sits next to Sophie. His arm rests on the cushion behind them. Not touching her, but close enough.

Erigan has seen this before. He moves in, gets close and then either rapes the women. The verb usually depends on when the woman comes to her senses.

Being a pretty big guy, it's hard to say no to Herc-slash-Behemoth, but every once in a while a woman will get the nerve to fight back. Very rarely does it ever matter in Herc's grand schemes.

The salty smell of burnt pepperoni distracts him for a moment until his hands slip on a grease spot on the wall.

When Behemoth doesn't say anything, he yells again. "Hey, fuck face! Get away from her."

Behemoth stands up from his seat next to Sophie. He takes both of her hands into his and he kisses them before he looks up and grimaces at Erigan.

"Really, pal? You want to play this game?"

"Don't you think this is a bit inappropriate?"

Behemoth shrugs. "What's it to you, Martha Stewart?"

Erigan shrugs. "Who?"

"Gods, I can't even make fun of you because you're so stupid."

"I'm the stupid one?" says Erigan. "Who was the one who thought he could bench press the Tower of Pisa?"

"Hey, it didn't fall down completely, okay?" Behemoth steps out of the seating area and takes only three steps to be right in front of Erigan.

Once again, he gets an up close and personal experience with Behemoth's bellybutton.

At least it's an attractive bellybutton. It could always be worse.

"You're going to get us both in trouble, Herc," Erigan whispers. "I'm trying to hide and you're trying to bed my neighbor."

"I'm a demigod."

"Ex-demi god. Remember? We aren't in charge anymore."

Sophie slaps the plastic behind her bench's cushions. "Seriously? Two guys fighting over me? That's awesome!"

"Just because we aren't in charge doesn't mean we stop being who we are!" growls Behemoth.

"But seriously guys," Sophie says. "Don't get in trouble, okay? Erigan! Don't get us kicked out!"

Brad walks by the two as Erigan and Behemoth face off. Or face-slash-bellybutton off.

"Lucifer's not really the forgiving type, and God doesn't want us up there." He pushes Behemoth back. Or rather, he tries to. Like an ant pushing a man-sized boulder. "So yes, it does mean we stop being who we are. You don't see me ferrying the dead back and forth into Hades."

"You're too domesticated." Behemoth jabs his sausage-thick index finger into Erigan's chest. Erigan takes a few steps back from the force. "And you know what? It's only going to get worse from here. You caught a lot of attention for that stunt you pulled down there."

Erigan gets the wild idea that maybe, just maybe, he can win this fight.

So he throws his first punch and hopes for the best.

His hands crunch underneath the pressure of Behemoth's rock hard, tight abs.

Behemoth, however, lets out a gasp. He must not have been expecting an actual tussle.

Behemoth reaches out and grabs Erigan's head. He lifts him up off the ground. "What are you doing, little man?"

Erigan swipes at Behemoth's face. He feels his human knuckles crunch again. Something snaps in his wrist. His shoulder cries out in exhaustion already.

Behemoth flicks Erigan in the chest.

Erigan feels his own chest tighten. This tension travels up his sternum to the back of his neck. He tightens himself up. Bracing for impact.

Behemoth's hand squeezes around Erigan's head. "You're not too smart about this," he says. "Is she really worth that much to you?"

"I have to," Erigan says and then cries out in pain. He reaches to pull Behemoth's hand off of his head but it doesn't work. "Find out," Erigan breathes out.

"Do you need us to call the cops?" says the boy behind the counter. From Erigan's vantage point, the boy just sits there. Frozen. His hands on his chest. His eyes gaping open almost as wide as his mouth.

Behemoth shakes his head. "No, I got this bro. Make sure you don't burn them pizzas, okay?"

The boy nods and takes a few steps out of Erigan's point of view.

"I have to. Find out. What happened. Why I'm here," Erigan manages to say. His hands grip the entirety of Behemoth's thumbs and index finger. He pulls himself free and lands on the ground.

Behemoth dusts off his hand and then smells them.

"I was asked to do that," he said. "I thought it was an assignment."

Behemoth straightens up. His shoulders tighten up and he raises an eyebrow. "Who?" he whispers.

Erigan shrugs. "I was set up. It was an accident. I

don't know."

"Seriously? You had a job that pissed off one of the biggest generals in Hell's Army, and you want to call it an accident?" Behemoth's laughter roars in the restaurant. "You're more screwed than you think. And worse yet, you are screwing *us*, too."

Us. The Olympians. Is he condemning them? Erigan feels the sudden pinch of fear around his heart.

"I am?"

"Oh boy are you ever." Behemoth grabs Erigan and brings him in close for a tight bear hub. "But you know what, bro? I got your back."

Erigan struggles to breathe. He slaps Behemoth's sides and chest to be released.

Sophie pops up from behind them, holding a piece of pizza that she appeared to be working on. "Are you guys okay? Not going to kill each other?"

"Yes, yes. We are fine," says Erigan. He takes a deep breath and takes in some of the spicy pepperoni smell. It lingers deep in the back of his throat. He coughs.

Behemoth slaps Erigan's back. The force lands him on the floor on all fours. Behemoth lifts him up and sets him on his feet. "Ya, we're good. Aren't we, buddy?"

"Mom!" says Brad. He comes out from the table holding his two plastic rings. On each one, a plastic spider wiggles its thin, angular legs. "You're not wearing your rings."

Sophie puts one on each of her ring fingers and holds them out to admire them. "Thank you, honey." She leans over and kisses Brad's forehead.

"Erigan helped me pick them out," Brad says.

Erigan smiles and closes his eyes.

"Thanks you," she says and taps him on the forehead.

The two humans return to their dinner. Behemoth and Erigan remain in front of the ordering counter.

"So who's watching, exactly?" says Erigan.

"Anyone and everyone," says Behemoth. "It's crawling with people looking for you."

Erigan peers around Behemoth's shoulder. "Is Lilith looking for me?"

Behemoth holds his hands out as if pushing away the idea. "You don't even want to know."

"But I want to know," Erigan says.

"No, you don't," Behemoth says. "Because if you did know, you'd run and never come back."

Chapter Thirty-Five

Erigan holds his head in his hands on the car ride back home.

It seems at every other stop sign, he catches Sophie smiling. Making fun of him. Hurting his feelings.

He makes a mental note to smite her somehow, when he can get a little flashy with his powers. For now, he's going to haunt her son a little extra tonight.

"How's your head," Sophie says. The car pulls into their parking spot at the far end of the lot.

"It's fine," he says. "Just like the last three times you asked."

"Does your head hurt?" says Brad.

Erigan looks behind him. Brad's shoes scrape across the asphalt parking lot. A rock in his shoe, which Brad seems to be enjoying.

Sophie laughs and lets them both inside the building.

Erigan and Sophie both wave at Maria, the afternoon office manager. Doing paperwork again. She was the quiet, less agreeable one. Peggy, on the other hand, she was the face and personality of the office.

Erigan had only gotten to meet Peggy, but by looking at Maria, he could tell so much about her.

If anything, humans were predictable.

Bad home life, or no home life. Spend time with numbers and offices because numbers don't lie. They're consistent. They always agree. And when they don't, there's always a solution.

"Is she here late a lot?" says Erigan.

Sophie waves again and then nods. "Ya, poor thing. Runs this place. She actually lives in this building. That's why she sneaks out into the office from time to time."

"She's weird," says Brad.

"Hush," Sophie warns. She grabs Brad's hand and pushes him along in front of them.

They walk up the steps. Erigan follows slowly. He watches as they turn down the hallway. He studies them for movements. Signs. Traits. Anything that tells him who the fuck they are and why he was led here of all places.

Why haunt this kid and then keep himself trapped?

The coincidences, it's too much for him to figure out. Oracles have been outlawed by order of God and the wackjobs that practice fortune-telling and magick up here aren't merely as accurate.

For this kind of job, he needs someone more adept. More available.

But everyone he knew was in Hell. The one place he can't go back.

Sophie stops at her door and waits for Erigan to stumble over to his.

With one hand on his head to calm the throbbing, Erigan reaches for his key and slips it into the lock. He waits. Cautiously turns his head to his side and winces in pain.

"So, I'll be seeing you around?" he says.

Sophie shrugs. "Sure, neighbor."

Erigan nods and steps into the apartment. He waits a second, putting his ear to the door. When he hears Sophie's door close shut, he finally closes his.

He tosses his keys in a black bowl with orange figures—naked figures—wrestling each other in a very geometric motif.

Erigan stops to stare at the bowl. Before he had just passed by it, not thinking anything of it. But now, it seemed different. Highlighted.

Was it here before?

Erigan steps into the room and sits down in the couch. He looks at the wooden shelves, stained a dark coffee color. They don't particular match the décor, enhancing the darkness of the room. Each is lined with books. When Erigan's eyes focus on the spine of each book, he reads the individual titles and smirks.

He's read these. All of these.

Hell, he's lived some of them.

Mythology by Edith Hamilton. *Odyssey* by Homer. *The Age of Fable or Stories of Gods and Heroes* by a Thomas Bullfinch. And then a bright green and blue book: *The Lightning Thief* by Rick Riordan.

Erigan smiles and takes the book off the shelf. The bright colors catch his eyes and he nods. A boy demigod, son of Poseidon tracking down the thief who stole Zeus's lightning bolt?

As if. His father would never be caught off guard like that. Never.

Erigan puts the book back and mutters something about lies.

It's not that Homer and Ovid were perfect, but they had help. As he fingers through the rest of the books, he wonders just where the Muses were. He hadn't seen them in Hell since he could remember. Were they in Heaven? Hell? Stay on Earth?

Erigan searches through the other three shelves that make up the unit and he stops.

Everything about mythology. Greek. Roman. Egyptian. Mesopotamian. All of his best friends are right here in story form.

He flips through the story of Gilgamesh. The pictures make him laugh, but they caught Enkidu's good side, he thinks. The long hair, braided down his back. The dark, curly beard that hangs down to his chest.

And in loincloths. Always with the loincloths. Erigan smiles. He puts the book back in its spot and he sits down on the couch again.

After he's done bouncing, he notices that the room smells different. Mustier. Even stronger. Stale.

Erigan sniffs the air and follows the trail to the bedroom. Or *his* bedroom, rather.

Though Erigan was technically paying for the place, he couldn't bring himself to describe the place as home just yet. He just felt it was a place to come to at night.

He pauses at the door. The stench becomes painfully familiar. Digging at his nose and poking around in his throat.

That strong odor. He opens the door and is both confirmed and horrified by what he finds.

"Where the hell did you get that?" he says.

Behemoth lies across his bed wearing only a white t-shirt and shorts that show off every bulge in his thighs. His strong, hairy legs are crossed, though Behemoth lies across the bed on his side.

On his finger, swinging around, is a silver hat. Disc-like, with tiny metal wings on each side.

"Remember this?" he says.

Erigan closes the door like someone's going to hear him. "Where the fuck did that come from?"

"I found it when I got here." Behemoth threatens to toss it to Erigan, but he refuses and holds his hands up.

"Why are you here?"

"You tap that yet?" says Behemoth. He rests the hat on his head and then points over to his neighbor's direction.

"No, I haven't tapped that. We just got home," he says. "Do I need to know why you're following me so closely?" Erigan takes the hat off his head and searches the smooth inside of it. "Were you followed?"

"I teleport up here," says Behemoth. He slides around and sits on the bed normally. He tries to cross his legs again, but his shorts won't let him. "Who's going to follow me?"

"You know damn well they have people who keep track of who leaves and enters Hell. Sooner or later, they're going to find out you're leaving and where you keep going."

"You're getting too paranoid," says Behemoth. "I'm fine."

Erigan thinks about putting the hat on his head, going so far as to let it gently brush past his curly brown hair. "You said you just found this here?"

"On your bed," his friend says. "I thought maybe you left it here."

Erigan takes the hat completely off his head and tosses it to the foot of the bed. He looks behind him and then behind the royal blue curtains that hang from either side of the rather large windows.

"Someone knows I'm here, then."

"Bullshit," say Behemoth. "Who would know?"

"You know," Erigan says. "Maybe you told someone."

"I haven't told anyone anything."

"Not Dio? Lilith?"

Behemoth shakes his head. "Please, I don't talk to

those assholes, okay? Your secret is safe with me."

Erigan searches for the truth in each of Behemoth's eyes. The problem with being in Hell as long as they have is they pick up how to lie pretty easily. It's practically in the orientation manual.

Welcome to Hell. Please read "How to Lie Effectively" in Chapter 5, page 282. Please come back prepared to lie about doing your homework.

"You are positively sure you did not talk to anyone?"

Behemoth stands up and outstretches his hands. "Who? Me?" He stands accused, his face twisted into both a smile and a look of insult. "Seriously?"

"Fine," Erigan says. He looks at the hat. Outstretches a hand, but pulls back just short of picking it back up. "I will trust you for now, but if you're fucking with me, I swear I will kill you."

Behemoth stands up and flicks Erigan on the forehead. "You can't even hurt me," he says. "What's for dinner?"

Erigan just watches Behemoth step out into the hallway.

He picks up the hat and rests it back on his head. It fits just as he remembered it. Loose around the top of his head. Resting just above his ears. He even feels the wings pick up air as he walks to the front door.

It fits like the proverbial glove. Whatever that meant. He closes his eyes and remembers the times flying in and out of Hades. Down to Tartaros. Up to Olympus.

Then, he opens his eyes.

This is not that time. It won't be that time. And Behemoth may be right.

He can't be that God anymore. The times, they have changed.

He rests the hat on the bedpost and walks out to the living room.

Chapter Thirty-Six

Erigan swears to himself when he wakes up on his own couch. His bare feet dangle from over the armrest and his head remains stuffed somewhere between a pillow and the mattress. He pries his head from the couch and hears the ripping sound of his sweaty forehead leaving the smooth leather couch.

Erigan rolls to his left and falls off the couch. His body thumps off the floor. His face comes within a hand's width away from scraping alongside the edge of the leather cube.

"Never again," he says.

When he finally manages to get up and walk around, he naturally heads to his own bed. The bed that Behemoth stole from him in a bet.

Drinking he was not known for. That was his brother's department. Even his father's from time to time.

But Hermes the drunk? There's a reason why mortals don't know him by that epithet.

"Next time you're getting the couch, you rat bastard." Erigan opens his bedroom door and sees only a nightstand, toppled over, and his bed in a mess.

There is a trail of dirty footprints along the floor that leads him to the apartment's front door.

"What is he doing now?"

He opens the door and peers outside. There's no sign of him.

Erigan wasn't sure there would be a sign of him. But a man that big, someone was bound to stop him. Or run from him. Or follow him madly in love with his muscles.

Erigan sighs and figures he probably went back to Hell.

Good old Hell. Home good-for-nothing home.

The door closes and an earth-shaking burp rattles his walls.

"Of course he is," Erigan says. He returns to his bedroom and searches the closet.

On television, he noticed that this is where the stylish mortals always hang their clothing.

But in this closet hung nothing impressive. Robes. White shirts. Black pants. Nothing that would be remotely close to his size.

So, he closes his eyes and imagines something similar to what he saw on television yesterday. This time, not in pink, but blue. With red stripes.

Opening his eyes, he checks himself out in the full-length body mirror by the bedroom door.

He finds it acceptable, though completely uncomfortable. He stretches out the shirt around his midsection and around his arms. The arms take some convincing, but soon they feel decent around his body. Sleeves seem to be a new invention among mortals. Besides the uniforms of Hell's Army, no one really wore sleeves in Hell.

It's just too damned hot.

But this shirt. Were they always so tight?

Erigan leaves the apartment, not bothering to lock up. After all, he doesn't go far. He's barefoot out in the hallway and doesn't regret a single part of it. He stretches his toes across the ceramic tiles. He likes the cold feeling—the so-cold-he-almost-feels-wet feeling along the bottoms of his feet.

Almost like that time he walked on water, and Jesus stole his trick.

Those mortals lost their minds over that. Erigan got a great laugh and Jesus got a chance to make history. Win-win.

Or mostly. Soon thereafter God was able to move in and usurp the throne.

Erigan shoves the image of packing up his stuff and moving with his family to the gates of Hell.

He taps on the door next to him. Apartment 1C.

The door opens swiftly. Sophie answers, wearing a pink tanktop, blue shirts. She looks cute, for lack of a better word. Her hair is pulled up behind her. She looks lazy, but relaxed. Not crazy after last night.

"We were wondering when you were going to get here," she says. She leaves the front door and pulls out a glass for him. "Margarita?" she says.

"No, thank you," Erigan says. Searching the apartment from where he stands, he spots a thick, hairy leg poking out from behind a glass door out in the patio.

"He's out back if you need to find him."

Erigan takes the suggestion. He opens the patio door and there is Behemoth, legs up on the patio railing. One hand behind his head, the other holding a glass with a frozen red drink. With his shirt off, his hairy chest and broad shoulders command much more attention than when clothed.

"I thought we talked about this," Erigan says.

Behemoth pulls his feet off the railing and sits up. He holds the glass out and pretends to tap it against Erigan's imaginary glass.

"Klink," Behemoth says and takes a drink.

"What are you doing here?"

"I was on my way out and she stopped me and asked me to come in for breakfast."

Erigan peers through the glass door. A white framed clock has a hand on the one and a longer one on the two.

"It's not in the morning any more," says Erigan. The actual time is unimportant. He has made his point.

"I promise," says Behemoth. He rests his empty hand on his chest and says, "I swear."

"You're from Hell," Erigan rolls his eyes. "You're word means shit to me."

The glass door slides open with a loud bang.

"So now that you both are here, can you tell me something?"

Behemoth stretches his hand behind his head again. Nice and slow, drawing extra attention to his bicep.

Erigan nods silently.

"So when you were fighting in the pizza place last night. You know, why you were," she pauses and appears to rethink her words. "How did you just pick him up like that?" Sophie showcases Behemoth's thick, muscular frame then Erigan's skinny stick of a body. "I mean. This. Then this. It's easy to believe, but. It still seemed. I don't know. Weird."

She slurps her pink frozen drink through an even pinker straw.

Erigan considers that she might have been drinking already. As is Behemoth. Again. For who knows how many times these past few days.

How far can he get without having to tell her the truth?

"I am a pretty scrawny guy," says Erigan. "And this guy," Erigan pats Behemoth on the chest. "Well just look at this guy. He has muscles on top of muscles."

Sophie's eyes narrow. She slurps on the drink again and smacks her lips together. "I thought you were a trickier type of person," she says. Her eyes meet Behemoth's and she smiles. "At least that's what he said."

Erigan feels like he's walked into the middle of a joke spider-web.

The two, they're having fun with him and no matter how hard he can try, he won't be able to scrape it all off. It's already beginning to linger all over his face.

"Are you sure you were even watching the whole time? I wasn't off the ground, you know."

"Dude," says Behemoth. He tosses his straw over the balcony and drinks directly from the cup. "She knows."

"What exactly does she know?"

"She knows about you and me. And Olympus. And Dad."

Words jackknife into Erigan's throat. They aren't sure if they want to be pissed off or finally relieved. Either way, they aren't coming out.

Sophie slurps again. "Listen, it's fine," she says. "I know you two are gay and it's okay."

Four words win the bout out of the flustered ex-god's throat. "We are not gay."

Behemoth smiles. "I tried telling her that."

"But you're Greek. Like gods, right? So you're gay."

Erigan puts his hands up and rests them on her shoulders. "Please don't judge us for the crimes of our father. Just because he consorted with both sexes doesn't mean we all do."

Behemoth takes a fast and quiet sip of his drink and stands up. "Whelp, it looks like I need more. Excuse me."

He motions for the door and pauses. "Do you have any beer?" he asks.

Erigan nods. "I have some. In the apartment. Door's open. Check in the cabinet next to the refrigerator."

Behemoth smiles and leaves.

As soon as the glass door closes, Erigan pushes the chair against the handle to prevent Behemoth from coming back out.

"Listen, what did he really tell you?"

"I'm cool with it, seriously." Sophie's words slip out of her mouth. Much the same they did out of Erigan's mouth last night.

"You're drunk."

"It helps the medicine go down, you know?"

"And you're really ready to believe this?" says Erigan. He coughs in disbelief. "That is unlikely. You people are skeptical of everything except for aliens."

Sophie sits down in Behemoth's chair. Her eyes widen and her hands search the chair. "This is really warm," she says and then laughs. "Ew."

"So you know. Everything?"

Sophie shakes her head. "Everything he told me."

"Everything Behemoth told you," he repeats to himself. "And you're okay with it."

"It makes sense, I guess." Sophie looks out over the town's tree line downtown. "This type of weirdness has always followed me."

Erigan rests against the railing. "It has? Like when?"

"Just around my life. Sometimes when I was a little

girl. A few years ago before Brad was born. Just some really weird shit."

Erigan tries to find what Sophie might be staring at across the town.

"When I was a little girl, I used to have an imaginary friend. A woman. Full grown. Silvery hair. She used to only show up when the moon was full. She was beautiful. Friendly. Bright red cheeks and always smiling. She was my best friend."

"What was her name?" say Erigan, already knowing the answer.

"Diana. It was a beautiful name," says Sophie. "It still is a beautiful name. And then when I turned thirteen, she disappeared from my life. At night we'd talk about everything. How life was going. About my mom and how hard she worked all the time." Sophie turns her head to look at Erigan.

Erigan feels awkward at first, the way she studies his face. Her eyes move back and forth, subtle lines, across his face. She studies his eyes, turning both blue and green and then back again.

"And then she just stopped coming. You know? And it was weird because when I was old enough to read the books, I learned about Diana and the goddess of the moon and it all made sense, you know." She takes a sip. "But imaginary friends are supposed to be imaginary."

Erigan nods. "It's funny," he says. "Artemis never mentioned any girls she visited."

"Artemis?" Sophie's face changes from a twisted,

quizzical one to having an "a-ha" moment. "Right. Greek name. Roman name."

Erigan sits down next to her. "So you've always suspected that we were out there?"

"I always knew, I guess. I don't know why, but after that I always felt like I was being watched. I even went to go see someone about it. A doctor in a big white and green hospital. I was on medication for a few months." She takes a sip. "Okay, okay, a few years."

She slaps Erigan on the shoulder and growls at him. "Fuck you guys for following me everywhere. My mom, she never believed me. She thought I was crazy. But you were there. You guys were always there."

Erigan doesn't want to confirm, but he knows it's possible. He keeps his mouth shut, pursing his lips and taking a rather large gulp of her pink frozen drink. The sugary syrup coats his tongue.

"And then right before Brad was born, I met someone. And he reminded me of Diana. He was sweet, friendly," she pauses and smiles. "Great body, and he loved to dance in the rain with me. We met a few times, never at my place or his place, but in public. We'd come back to my apartment. Until one day, we didn't."

Sophie looks out at the tree line again. Wipes her eyes. "He just didn't show up anymore and I was left with a baby."

"And you suspect," says Erigan.

Sophie nods. "Yes, it was one of you," she says. "One of you is my son's father."

Chapter Thirty-Seven

Erigan opens his apartment door and begins the yelling, "You stupid, stupid son of a bitch!"

Behemoth stands in the kitchen with all of the drawers and cabinets open. "Dude, I don't think you have any beer."

"Of course I don't have any beer. Or if I do, it's not mine and I have no idea where it is." Erigan grabs an empty bottle left on the counter from last night and launches it at Behemoth.

"What the fuck?" Behemoth begins to show his teeth. His throat grumbles, a low growl escapes his vocal cords.

"Why did you tell her everything?" Erigan says. "We'll be royally fucked if she says something to the wrong person. You said yourself that Hell's got its eyes peeled, looking out for me."

Behemoth shrugs. "What? She asked." Behemoth dodges another brown glass bottle. "You better watch it."

"If I get found, and brought into the Ninth Circles for this, I'll make sure your dumb ass goes right along with me."

Behemoth kicks aside the shards of broken glass. "You and what army?" he says.

"We both know I can get one."

"Dio is no help, and the rest of the other gods have gone into hiding. You were the only smart one, smooth-talking yourself into the new regime for security." Behemoth walks through the rest of the broken shards. His steps don't falter as the glass crunches underneath his feet.

"Get out," says Erigan. "Don't come back."

"I did you a favor, you fool." Behemoth walks around the kitchen to the hallway by the front door. "She's okay with it and you don't have to stop being who you are anymore. See? All of your problems solved and you're not lying to her."

"Do you realize that she's been followed by us since she was little?" Erigan grabs another bottle.

Behemoth braces himself for another attack by sticking out his chest. Holding his ground.

"She thinks that one of us is the father of her child."

Behemoth nods. "I know."

"But then why here? Who sent me here?" Erigan rubs his face but stops when he smells the stale scent of hops and beer all over his cheekbones. "Whose fucking place is this?"

Behemoth shakes his head. "You've fucking lost it." For the first time since this argument started, Behemoth's voice is calm, mellow. "You need to get your head straight and stop thinking so much. Let this all blow over. It'll be for the best."

"What do you mean by that?" Erigan says.

"Just trust me on this one, okay?" Behemoth opens the door.

"Be the best? For who? What's going on?"

When the door opens completely, the outside world is replaced with a portal. A view into Hell sits like a window in front of them. A window covered with a hazy appearance like looking through a hundred spider webs layered together.

Deep inside the picture, Erigan spots shadows moving about slowly across the scenery. He's watching the outside walls of Dis. The guards sit atop the walls and the shadow guards' motion from side to side on duty.

"Where are you going?" Erigan reaches out to grab Behemoth's hand.

Behemoth withdraws his hand and nods at his friend. His large body walks through the portal quickly. The door closes behind him.

Erigan grabs the gold-painted handle and swings the door open. He's greeted by the puffy, just crying face of Sophie. And she brought the rest of her body with her.

"So, did you guys find the beer yet?"

Chapter Thirty-Eight

When Sophie walks into Erigan's darkened apartment, she pinches her nose. "What smells like rotten bread?"

She turns the corner into the kitchen and spots the shattered glass bottles all over the floor. "Oh."

"We got into a little bit of a fight," says Erigan. "He left, I'm left to clean up."

"Are you sure you guys aren't gay for each other?" Sophie looks at her empty hand like she wants to take a drink.

Erigan doesn't answer. He snaps his fingers and the room blinks. Nothing out of place. The shattered bits of brown glass no longer speckle the walls. But the smell still lingers.

Sophie lets go over her nose. "Can you please do that at my place? I'll pay."

Erigan shakes his head. "It might be better if you just

go," he says. "For both of us."

Sophie grabs Erigan's hand. "Okay Hermes. You have thirty minutes to get ready and meet me out in front of my apartment. We're going to go talk. Get cheered up. Okay?"

Erigan snaps his hands back to his side. "Not a good idea."

"I won't take no for an answer." She walks backwards toward the door. She's overly confident that she won't step on something and slip and fall.

"You are really going to have to this time," says Erigan.

"No," she says. "No, I don't. Thirty minutes." She taps at a wristwatch that doesn't exist. "Tick tick tick."

Erigan sits on the steps in front of Sophie's apartment door fifteen minutes early. He only left earlier because he knew there would be nothing of interest on the television.

His almost favorite show, The Real World, was only showing reruns from last night's episodes.

In the hallways, he counted the steps and then paced back and forth.

Finally, the door opens and while Erigan stands up expecting Sophie at the door, Brad stands there instead.

"You can come in if you want."

Erigan smiles and declines. "Your mom said I should meet her here."

"But it's boring out there," he says. "You can come inside and watch television with me while she's waiting for the babysitter to come over."

Erigan looks out at the halogen-lit hallway. He looks at the white-yellow twelve-inch squares that line the floor of the hallway.

"Well, there are so many different ways to count tiles," he says. He follows Brad's motions into the living room.

Erigan chooses the side of the couch furthest away from the TV. It's not an accident that it ended up furthest away from the kid, too.

"So, um, is your mom going to be ready soon?" he asks.

The boy's attention stays fixed to the cartoon family chasing each other round their colorful kitchen table. A white dog leads the pack as being the loudest.

Erigan sits back on the couch, resting along the armrest. "Okay then. Good talk."

From this view, Erigan searches the boy's looks. He's gotta look like someone he knows.

The boy's ears look average. Not pointed, earlobes attached. His eyebrows don't arch. Almost flat along his brow line. His cheeks look round. A little chubby, but the kid is eight. Not much he can do except go run around.

The key is always in the eyes. And Erigan itches to try to just reach around, search the kid's eyes and figure out just where and who he came from.

But that, well, that would be awkward.

"Hey Brad," says Erigan. "What's your favorite TV show?"

Brad turns around and smiles. "All of them," he says. "But I like Iron Man the most."

His eyes are blue. Almost an electric blue. A thin line of a pale blue circles around the darker blue irises, giving them a haunting glow.

Apollo's golden hair, maybe? Too blond for Ares?

Erigan shrugs. "Sure. He's cool."

Iron who?

"I'm sorry, who are you?"

Erigan turns around to meet the voice.

It's an elderly woman. She adjusts her glasses, peering just over the frames. Her soft yellow shirt hangs tight against her body. Gray slacks, no shoes on.

Erigan guesses she is close to dying in a few more decades. Or something. Erigan was never that sure of human mortality issues.

"I'm Herm–um–Erigan. Nice to meet you."

The woman adjusts her glasses again now that she's closer to his face. "Hrm. You're a cute fellow." She smiles. Her skin looks baby soft with barely visible peach fuzz hairs along her pink blushing cheeks. "Would you like something to drink, Mister Erigan?"

She walks confidently into the kitchen and disappears behind the walls.

From outside, Erigan hears the slamming of drawers and cabinets.

"Where are those damn glasses, anyway?"

"In the cabinet by the fridge, Gramma."

"Thanks, boy." Gramma emerges from the kitchen with wet lips and hands on her hips. "And where are you kids going off to?"

"Don't call us kids, mother. I'm almost thirty years old."

High heels clip-clop out of their shortened hallway and into the living room.

"You're twenty-seven, dear." Gramma rolls her eyes. "Hardly thirty."

Standing at the entryway, Sophie's hands still adjust finishing touches in her hair. Her white T-shirt leaves little to Erigan's imagination. The short black jacket makes her shoulders look bigger than Erigan's. They might just be without the pads.

Between her shirt and high heels are a pair of black pants, cut off just before they meet the ankle.

For a moment, Erigan feels a little underdressed for this outing.

"She looks like you have expectations, sir," says Gramma to Erigan.

"What?" he shakes his head. "No. This was her idea."

"Figures." Gramma sits down on the couch behind Brad. She rubs over his soft blond hair and tries to concentration on the television.

"Mom," Sophie comes out of the hallway and digs through a black box she has sitting on the breakfast nook. "What is that supposed to mean?"

She brings both of her hands near her left ear and then her right, attaching something to them.

"You just have a history, dear. You know that."

Erigan assesses his khaki pants—left in the closet—and the pink collared shirt he chose because it was the closest thing that fit his narrow shoulders.

"Is this okay?"

Sophie's look goes blank. "Yes, yes, you're fine. I like the pink," she says.

She takes off her high heels and tosses them off to the side. She uses her foot to push around a pile of shoes near the front door. Finding another set of black heels, she pulls them closer to her and kneels down and picks them up. "It's a good color on you."

Is that a compliment?

"Don't let him watch television all day, Mom," says Sophie. "Did you hear Mommy?"

Brad's eyes don't leave the television.

"Honey!" Sophie claps the near the boy's head.

Brad flinches, rubs his eyes. "I don't know, mom. Honest."

Sophie smiles.

Her mother groans.

Erigan watches.

"I said you're not watching television all day, got it?"

Brad apologizes with a whimper. "Yes, Mom." He gets up to give her a hug.

Without any prompting or a hint, he gives Erigan's leg a hug, too.

Erigan's hands go up to show he's empty-handed and not touching anyone or anything.

Instead of being alarmed, Sophie says, "He's taking a liking to you," she says. She grabs the keys off the kitchen counter. "We'll be back soon, Mom. We're just going out for a bite to eat."

Her mother waves them off. "Go. Have a good time. We'll be fine."

Chapter Thirty-Nine

She picks a local place to walk to. A sandwich shop. Red booths, chipped paint, and white walls decorated with monotone pictures of vegetables all around them.

Erigan considers for a moment if he's ever had a "submarine" before.

"It's just a nickname," says Sophie. She unwraps her sandwich from the butcher paper. "It's because it looks like a submarine."

Erigan shrugs. "I didn't know you could eat subs." Then bites into the sandwich.

The tangy horseradish burns his tongue at first, then leaves him feeling like he can breathe fire through his nostrils.

Licking his lips into a smile, he takes another bite.

"Good?" says Sophie. She doesn't wait for an answer. "So I want to ask you something."

The oversized bite of bread and meat in Erigan's mouth keeps him from telling her to not ask then.

"So what's Heaven like?"

It takes some effort, but Erigan finally swallows it all down and takes a drink of his dark and sweet soda. "I do not know," he says. "Now that you mention it."

"How do you not know?"

"I'm from Hell."

Sophie opens her mouth wide enough for Erigan to see the white bits of bread hanging between her teeth. "Bull shit."

"So do cows," says Erigan. "You do not hear them bragging about it."

No reaction from Sophie. "So all of you old gods are down in Hell?"

"After the regime change, ya. Otherwise we'd be competition." Erigan uses air-quotes to put extra emphasis on *competition*.

"That oddly makes sense," says Sophie. She put down the half-eaten sub in mid-sentence and seems to forget about it completely. "So what? Some guy comes in and tosses you out on your ass?"

"Isn't that what happens here?"

Sophie slurps her drink. Makes a face like it's sour or cold. "Well, ya. But sometimes they're elected."

Erigan smirks wider. "Ya, we do not get elected. We are either in or we are out."

"And when you're out, you just go to Hell?"

"Depends on who wins," Erigan says. "So you are sure

you don't know who Brad's father is?"

Sophie doesn't bat an eye. "So this time you end up in Hell? And no, no idea." She swallows. "You guys can shape change and all that. I read my mythology books."

"It's not really that simple. The books only half get it right." Erigan looks at his sandwich, but he has to give up. He can't eat anymore. "Listen," says Erigan. He takes a long breath. "When someone else takes over, there is a new major religion down here. It is wonky and hectic, but that is how it really works. When God's forces gained ground down here, he earned his new place among the older gods."

Sophie blinks in disbelief. "Gained ground?"

"When he becomes popular. So when he takes over—a regime change—then the rest of us have to go packing. In our case, we were dethroned, tossed out of Olympus, and relegated to Hell so we wouldn't become a problem."

"Why not just kill you?"

Erigan blinks. It wouldn't be the first time that question has come up. "Because we are still being worshipped, albeit in small numbers around the world. Thank you to all those pagans out there."

"And so then if you still have powers, why not just go kill them first?"

Erigan snorts. "A joke? Funny," he says. "Our powers come from those who believe in us, so I have some of my older god-like abilities. My wings, my golden voice, my good looks."

Sophie rolls her eyes, but still has a smile and a glimmer.

"But beyond that, we pale in comparison to the ones who are really in charge." Erigan points upward toward the ceiling and downward at the same time.

"Fascinating and strange and weird," says Sophie. "How come we never find out about this?"

"Because God does not want you to. That is why we have stories. To help you believe what we want you to believe. To set humanity on its new intended path. The winners get to tell the history." He raises his white paper cup. "Cheers to that."

"So then why are you named Erigan? Why not keep your old name?"

He gets tired of waiting for Sophie to tap his cup with hers.

"Can you imagine the Bible, with mentions of all the little gods and goddesses from the past, running around and exacting their will on a monotheistic world—mono meaning one, mind you? Can you imagine how things would be different? It undermines God's whole conquest idea, does it not?"

Sophie sits back in her chair. Her mouth does this thing with the tongue sticking out. Thinking, maybe? "But you just get a new name so you don't exit anymore? That's so cruel," she says.

He continues, "From what I see, it is not too different up here. Your new governments take over, old governments are sent into exile—"

Sophie smirks. "Or killed."

Erigan bites his tongue for a split second to calm down. "Or killed. And then new rules and new beliefs."

Behemoth's big burly hands nearly consume the back of a chair and slides it over to Erigan's table. "Hi, guys."

"What are you doing here?" says Erigan.

"I need to talk to you," Behemoth says. He eyes Sophie. "Alone."

"About what?"

Behemoth eyes Sophie, who finally gets the hint.

She shakes her cup. "Fine, I'll go get a refill."

Behemoth takes Erigan's sandwich and sniffs it first, then takes out a small bite. He chews the pieces in his bearded mouth before finally swallowing. "Wow. Spicy." He licks his lips. "I like it."

"You didn't come here to eat my sandwich. What do you want?"

"She knows you're here," says Behemoth. "And she's pissed."

Chapter Forty

Erigan can't tell if Sophie is behind him or not. He just knows that he can't waste any time just yet.

Sophie cries out behind him. "Can't you just teleport us or something?"

"Not humans," Erigan says between exhausted huffs and puffs. He grips the door, thrusts it open and lets it bounce off the wall and back into his side. "You guys ca not survive the trip. Too fragile."

"Lucky us, then."

Running here, the town looked quiet. Serene. Same as they left it before going to talk.

Which means no army. No show of force. This is meant to be covert, or not sanctioned by the generals.

"The apartment building looks okay," says Sophie. She stops, grabs her hips and bends over at the waist.

She could be inside, he thinks. She could already

have her hands all over the boy. Probably even taking him, torturing him.

All to get to him. Because somehow, someway, he's pissed off everyone.

"Hush," Erigan commands.

Erigan takes one quiet step inside.

Sophie breathes louder, puffing to catch her breath, than Erigan.

He closes his eyes, wishing she could just be quiet.

But to say anything would incur the wrath of a woman he's not had a chance to assess. Ex-god or not, women were nothing to be trifled with.

"Who is this again?" Sophie attempts to take a step forward, but Erigan's outstretched arm seizes her waist.

Her breaths are deep, slow, and chaotic.

"Lilith," Erigan whispers. "Evil. You don't want to know more."

"And she's after my child?" she says. "Why?"

Erigan looks back at her. He rests his index finger against his lips. "No time to enough to wait and explain," he whispers back to her.

Erigan already knows what Sophie is looking for. He senses her behind him, searching the front door for break-ins, busted locks. Violence of the physical kind.

"No use," he says. "No signs of forced entry means she used otherworldy means."

"That bitch," says Sophie.

Erigan nods. "Indeed."

They move with the coordination of a paraplegic

orangutan down the hallway. For every one of Erigan's steps, Sophie runs into him no less than three times.

He grits her teeth and runs the phrase "Back the hell off" in his head over and over again.

But that's where he keeps the words—in his head. To say them out loud would only complicate matters.

Sophie taps Erigan on the shoulder and tiptoes to the kitchen. She reaches out for a pot or a pan.

Either way, he knows that it's too much noise.

When Erigan turns around and peeks around the corner, he sees feet, toes pointed to the ceiling.

"Stay in there," says Erigan.

"What?" whispers Sophie. "Not a chance." She wields an orange heavy bottomed pot like an axe. "I'm ready."

When Sophie gasps, Erigan knows that she's already found her mother.

"No," Sophie gasps. She pushes Erigan out of the way and runs to the side of her mother's body.

She rests her head against her mother's chest. She holds her ear over the mouth, listens, feels. Searches for life.

"It's a waste of time," he says.

But Sophie searches. When she looks up, Erigan watches every new wrinkle pull Sophie's face in every direction.

Pain. But not from his own hands.

This feels...different.

Not a good different.

"Sophie," says Erigan. "I'm."

He can't finish the sentence. His mouth remains open but everything seizes in his throat.

This feeling is new to him. Hasn't bothered to feel it in generations.

What the humans call regret. Sadness.

His time in Hell, Erigan thinks. He regrets it all.

It's removed him from the humans he's loved to tinker with. To play with. To romance and to tease.

"She will pay," Erigan whispers. He leaves Sophie at her mother's corpse and runs down the hallway. He phases through the door as a shadow.

The fibers of the door pull at his wispy form until it all disappears before him.

He's in the room, his bed empty and decidedly clean. Even neat and tidy except for one spot.

On the soft baby blue sheets, a shard of something white.

Sophie opens the door. Despite her tears and sobbing, she manages to say, "He's not here, is he?"

Erigan says nothing. He steps forward, takes the item off the bed and clenches it tight in his fist.

"What is that?"

"It's mine," he says. His fingers turn red, first from blood rushing to his hands, then from his change of form.

He doesn't see the look on Sophie's face as he does this.

His concentration. The care he took to protect himself. Fuck it all.

There is the slight airy gasp when Erigan completes his change.

Black tunic, leather boots, red skin and a single horn along his left forehead.

Taking the horn, he pulls his hand up to his right temple and holds it still.

The piece fits perfectly in the jagged ridges of his horn. Long lost in a battle ages ago.

"Shit," says Sophie.

Erigan turns around. His once green eyes and brown curly hair are replaced by onyx black eyes set against a sea of white and black hair with tight curls.

"I know who is after your son," he says.

Chapter Forty-One

Sophie's hand caresses the side of Erigan's new demon face.

He frowns, but grinds his teeth behind tight lips.

She hasn't run. Yet.

But that could be any minute now.

Sophie's eyes study the once soft curves, now turned into hardened, sharp edges. His soft cheek and high cheekbones now replaced with sunken eyes and rough, almost leathery skin.

"Is this—you?"

Erigan nods. He says nothing. Takes in a deep breath. Any minute now.

She'll run.

Sophie's eyes begin to water.

"Is this what took my baby?" she whispers. "Someone—like you?"

Silence.

Any answer could be the wrong one. But Erigan goes with his gut instinct on this. "Yes."

Sophie bites her lower lip and falls to the bed. She grabs his pillow, sniffs it and then clutches it tight against her chest.

For the first time he's known her, watched her, Sophie sheds a tear. It darkens the pillow's fabric. Once a light blue, now the color of a dark, midnight sky.

"We'll get him back," says Erigan. "I promise you."

"Do demons keep promises?" she says.

"I'm a god first."

"No," she says. "Not any more. You said."

Erigan takes a step back. If she's going to be this way, he won't take the time to reason with her.

She is, after all, human.

Sophie slams her foot down in her son's bedroom. The light blue of the Olympian sky against Brad's headboard catches her attention.

"I'm coming with you."

Erigan's tail slaps at Sophie's leg. "No, you're not."

He takes the piece of his broken horn and tucks it deep into his black tunic against his chest.

"But they have my son."

"And I will get him back. You stay here."

Sophie grabs hold of Erigan's tunic and thrusts her face into his. He had expected more of a reaction from her, his transformed, Hellish presence usually scares most humans.

But both Brad and she don't seem afraid.

He raises an eyebrow and wonders if she's even noticed that he looks different.

"And I told you. Not without my help." Sophie wields the pot in her hands. She begins to rattle it about in front of her, pretending perhaps to hit some "bad guy" on the head.

Erigan can see her knuckles turn white. Her lips push tight together. Her breathing slows.

"I cannot do this with you," he says.

"Well tough shit because you are."

Erigan grabs her shoulders tight at first, then lightens his grip. Her looks of surprise make Erigan feel better about this. Maybe she is human after all.

"Herc!" he cries out.

But no answer.

"Why are we waiting for him?" she asks.

"Because he knows something." Erigan could slap himself. His warnings. The pleadings to stay on Earth. To stay away.

Take a fucking vacation.

"Fuck you, Herakles! Now get your ass up here!"

Erigan listens close to the air. Nothing crackles between the molecules. No wavering or vibrations.

"He's not here," he says. "Come on."

"Where are we going?"

"We cannot stay here," he says. "If we do, they might come for you, too." Erigan seizes her hand, pulls her forward.

"So we go next door?"

Erigan tries to take a step forward, but he's pulled backward.

"No."

Erigan feels his hand grow cold from where Sophie pulled form his grip. "What do you mean no?" He snarls through his jagged teeth.

Sophie crosses her arms. "No, we aren't running."

"This isn't funny. This is not some sort of game," says Erigan. "If they took him, they can and will come for you. Or me."

"Is that what this is all about?" says Sophie. "About coming for you?"

"No," says Erigan after a beat. He pauses and looks past Sophie to the painted Mount Olympus behind her. "I mean yes. I do not know yet."

"Well that's not going to help get Brad back."

Erigan stomps into the ground and roars. "Do you not think I know that?"

"We're getting my son back," Sophie says. She stares directly in front of her. She studies the wall in front of her, as if some sort of plan or map lie hidden from Erigan's view. "Now let's go."

Erigan waits for only a moment. She is missing a vital piece of information. So, he taps his sandaled foot against the hardwood floors. "One. Two."

Sophie's head pops in from the hallway. "So how do we get to Hell?"

Chapter Forty-Two

The sky outside feels particularly bright today. Erigan could not notice how bright until he no longer felt the need to squint.

A light breeze carries with it the smell of rain. Darkened clouds lie just over the horizon.

All of this, Erigan sees while Sophie insists on embarrassing herself in the front office.

"But you said you didn't see anyone?" says Sophie.

Peggy rests her index finger against her chin and looks up. "No, hun," she says with a smile that seems permanently chiseled into her face. "Nope. No one left with the little boy."

"And you were here all day?" Sophie says. Erigan hears the quivering in her voice. She wants to yell but hides it.

Erigan steps up. As he does so, there's a smooth,

shadowy transition of red horned demon to smooth, baby-faced human. "Hi, sweetheart." He tries his best at a southern accent, but can't quite get it right. "You were here, right? All day?"

Peggy's eyes dart between Erigan and Sophie's exasperated eyes. "You want me to call the police?" she says. Peggy's shaking hands grasp at her necklace and she twirls the Star of David between her fingers. "I mean, I could get fired if word got out that a child rapist just took a young boy while I was watching over the place."

Sophie gasps. Her mouth won't close. Her left eye twitches,

Erigan can see she's angry and sad at the same time.

What do you do when a stranger suggests something that might be worse than death?

Peggy's hands reach out for Sophie's, which rest against the counter. "I didn't mean nothing by that, hun. Just, you know. You can never tell."

Sophie just walks away. Her mouth still open. "Take care of this, please."

Erigan tries to smile—and manages something passable at least—and says, "Listen, Peggy. Don't call the police. We cannot have you get fired because of a misplaced kid."

"Misplaced?" Peggy says. She whispers the word to herself, trying to convince herself.

"So if you call the police, it'll only make things awkward. You know what I'm saying?"

Peggy nods first, then shakes her head. "But I should tell somebody."

"What you should do is your absolute best to keep this secret, okay?"

Erigan's hands reach around and grasp Erigan's hands. He looks into her eyes. His eyes change colors slowly in the light until he sees Peggy's irises dilate. He rests on something like a green-hazel combination.

"Now that I have your attention," he says, "what are you going to do?"

Peggy nods.

"No, Peggy. Say it."

Peggy shakes her head.

"Peggy, dammit, if you don't say something, I'll have to be mean, and that will not be very nice."

Erigan feels a tug on his belt. "Did you hypnotize her or something?"

He shrugs her off. "Peggy, are you with me?"

Peggy shakes her head. "Yes."

"Good. Now who are you going to call?"

"Ghostbusters?"

Erigan looks over at Sophie. "Who is that?"

Sophie's hands cover her mouth, but Erigan can still see the thin edges of her lips as she tries to hide her laughter.

He rolls his eyes and pulls tighter. "Peggy, you need to get that, okay?"

Sophie mumbles, "Get what?"

The phone rings.

Peggy's eyes open wide. "Can you hold on a minute?" she says. "I need to get this."

Erigan waves her off. "Sure, go for it."

When Peggy is midway between the counter and phone, Erigan shouts out to her, "You know what? Don't worry about it. We'll be back later."

Peggy nods and lifts the receiver to her ear. "Saraday Apartments, Peggy speaking. How may I help you this beautiful afternoon?"

Sophie grins. "You did that."

"She'll be on the phone for the next twelve hours," says Erigan.

"How do you know?"

"Little god things," he says. "Every time she hangs up, the phone is going to ring and she'll feel compelled to pick it up."

"Wow," says Sophie.

The sun welcomes them both.

In this form, Erigan squints and shields his eyes with his palm.

"So what now?" Sophie says.

"Come with us," says a voice.

Erigan recognizes it and turns around. "Jason."

"We told you to keep out of sight and not cause any problems." Jason steps from beside the building. His tall friend Bell steps forward.

Bell keeps his arms cross across his chest. His wide shoulders fill out his white button down dress shirt. His gray slacks and black shoes look flawlessly clean. Fresh out the store.

"You just got here," says Erigan.

Jason smiles. "You're perceptive."

"How long have you been watching us?"

"Since you got here, Hermes."

Sophie steps forward and grips the pan. "You could have saved my son!" She takes a wild swing at Jason's head but misses. The force of the swing brings her down onto the grass.

The pan slams hard into the ground and grinds against the rocks as it slides away.

"Control your human," says Jason.

Erigan makes no sign to pick her up despite her reaching out to him.

"She's not my human, Jason. Why are you here?"

"We're here because we need you to lay low. And now that the child is taken, you need to come with us."

"Where is he?" Sophie cries. Her face turns red. She bares her teeth as she spouts her commands. "Take us to him!"

"If I could do that, human, you'd know about it."

"She has a name," says Erigan. "This is Sophie, the boy's mother."

"I know damn well who she is." Jason eyes her down. "I don't know what he sees in you anyway?"

Sophie peeks over at Erigan.

Erigan looks away, fidgets with his hands before thrusting them into his pants pockets.

"Where are we going?"

"Get in the car."

Sophie looks down the road. She rushes to Erigan's side and pulls on his shirt. "Down there."

Erigan doesn't have to look down to feel the presence of something magical coming his way.

"Where are we going?"

"If you'd just get in the car, we'll find out."

Sophie's arms wrap around Erigan's right arm tight. Her nails claw into his bicep out of fear.

It had been a long time since he had felt a human's body heat this close to his skin.

Part of it led him to fantasies, images of her soft skin in his mind.

The brown Lincoln Continental pulls up. The vehicle looks boxy when compared to most of the sleek and rounded metallic chariots he's seen parked along the streets.

Erigan peeks down when he hears Sophie whisper something to herself.

"Jason?" she says.

Erigan turns to face the vehicle and nods.

A white vanity license plate screwed into the front of the car reads in red letters ARGO.

Chapter Forty-Three

Though Erigan will concede that though he has not been in Saraday, South Carolina very long—or Earth, for that matter—none of this looks familiar at all to him.

"Where are we?" Sophie whispers to Erigan.

Both men at the table turn toward Sophie and raise their eyebrows.

A not-so-universal sign for shut the Hell up.

Despite the subtle connotations, Sophie gets the hint.

The room is surrounded in green paint. A dark green like the needle-like leaves on the pine trees that surround the Saraday library.

Erigan thinks this is a restaurant, but there's nothing that reminds him of food in the air. It smells fresh, like regular clean air.

No customers sit at any of the booths or table around him.

There is not even a bar where one can get deliciously flavored alcoholic drinks. So it cannot be a restaurant, right?

"I don't recognize this place," says Sophie. "So where are we? And just how fast were you driving? Do you know where my son is?"

Jason pulls his disappointing gaze to Erigan and takes his pointed fingers and slices across his throat.

Erigan nods and snaps his fingers. As he does so, Sophie falls gently onto his shoulder.

"Thank you," Jason says.

Bell smiles and then peers behind Erigan's left shoulder.

Erigan shrugs. "And we are here because?"

"Because we need help," says Jason. "And you need our help. It's a win-win scenario."

"I never said I needed your help."

A dark voice coughed behind Erigan and Sophie. "That's because you are, and always have been, stupid."

Erigan sat up and turned around.

Sophie, still asleep, nuzzled over to the table and began snoring.

"Just who the hell do you think you are?" Erigan stands up from the table. His body shifts, covered with shadows like a silken curtain. It swirls around his body as if made of liquid. Soon, it drips off his skin and he emerges with his demon red skin, black eyes and hair.

"Sit down, son, so we can talk this over." Standing at the edge of the tables one row over is a tall man. He stands proudly, shoulders high and white hair falling from his remarkably smooth, pale white skin. His snow white beard has streaks of black that strike like bolts from the edges of his lips, tracing a shape somewhat like a goatee down to his chin.

He holds a white gold cane in his hand, using it to walk over. In the light, an untucked white button down shirt becomes visible.

"Zeus?" Erigan kneels, bows his head and closes his eyes. His form does not change.

"You continue to keep this form they gave you?" says Zeus. He taps Erigan on the shoulder. "Get up. I'm your father, for Christ's sake."

Erigan recognizes the irony of his word choice but says nothing. He smiles and gives his father a giant hug.

The hug feels like it's over in a blink of an eye, but the others in the room—Jason and Bell—both stand at the table and have their heads facing downward. Bell reaches for his forehead and massages it, trying to look away.

"I thought you were killed?"

Zeus motions for them all to sit down. "Is that what they're telling you?" He grins and strokes his beard.

"Those were the rumors." Erigan smirks. "It is Hell. There are millions of rumors all the time."

"I left," says Zeus. His voice rings deep, full of a bass that shakes Erigan's chest even in his hellish form. "To regroup. To plan."

"Plan?"

Zeus waves it off. "The girl," he says. "Her son is taken."

Erigan nods. "Yes, it was my job to find him. But things got—complicated."

Zeus sighs. "They always do with you."

"What is that—?"

Jason slams his fist on the table. This silences Erigan.

"I'll be honest. We need you. If you can help me out, then we'll help the boy."

Erigan searches his father's storm gray eyes for a hidden meaning, a secret somewhere. A god of communication, Erigan has always had a knack to sense deceit.

But as of late, it seems that he's off his game. Everything falling apart at the seams.

"Fine," says Erigan. "I'll play. What do we do?"

"First," says Zeus. "We get you into Hell. Then, we take what's ours."

Chapter Forty-Four

Erigan watches as Sophie's eyelids flicker just before she opens them.

"Were we kidnapped by the Greek mafia?" she says.

Erigan says, "Worse."

Sophie rubs her eyes and then tries to sit up. Erigan grabs her shoulders and pulls her forward. "Where are we?"

Erigan looks around at their makeshift holding room. The room is small, dusty. Probably meant to be a private dining area in an old restaurant. The walls here are painted a maroon color. Chipped and faded in some areas. The air still feels fresh, not tainted with food or mold.

"I have no idea," says Erigan.

"Is it the Italian mafia?" she says. "When did I fall asleep?"

"My fault," says Erigan.

Sophie nods and holds her head. "Is my head supposed to hurt?"

"Probably," says Erigan.

"What's your fucking problem?" says Sophie. "My kid's the one that was taken."

Erigan stands up and look out the doorway into the rest of the restaurant. Bell and Jason both surround his father as the two appear to concoct some plan, a plan that will remain hidden from Erigan.

"Blood is thicker than water" be damned.

Erigan feels his sharpened nails dig into the leathery red skin of his palms.

Sophie stands up like a new foal learning to walk. She wobbles at first, then grabs her chair. Steadily, she stands up and smiles at Erigan, looking for approval.

"What did you guys do to me?"

"You were asking a lot of questions and we needed you to be quiet."

Sophie says, "And you couldn't have just told me to shut up?"

"Would you have?" Erigan says.

Sophie shrugs.

"Then I was justified."

Sophie goes to stand next to Erigan. He feels her arms reach for his. For security, he feels.

But he doesn't need security.

He pulls away and crosses his arms.

Sophie take a step back and returns to her chair.

"Now what?"

"Now we wait and see what their plan is."

"Meanwhile they rape and kill my child?" Sophie stands up again. Quickly at first, but then returns to sitting down when her head spins. "Seriously, what did you guys do to me?"

"I put you under a sleep spell. Your body is resisting. It will pass."

Sophie grabs her head. "Jesus Christ. Fuck you guys."

Erigan looks over his shoulder where Sophie sticks her head between her legs. She coughs a bit and then spits onto the ground.

"You'll be fine. I promise."

Sophie looks up. Her eyes are red, bloodshot, he thinks it's called. "But what about Brad? Why him? Why not me? What do they want?"

"I don't know," says Erigan. "We need to figure—"

Something knocks on the door behind him.

"Is that you?" says Sophie.

Erigan shakes his head. "I thought it was you." Erigan takes a step toward the back wall, but stops. He returns to the doorway and peers outside at his father, still in heavy conversation with his henchmen...if that's what they're called these days.

They make no movements. Not even looking back here.

They don't hear the sound.

"It's no one they know," says Erigan. He walks to the back wall and knocks.

Another knocking from the other side.

Erigan takes a step back. "Come out, Herc."

Behemoth materializes through the wall, fading in from a blurry humanoid shape to a solid man-shaped tower of muscle.

"How did you know it was me?" says Behemoth.

"Where the fuck were you?" Though Erigan is almost half Behemoth's size, it doesn't keep him from pointing a sharpened fingernail into his chest, jabbing deeper and deeper with each successive poke.

"I had to lay low," says Behemoth. "I told you she found him."

"And you couldn't help?"

"Dude, they are after me, too."

Erigan's claws dig into Behemoth's green and white Hawaiian shirt. He presses him against the wall, careful to not make a sound and catch the attention of his father.

"Speak. Now. All of it. Where is the boy?"

"Lilith has him. Don't know why."

Erigan thrusts him into the wall again. The look on Behemoth's face turns from a stoic calm to legitimate concern.

Erigan lapses for only a split second as he wonders where his strength came from.

"You know more than you speak," says Erigan. "Now talk." Erigan speaks calmly, slowly. This appears to frighten the demigod much more than yelling.

"All I know is she wanted the boy, but we're not sure

why. Ba'al may be involved."

"Tell me something I do not already know," says Erigan. He keeps one hand on Behemoth's chest while reaching into his vest and pulling out his horn. "He left me a present."

Erigan tosses it to the ground with a thump.

Behemoth's eyes widen. And though he is literally backed into a corner, he apparently has nothing to say.

"I need you to find out where they are keeping the boy, and why they need him."

Behemoth shakes his head up and down quickly. "Y-yes."

"Good. And when you are done with that, you come find me."

Erigan and Behemoth both seem to hear Sophie's muted but impressed whistle at the situation.

Then, footsteps.

"Now go," says Erigan. "Remember. Find him, then find me."

Behemoth nods.

When Erigan releases Behemoth from his grip, the man-giant disappears gradually into the wall, dispersing into the air.

"I don't think I can get used to seeing that."

Erigan turns and smiles at his father. "So, what is our great plan, Lord Zeus?"

"Why did you not tell me that you cannot return to Hell?" asked Zeus.

"You did not ask me, Father."

Zeus raises his right hand and with great speed, he backhands his son.

Erigan's body drops to the floor. He holds himself up and rubs his cheek.

Erigan's red, leathery cheek turns purplish, then black. A bruise.

"Do not play semantics with me, child. True you are a god of communication, but you will not play word games with me. Now speak. Why did you not tell me?"

Erigan looks down at the ground. "They locked me out. Someone did, anyway."

"And why?"

Sophie steps forward, between herself and Zeus. "Lay off him, will you?"

Zeus pauses. His hand raises up at first. All in the room no doubt believe that he will punish Sophie as well.

But his shoulder relaxes, dropping. The back of Zeus's muscular hands gently rubs Sophie's cheek. "It's been a long time since then, but you need to get out of the way, child. There is no reason to make your son an orphan."

Sophie steps down. She falls to Erigan's side. "Are you okay?" she asks.

Erigan nods and wipes his cheek.

"Do not take that demonic, Christian form with me, child. Be who you are."

Erigan's form fades from red to white. A dark, olive complexion with dark green eyes and curly hair.

He looks to Sophie for a reaction.

Sophie takes a quick breath in and then lets it out slowly.

Erigan feels the pressure of her breath against his skin. Finding that she seems to be smiling, he finds the side of his mouth curling upwards into a smile.

Even in this restaurant and in this stress, she still smells like flowers. And vanilla, maybe.

"There," says Zeus. "That's so much more refreshing, isn't it?"

Sophie sits cross-legged on the floor. Her eyes, wide open, she watches as Zeus kneels down in front of his son.

"No longer are you Erigan, demon of lies. You are better than that. You are once more Hermes, Messenger of the Gods. God of commerce, communication, and travel. And my trickster son."

Zeus stands up and then turns around. He extends his arms out as if to hug someone, anyone.

Erigan watches as Zeus eyes him, telling him to stand up and hug his father, but Erigan refuses, remains on the floor.

"We will be great again, son. We will take back what is ours."

"And how are we going to be great again? We hold no power."

"If we cause an uproar, raise an army, we can storm Olympus once more and take what we need." Zeus speaks so slowly that Erigan thinks himself to be deaf.

"You do realize what will happen if you succeed? You will tear the Christian world apart and go against Jehova himself. You cannot be that stupid. You will cause both Heaven and Hell to wage war on us all."

"You have no faith in me, child. All of the trust I put in you, and you will not return it when I need it so? We will be great again, son."

He crosses his arms across his chest. His smirk reminds him of the coy, stupid smiles of Behemoth. Those same ones he has wanted to choke off of his face time and time again.

This smile causes the same reaction, so Erigan rests his hands behind his back.

Zeus approaches Erigan and grips his shoulders tight. His electric blue eyes blink once, twice, then he says slowly, "As I said, we will be great again. But first, I must send you out to one slight errand."

Chapter Forty-Five

Upon leaving Mount Olympus, all of the Greek gods were warned: Do not return to Greece.

It was the ultimate insult to the Greek pantheon. To never return to their old stomping grounds. Their home. Their loved ones.

Instead, they were sent packing to their new home in Tartaros.

Today, the Christian world calls it Hell. The truth is, only part of it belong to Hell. The other part is where people in Hell get forgotten about.

Every major religion has their own version of it. A place of suffering for those who led horrible, immoral lives while under the watchful eye of the predominate deity. A prison for souls, if you will.

And though Erigan has made the trip millions of times back in the days of Ancient Greece and Rome, he feels his stomach churn with anxiety and perverse wonder.

If anyone were to ask him, however, he would deny it all flat out.

Erigan's winged sandals carry him to Greece in record time. His destination is in the northwest of Greece. A river named Acheron, the gateway to Hades.

The river has changed much since he has been here last. In nearly two thousand years, there are many more people settled around its shores.

A house buried deep into the wooded areas to the south.

The small village of Ammoudia to the north.

The soft crashing of waves against the rocky shores around him, it all makes Erigan take in a deep breath of salty air and smile.

"It is so good to be home," he says.

He lands in the water, near the mouth of the river that pours into the Ionian Sea. The cold water chills Erigan's legs. He misses these moments, and the deep blue green that would make an emerald jealous.

He wades through the water, distracted by the scenery and the knowledge that the human settlements have made this job much more riskier than it should be.

In the distance he hears the sounds of boats against the waves. Nothing motorized this late in the afternoon, in this heat.

But up the river, white boats, flat and wide, bob along the river's edge.

Rich humans. Treating this sacred river as a spot of relaxation.

If they had only known.

He steps out of the water and walks along the surface. His wings flitter loudly to keep him above the surface.

If one were to watch from afar, Erigan would appear to be walking on the water's surface.

Thick bushes with thin, green leaves jut out into the water's surface. These plants have learned to thrive off the moist, nutritious soil along the riverbed. Opportunists, Erigan thinks.

He can respect that.

If he ever sees Demeter again, he'll have to compliment her on their incredible resiliency.

Their cattails, these thin and light tan straws poke out of the bush like arrows buried in the wooden wall of a fortress. At the end of each straw hangs a thin line of delicate feather-like leaves. So soft against his skin as he brushes past them, it feels like a slow dip into the Ionian Sea.

A rather large part of him wants to just sit down, dig his feet into the soil and relish in this opportunity.

But a bigger part of him wishes to see Hades and Tartaros again. If only to relive old memories.

Erigan brushes past the bushes. His toes sink into the thick, wet soil. Rather than feel uncomfortable, he smiles.

Home sweet home.

Erigan presses on down the river bed, following it as it curves south, then north into the heart of Greece.

The people around these areas make much more noise than he remembered. Gas-powered engines and screaming groups of people.

And tourists.

Oh, the damned tourists.

All of these things disrupt his line of thought. Like a constant poking—no prodding—into his brain with the trident of Poseidon himself.

All of this to get away from Hell. To get out of responsibility. Now that he's finally out, he's forced to go back in and rescue a boy he doesn't know.

Yet a boy that seems too important to everyone except him.

The cliffs along the river grow steeper along the northern shore.

A sign, he believes. Growing closer.

Something rustles the grass and straw-like bushes behind him.

"Just where, exactly, do you think you are going, Hermes?"

The voice sounds familiar, but the tone does not.

He looks over his shoulder then turns around. A girl child, dark brown hair and thick eyebrows stand out on her face. Her skin is dark from sun exposure, her eyes a light green.

"That's brave of you," he says. "Hiding behind a child."

The girl smiles and rests her hands against her hips. "What's the matter?" she says. "Don't you love the new me?"

Erigan takes the three steps toward the girl and he grabs her neck. "Where is the boy? Tell me or I kill this body."

"I've been in Hell longer than you can imagine," she says.

The girl's appears to cough up blood but still continues to smile. When she blinks, her eyes turn empty, completely white. Her smile stagnant and lifeless.

"I've grown in powers, you pussy. Besides, I saw the way you look at that girl and this boy. You have gotten soft and domesticated. You don't have the stones to destroy this child."

Erigan's grip grows tighter around the girl's neck.

Her cheeks swell and puff out, her eyes turning red. Soon her forehead turns white then a bright red.

The girl continues to smile. "So you do have stones."

A pause as Erigan studies the girl's eyes, looking for a sign of Lilith. Maybe he can pull her out. Scare her.

"Good," says the girl and she kicks Erigan between the legs.

Though still a demon, he feels the surprise jolt of pain travel through his thighs and up through his stomach.

His grip weakens and the girl lands on her knees.

For a moment, she cries then stands up and kicks

Erigan in the face.

"You're a fucking pussy," she says. "Always will have been and always will be."

The girl leans over into the riverbed. She grasps a smooth gray rock as thick as her hands. Her smile steadies, even widens a bit until it almost takes over her face.

"Your beloved boy is already dead," she says.

The rock goes into her forehead. Blood drips from her temples. The smile continues.

"And there's nothing you can do about it," she says. The rock goes into her forehead again. This time, the girl staggers backward for a split moment. Then her stance steadies.

Her lips become traced with the blood that drips down the ridges of her nose.

"We already have what we want." The girl's voice fades and cracks. Though Lilith inhabits the mind, the body grows weak from the abuse.

The girl's hand thrusts the rock further and further into the front, then side of the head of the girl.

Erigan rushes to his feet and straddles the girl's waist He tries to pull the rock from her tiny little hands, but it's no use. Her arms keep with the repetitive motions, banging the rock into the girl's head.

Erigan seizes the girl's arms and pulls them down. When they are down far enough, Erigan rests his knees onto her wrists to paralyze her.

Dark black and purple splotches grow quickly over

the child's face. Still, she smiles and even winks at Erigan.

"You always were a sap," she says. Blood drips down the side of the girl's head and into the river. The water around them turns a murky, muddy red an then dissolves to its pure blue green color.

"You're being led into a trap," the girl whispers. "And Ba'al is pissed."

The smile begins to fade on the child's face. Erigan's grip on her wrists weakens until he's convinced she's no longer a danger to herself.

He stands up and looks over the girl's body.

Lilith's presence fades from the girl's body.

What's left is a screaming, crying husk as the girl realizes her last moments.

Erigan leaves the body and continues walking down the river. Though he feels a presence behind him, he doesn't turn around. Keeping his gaze forward toward his destination, he catches the faint spirit.

The little girl.

She runs behind him, eventually passing him by and disappearing into the trees to the south.

Chapter Forty-Six

Erigan pushes aside the overgrown bushes. The shade cast over him from the high walls feels good in the salty heat that beat down on him from overhead.

The light brown wall in front of him looked solid, packed tight. It looked to be made up of the packed dirt from the surrounding riverbed and beaches. The miracle is that it stayed up at all.

After all, this is relatively shallow cliff. Any reasonable weight can cause it to collapse. It was a miracle at all that it never did these last two thousand years. A true testament to Hephaestus's handiwork. It was a simple mass of land that looks unassuming to most human eyes, unless you knew what you were looking for.

Erigan pushes the bushes further aside to his left. There, hidden in the deepest heart of the bush, stands a statue of a three-headed dog seated as if guarding an entrance.

"Kerberos, my good friend." Erigan's hand taps the top of the head and scratches behind the stone ear.

Erigan smiles, half expecting a real dog to spring out of the rock. The statue, however, is only that.

His real gigantic furry friend was moved during the takeover. His new role is that of torturer and guardian of the Third Circle of Hell. His daily meals are made up of gluttonous souls.

At least most of the souls are fat. He certainly cannot starve with a job like that.

To Erigan's eyes, it is not even a reasonable fake. All of its features were cut to make it boxy and angular. The statue itself only stood maybe four feet high, but the rest of it was worn thin from the dirt that blew in the winds. What still remains of the statue is smoothed out. Almost featureless. Everything except Kerberos's most prominent feature: his mouth.

"That's one," he mutters to himself.

He searches his right and pushes back on some branches. They fall away easily. Loose.

Was this area still being used to get in and out?

Erigan kneels in the dirt and searches the grounds in front of him.

"There you are," he says.

The second stone guardian, a snake curled up into a tight ball on the ground.

The two statues were meant to be only threats and warnings. A superstition that kept most of the looters and would-be heroes out of Hades and into the realm of humans where they belonged.

Too many humans in Hades and things get confusing and messy very, very quickly. So, they needed a simple message: "Do not cross here" these statues demanded of any potential trespassers.

The stone Kerberos warned them of what was to come. The snake represented Death.

It's not what Hades had wanted, but the people will be people after all. And it was their superstitions that helped them have power.

While some of the gods and goddesses remained pissed at their representations, Hermes found himself flattered by the attention.

"If they think this much about us to create all of this, then they must love us," he told Eros once.

Eros never bought the same philosophy himself. "Can't those idiots see that I do not even have wings," he said. "Where did that even come from?"

Erigan smiles and nods. Resting his hands against the wall in front of him, he presses forward.

The wall gives way and Erigan stumbles forward. He shakes the surprise off of his face and steps forward into the tunnel.

The lake pours in around his feet soon after the door is opened. The familiar smell of moist dirt and stale shit lingers. Erigan takes one long sniff and wipes a tear from his eye.

"It is so good to be back home," he says.

Chapter Forty-Seven

Erigan flies over the River Styx and the surrounding boats and docks. Each of the docks is really nothing more than a rocky peninsula. Just wide enough for a human or two to stand side-by-side and wait for Charon to come pick them up.

Lucky for him, Charon was forcefully "retired" a thousand years ago. Now he resides in one of the circles of Hell. No one seems to know which circle, nor for which sin.

But as Erigan flies over, he takes a moment and lands in the boat that Charon used most often. The boat was narrow, made of a solid dark wood not from the earth above.

Another example of the gods' amazing creativity and ingenuity. If there were something needed, they always had the power to make it happen.

So then how could it all just go to shit so quickly?

Erigan legs begin to twitch, so he flies up into the air. The rocky ceiling is dark, jagged, and threatens to scrape the top of his head if he were to fly too close.

It was easy to do, fly too high up. The entirety of Hades was something of a darkened maze when Hermes's young eyes had first seen it. It was a new realm, just given to his uncle from a rigged game.

If you were to ask Hades, both Poseidon and Zeus conspired against him. He just couldn't prove it.

So, he terrorized the souls whenever he could.

Hades wasn't all bad, Hermes felt. It was cool at this level, a refreshing getaway from the warm humidity on the surface. It was also quiet.

The souls knew better than to cause any problems, for Kerberos was a huge, terrifying dog.

And he had an appetite to match.

Erigan's eyes survey the entirety of Hell from his floating position over the mouth of the River Styx.

"You'll know him when you see him, son." That was Zeus's message to him before sending him off on this ridiculous mission.

"But seriously, what am I doing back in Hades?"

Zeus remained silent at first, then took his hands and grasped Erigan's shoulders. "You are my son, Hermes, and although I hate to put you in this kind of danger, I must ask you to take one final trip into Hades."

At that, Zeus turned and disappeared out of sight.

It's a nasty habit that he, too, shared.

When the conversation gets too awkward, when the humans ask too many questions, you disappear. Let them figure it out.

"Let them learn," Apollo often said with a slight chuckle in his golden voice. "If you do everything for them, they will not be stronger and better when the time comes."

Erigan felt his hands come to a tight grip.

He was not human.

He refused to think of himself as human.

And yet, this was what he was teased for. Both Behemoth-slash-Herakles, Lilith, and the all-mighty Zeus, his own father, had made note of it.

"You're too soft," they said.

Were they right?

As Erigan continues down the path watery path, the light grows dimmer. The last source of light comes from the illuminating glow of the entrance and exit...the only one in these parts of the Underworld.

But for now, Erigan flies still. Light echoes of his winged sandals reach his ears.

Beyond that: Silence.

Erigan, lacking worthwhile directions, flies to the center of the Underworld and finds the River Phlegethon—the river of fire. This river was vast, circling around the Underworld until finally delivering its waters to the world underneath: Tartaros.

He begins his flight upon the river of fire, moving higher so the tongues of flame just miss the bottoms of his feet.

Anything higher than that, and he risks being run through with the solid black stalactites.

The path grows darker, the walls closer to his physical self as he delves deeper into the caves. To keep his mind off the mysteries and wonderment, he tries to determine whether he is colder or hotter here than in the Underworld.

He concedes that he is both.

As messenger of the Gods, it was not customary for him to deliver any souls to Tartaros. Anyone going there was delivered straight to their prisons by Zeus himself.

The last known occupants were the Titans—his grandfather and great uncles. Now, he knows not what he will find.

And for all his time in Hell, this thought frightens him more.

Soon upon the cave, through a hole no bigger than a human child, comes in a strip of weak light.

These were the only sources of light in Tartaros.

Erigan holds his arms and legs tight together to make himself slim and small and he flies headfirst into the hole.

Emerging into the other side, he feels a chill crawl up his lower back to his neck.

Only three tracks of faint light circled around him like collars around a dog's neck. The light only gives enough vision, even for a god used to the eternal darkness of Hell, for him to spot giant roots in the ceiling miles above him.

The roots hang from the ceiling in much the way that clouds hang in the sky above the land of Earth.

Erigan shivers again. He looks down below and spots a familiar spot: the once eternal punishment spot of Sisyphus. The only king who swore he was more clever than Zeus and worthy of being a god himself. He was punished with his boulder, which still stood in its resting place at the bottom of the hill.

Sisyphus had escaped nearly three times in his time in Tartaros. The third time, Hermes was charged with dragging his pathetic ass back all by himself.

That seems like a lifetime ago, as Erigan flies down to the ground. Near his feet, he kicks manacles—empty and opened—that lay on the ground like forgotten waste.

Now Sisyphus is rewarded with a new position in Hell. Lucifer, a being of much pride himself, found a kindred spirit in Sisyphus and stole him from his chains, awarding him a high position in Hell.

His name—like all of their names—have been changed to keep the humans from recognizing them. But Sisyphus still lived, much to the anger of all the original Olympians. This time, they just called him Ba'al.

Erigan is pulled from his deep thought by the rattling of chains in the deep distance.

It is the only thing he hears except for his own swallows and winged sandals.

Should he go toward it? Is this what Zeus had wanted him to find?

"Hello?" he calls out.

The words echo into the empty walls and refuse to come back to his own ears.

He flies closer to the ground, still away from the freezing cold, gray, and rocky land mass.

"Hello?"

More rattling.

Going against his better judgment, Erigan flies closer to the sounds. The rattling grows more restless. These belong to chains.

"Someone is still down here?" he calls out.

It is as much a question as it is an answer.

The chains stop their noise for a brief moment. Then coughing.

"Hello?"

Erigan closes his eyes and follows the sounds. He hears the sounds grow louder, returned and echoed off the solid gray wall that cover all of his view in the distance.

A voice coughs again.

For a moment, Erigan considers that he may be losing his mind.

Perhaps a spirit wandered in here. The entrance was hidden, but not *that* hidden.

But still, who could have possibly made it down here?

Who would even want to be down here?

He gives it one more call. "Hello?"

A weak voice calls out to him from down below.

"Hel-hello?"

Erigan follows the voice with his eyes closed.

Trusting his gut, he lands on what seems like a floating island amidst a sea of darkness.

The island is small, maybe only two human lengths long. Ten humans lengths wide. He opens his eyes.

"Why have you come?" says the voice.

The figure before him has thick black hair that grows into a fierce beard that hangs from his old chin, strong as the stalactites above him.

His eyes are black as onyx, his skin a light blue. And immediately, Erigan recognizes his own uncle.

Chapter Forty-Eight

"Hades?" Erigan's ankle wings drop him to the ground without much of a warning.

When Erigan's mind wanders, he finds the wings have a tendency to do whatever the hell they want.

"Is this where they kept you?"

Hades struggles to stand from his knelt position. A thick black cloak hangs off of his body. Nothing but his knees—hairless but strong with thick muscles—and hands are visible from the dark shadowy cloth.

"Why are you here, nephew?" Hades holds up a shaky hand and stops whatever Erigan may want to say. "He sent you, didn't he?"

"You knew?"

Hades nods. "I knew he would send for me again. Eventually."

Erigan drops to his knees. He examines the manacles

that hold his uncle in place. In the little bit of light that glows dimly over them, Erigan can barely make out what might be holding his uncle to his prison.

"You are wasting your time," says Hades. He growls as he says this, his lips pulling away from his teeth. "Go back and tell my youngest brother that I will not join his army."

"Army? What army?" Erigan releases his tight grip on the manacles and falls back to sit on his heels.

Hades chuckles. His head falls forward. His hair drapes down over his forehead, down to his chest. Without looking up, Hades says, "He even keeps this , his big great plan, from his own kin?"

"What army?"

Hades lets out a sigh that turns into light chuckles that shake his shoulders. "Your father thinks himself to be another revolutionary yet again."

Before Hermes and his family of Olympians were overthrown and evicted from their beautiful Mount Olympus home, Zeus had worked with his siblings to rid the human world of the Titans. He went so far as to exile his own father, Cronus, into Tartaros.

"He just wants his respect," he says.

"Your father is ignorant and naïve. He cannot win because it is not his right to win!" Hades thrusts forward from his chains. His hands, cuffed together and held at his side by chains that extended a body-length away from their points in the ground. "And he will get you all stuck down here."

"Is that what happened to you?" says Erigan.

After the takeover, the new "regime change" as Erigan affectionately calls it, some of the old gods were rounded up and cast into Hell. The ones that went missing—well, everyone assumed they just didn't make it through the war.

"I was cast here out of fear. Do you know how many rulers of an Underworld the humans need? Turns out two is a bit more confusing than those idiots upstairs can understand." Hades twitches his hands first, then moves them around in a small circle. "I grow restless," he says.

Erigan grabs hold of the chain and grips them tightly. "Then let me free you, at least."

"No," he says. "If you do that, I'll be in even more trouble."

"The Great Dark Lord of the Underground, Hades himself, is afraid of a little trouble?"

"A little trouble?"

Erigan takes a step backwards as he notices Hades' body shift from completely kneeling and leaning forward to sitting up. Hades' hands rest by his body, supporting him as he attempts to stand up fully.

"You've seen what he can do, I presume. What they are capable of. The Lightbringer is pissed off because he's playing second fiddle to the man upstairs. It's a battle he cannot win, but he won't stop trying." Hades' tall and thin body towers over Erigan. "And, young Hermes, your father is about to do the same damned thing."

"So you cannot be freed?"

"Have you noticed that the punishments—the Nine Levels of Hell—are all derived from the punishments down here? That ignorant asswipe of a deity hasn't had an original thought since he was created. Even that so-called supreme being God Jehova has taken Zeus's appearance. All in the name of subjugating the masses."

Erigan's ankle wings flap, causing him to take flight.

"Our power is based on beliefs, young one. Surely even you know that."

Erigan notices that Hades' hands form tight fists with knuckles that crackle as he flexes them.

"What do you think those two will do when there is a challenge to their right to rule? You saw what that forgiving God did to one of his own. Cast him out, forced him to take my title and my realm." Hades' cheeks create deep, dark dimples in his cheeks as he smirks. "So, no. Leave me right here."

Erigan's sandals touch the ground once more.

"Tell me more," Erigan says. "Then why would Father threaten his family and his own life so?"

"Because he sees hope in the future. Maybe hope in you. Maybe hope in another."

Erigan freezes still. "Brad?"

Hades shrugs and brings his hands forward. "You can't leave here. You know too much. You cannot feign ignorance, Hermes. He will see through and cast you here too."

The chained god's hands make tight fists.

"My brother will fail because he has to fail. Our time is over, young Hermes. He must be allowed to fail and die for leaving me down here. For casting me out of Olympus and into the Depths."

"I must warn my father." Erigan turns to fly but feels something tug on his tunic. "Uncle, what are you doing?"

"You cannot leave me here. You cannot warn him!" says Hades between snarling teeth.

Erigan feels his neck grow cold, then warm, squeezed tightly. Hades' chains wrapped around his neck.

Erigan reaches for his neck. His fingers slip in and out of the holes of the rings around his neck, but never able to get a solid grip on them.

He pulls at his uncle's arms and hands. Then slaps about his own shoulders.

He feels his own breath leave his body in smaller and smaller breaths.

Erigan fears closing his eyes. He fears what he may see if he should do so. Down here in the depths of Tartaros, he may see anything. Or nothing.

Nothing forever.

"Uncle," Erigan tries to say but it only comes out in gurgles and stray pieces of spit.

He falls backwards and lands on the ground.

Hades's thin but deceptively strong body buffers his fall.

Erigan thinks he hears something snap. Maybe a cracking noise in the middle of the tussle. He does not stop to listen further.

He attempts to turn around, grab his uncle's cloak and maybe return the favor. He fails at all costs. Hades is just too fast for him. Even now.

Erigan feels his shoulders fail, weaken and droop to his side.

"I'm sorry to do this," says Hades. "But he must die so that you can all live. My brother must fail."

Erigan's eyes close. The sounds of rocks falling, maybe crumbling off the island blend together and then silence.

And for a moment, Erigan doubts he will ever wake up again.

Chapter Forty-Nine

When Erigan takes what he believes to be his last breath, he feels the cold, dank air rush around his neck.

The chains, they loosen around his neck and he's able to take in a deep breath yet again.

And another.

His hands grip his neck to validate the obvious. Yes, the chains are gone.

Erigan sits up and looks behind him. His uncle lays unmoving underneath him.

"You're welcome," says a female voice. A white hand with blue fingernails that remind Erigan of a suffocated corpse extends into his blurry field of vision. "Need some help?"

Erigan rubs his eyes and waits—and hopes, really—that his eyesight will return to normal. As he sits in silence, the blurry image of white gradually takes a human shape.

Or half of a human shape. The bottom half of the body appears to be stuck, maybe even merged, with the stone wall behind her.

As Erigan's eyes begin to focus, the details fill in and he's greeted by a friendly, albeit saddened face that looks pale compared to the dark, almost shadow-like rocks around them.

"Persephone," says Erigan. "You are held captive, too?"

"When my husband was cast down here, Lucifer thought it a bad idea to separate us." A thick rock drops from the grip of her left hand. "How nice of him."

Erigan stands and kicks his uncle. "He is out cold. I do not know how to thank you."

Persephone looks up at her hands and extends her chained wrists to Erigan. "Free me?"

Erigan searches her manacles for a weakness but finds none.

"Looks like Hephaestus's work," he says. "I don't know that I can do anything to help you."

Persephone's face turns downward. From this vantage point, Erigan can see patches of hair missing from her scalp. The little bald spots are few and far between, but big enough to make it look like she may have pulled them out herself over the millennia.

"You will get me free," she says. "I helped you. You must."

Erigan's feet took flight. "I am sorry. You would be

another mouth to feed and get in the way."

"You wretch!" she scream.

Her powerful voice echoes in the dark caves. "You miserable, fucking wretch!" She screams something that Erigan does not hear—or want to understand. Maybe ancient Greek. Maybe a long-forgotten language.

He shrugs and manages something of a smile.

While he means it as a smile of hope, Persephone apparently takes it as a snub. A happy-go-lucky "fuck you."

She grabs the rock that she had used to subdue her husband and launches it into the air.

Erigan watches the rock fly toward him.

All of his time in the air, able to fly around at will, and he misunderstands just how fast and far that rock could fly.

Erigan looks upwards, his goal to dodge the rock and fly toward the ceiling.

His wings, however, have a different idea altogether.

He reaches down toward the veil of fire that radiates from his foot. His ankle feels slick, warm.

Blood?

"Bitch," he says to himself and only himself. He dare not piss her off again.

He lowers himself down only a little. The other foot has to take most of the weight, and carrying himself outside will take more than he thinks his little sandal wings can handle.

After all, his sandals only go as fast as he tells them.

And when he's in pain, he has a tendency to not think so clearly.

He moves backwards slowly—almost crawling—as he faces the crying and shrieking face of his aunt.

Or is that niece? Or maybe it was sister?

Is there a name for all three at the same time?

These thoughts entertain Erigan's brain, forcing him to pay attention away from the wincing pain and into the moment. Get out of the pain head. Focus at the task at hand.

However, a realization hits for Erigan in the gut: his family tree is turned in on itself, twisted with the various trysts and inbreeding to keep the powers of Olympus within the same family.

Centuries of human families attempted the same thing in Europe. Mostly with great successful, he remembers. He watched with amazement as the royal cousins, the King of England, Tsar of Russia, and Kaiser of Germany, all started World War I amidst their family issues.

Erigan smirks as he passes over the fiery River Phlegethon. He may not condone the killing of family members, but he certainly understands.

He comes to an open area just before the connecting to the River Acheron—the river of hate.

As he does so, he pauses and hovers in the air. Below him lay gray rocks, dark as ash. A solid floor with dust that penetrates the clothing and stays forever.

At one time, this part of the Underworld boasted

over a million souls. Easily a billion after the wars that tore the city-states apart.

And now, nothing. No new souls. No old souls. No nothing.

He says a name. "Hades." As if by some magic, it will bring everything back again.

His words fall on empty walls.

They feel weak, even deep down here. The eternal resting place of spirits—both good and bad—is now nothing more than a wasteland. A ghost town minus the ghosts.

He flies closer to the edge of the river and follows it out into the Ionian Bay. Here, he pauses and takes in the fresh air.

He smells the sweet, herbal scent of daffodils and wet grass. The salty air kisses his nostrils and he realizes, this could be the last time he gets to see this yet again.

"How many more years?" he asks himself.

He doesn't expect an answer, but it would be nice if someone, somewhere, was able to answer.

Chapter Fifty

His ankle throbs even with it bearing no weight as he flies. He knows touching it and grabbing won't help—it rarely does—but he does it anyway.

He flies high over the town of Saraday. Clouds tickle his hair just above him and down below, he notices that the town seems quiet, even in the afternoon.

The orange sun sets into a pink sunset. A blend of pink and light blue swirls in the sky directly above him.

In the middle of the air, he manages to bring his foot up to his navel and clutch his ankle in his hands. It feels warm in his grip. The bleeding has slowed, but down below it rains tiny droplets that drip slowly off his toes.

How to tell your father that you've failed? That his brother wants him to fail, to die, and suffer because he has to?

Erigan flies back to his building and lands just

behind it. With a lack of people around, he considers it safe to do what he wants freely. Who cares about hiding his identity now?

He walks into the foyer and directly up the stairs in front of him. He doesn't turn around when Peggy tries to catch his attention.

He waves her off, listening to her try to step away from the phone only for it to ring again.

"Thank you for calling Saraday Apartments," she says—or rather slurs after these few hours—"This is Peggy, how may I help you?"

Erigan opens the door and enters.

It isn't until he's already stepped inside and witnesses his father's feet up on the black leather cube coffee table thingy that he realized the front door was unlocked.

"Why are you here?" Erigan says.

"What's the news?"

"First you answer my question, then I answer yours."

Zeus stands up and rests his hands against his side. "This is my place," he says. "I lent it to you. For safekeeping."

"You put the statue in the box. You knew I'd be here."

"I wanted to catch your attention," Zeus says with a smirk. "I trust I did?"

Erigan limps to the couch and rests on the arm.

"You're hurt," says Zeus, watching his son pace to the couch.

Erigan raises his foot, placing it on the black cube.

"Courtesy of your daughter or sister-in-law." Erigan rolls his eyes. "Whatever she is."

"Persephone?" says Zeus with a smile. "She's a good shot."

Erigan looks up to his father and snarls.

"So you found my brother?"

"He politely said you could go fuck yourself, dad."

Zeus strokes his beard and turns to face the windows. The shades are drawn open completely, letting in the sun and all of its wondrous colors.

The floor of his apartment—or his father's apartment if he can be believed—glows with an orange hue from the setting sun outside.

"I'm tempted to say you really have no plan," says Erigan. When the bleeding stops, he sets his right foot down and puts some weight on it. To his surprise, he does not feel pain. Just a little soreness.

Testing further, he stands up and cries out. "Ow."

"For far too long we've been under the heel of that thief and his fallen servants." Zeus turns around and rests his hands behind his back. "Tell me, Hermes. Is that really what you want? To live a life of servitude?"

"How is it any different from working for you?"

Zeus smiles and turns to face the fading sunlight as it disappears behind the low hills.

"I figured you'd say that," he mutters.

Erigan finally manages to stand up properly on his foot. The wings on his sandals flap quickly to test for pain.

Erigan nods in approval. "There," he says. "Better."

"No," say Zeus. "We're doomed if we cannot win back our realms." He closes the curtains with a wave of his hand and then he turns around in the darkness that consumes the living room.

"Tell me why here? Why this apartment? Why this pathetic town?"

"Because my son lives here."

Erigan nods.

Zeus continues, "And by leading you here, I can keep my family in one place. Get you to work together and recreate the pantheon."

"And what do you hope to do with a little boy? He's only eight years old. He knows nothing of the world, let alone us."

"His mother will come around," says Zeus. "Or she goes away."

"You will kill Sophie so you can secure your next-of-kin?"

Zeus makes a tight fist and holds it up in front of his face. It begins to crackle, glowing a bright blue color that zaps the air around it. "I will do what is necessary to ensure the survival of our family, Hermes. Don't you forget that you, too, are a part of this pantheon."

A stray bolt lashes out and flicks Erigan's chest. He gasps in pain and rubs the singed part of his tunic.

The blue light allows Zeus's beard to glow a bright, snowy blue. "I really expected more from you."

"What about Hera? Apollo?" says Erigan. He takes

a step backwards toward the door. If things should get ugly...

"They've been placed into the ninth level of Hell. Don't they tell you anything at those upper levels?"

The cool of the door against his back conflicts with the warmth and crackling of the air before him.

"Where do you think you are going?" Zeus asks.

The door behind Erigan locks shut and feels warm. Tingly.

"You will not leave until I permit it."

Erigan stops paying attention to the ramblings of his father. Something cracks behind him. A stomping, maybe?

Erigan's cheeks feel a slight wind, the shifting of the air behind him.

Something is pushing through the door.

"Dad?" Erigan whispers.

"So we have one decision to make and one decision only. Will you or will you not help me help our family?"

Erigan feels his legs lift off of the ground—his wings have begun to react before his brain knows what's going on.

He finds himself pushing off the doorway and throwing himself headlong into his father's chest.

The ball of electricity that encircled Zeus's fist burns at Erigan's shoulders and chest and he cries out in pain.

All of this forces him to pull himself into a ball, his head tucked deep in his chest, his arms wrapped around the back of his head and neck.

The door explodes into the room. The walls rattle like children's toys. Splintered pieces of the door rain down upon the fallen Greek gods. The wooden shards tap softly against the hardwood floors.

"What—what happened?"

Zeus's lightning ball fizzles out of his hand as he collapses backward.

Erigan tries to raise his head to see what had caused the explosion, but dust covers his view.

"I told you to mind your own business, Hermes." The voice is gruff, bull-like. A massive shadowy figure steps forward through the dust. Red eyes glow from the shape's head, and the grinning white teeth form a stark contrast to the deadly figure.

Chapter Fifty-One

Erigan rolls to his side. He feels a tight pinch his left side as he is lifted from the ground.

A short blast of air around his head. Then a bony shoulder underneath his stomach.

And though he can't see anything around him—white dust has covered his eyes—he instantly knows who is giving him a ride.

"Let me down, Behemoth," Erigan says.

Behemoth headbutts the top of the doorframe. It crumbles into thick grey and white powder.

"Can't do that," he says. "I need to get you out of here."

Erigan wipes his eyes and stares up. Thrown over Behemoth's shoulder, he gets a perfect cloudy view of his old apartment. Inside, his father, Zeus the King of the Olympians, on his knees and coughing, gasping for breath.

"But Zeus!" says Erigan. He slaps his ride's back. "He's alive! Look!"

Behemoth nods his short head. Well, short compared to the rest of his burly, muscular body. "I know. Why don't you think I told you to go on vacation."

"But I found Dad!" Erigan starts to kick. "What is going on here, anyway?"

Behemoth turns down the corner and takes the steps.

From their descent, Erigan watches figures—horned figures—come out of shadows and grab his father.

"Wait," says Erigan. He kicks and pounds Behemoth in the chest, back, shoulders. Nothing slows this man down.

As they head down the hallway to the foyer, Erigan hears the telephone ring yet again.

"Thank you for calling Saraday Apartments, this is Peggy..."

Outside the sky feels dark with thick clouds and a wind that begins to pick up.

"Someone is taking him. I think he is in trouble," says Erigan. "We have to go help."

Behemoth sets Erigan down, but grips the top of the little god's head. His palms are so wide that they allow Behemoth to take all of Erigan's head—from ear to ear—with his entire hand.

Erigan's feet try to fly away, but fail. The grip on his head is too tight. Moving too far or too fast in any direction would only snap his neck. And if anyone could snap the neck of a god, it would be Herakles himself.

"You know something you are not telling me."

Behemoth's mouth presses tight. "I'm sorry," he says.

"What are you hiding?" Erigan says. He stamps his foot. "What are you doing?"

Behemoth's fingers squeeze, applying pressure on Erigan's head like it's a watermelon or avocado.

"I'm not listening to you," he says with a grin. "That's what I'm doing."

"You are going to get Zeus killed."

Behemoth nods.

Erigan freezes. "You mean?"

Behemoth nods again. "Now stay here until we're ready for you?"

"We?"

A giant, winged shadow cast over Behemoth and Erigan as they stand in the alley next to his apartment building.

"It's about damned time I got my hands on you," says a sexy, bewitching voice.

Erigan's eyes shift to Behemoth. "Lilith? Really? How could you?" he says.

Behemoth lifts Erigan into air using only the grip on his friend's head. "Shhh," he warns.

The shadows grow bigger, bigger, until they reveal the physical forms of Lilith. Her darkened hair lays flipped over hear head, covering her left shoulder. The rest of her clothing leaves little to anyone's imagination. A black dress, deep cut in the front and sleeveless. The black frills on the dress extend into shadowy clouds, disappearing and then reappearing just out of view.

"You are a stubborn, stubborn man," she says.

Lilith approaches Erigan and traces her finger across his softened human cheek.

"I trust you got what you wanted back at the caves?"

Erigan's eyes begin to water from the pain and pressure.

"Good," says Lilith. "Now you're coming home with me."

Erigan tries to say something, but words won't come out. Every thought in his head is replaced with pain, searing, fire, burning.

Behemoth's hand releases just slightly.

Erigan's curly brown hair remains wrapped around his captor's fingernails. "I am exiled. I cannot return, or have you forgotten?" he says.

Lilith smiles. "No, you're not," she says. "Now come on." She snaps her fingers and closes her eyes. When she opens them, she realizes that they both stand there.

Having been released from Behemoth's grip, Erigan kneels on the ground, clutching his temples and trying to find the energy to stand.

"What in the nine circles is this?" Lilith exclaims. "What did you do?" Lilith's hand wraps around Erigan's neck. Her black nails prick into Erigan's neck.

Pressure in his windpipe, then a sudden release of warmth—same as he felt on his foot only hours ago. "What did you do?"

Erigan shakes his head as much as the pain will let him. "Nothing."

"Why are we not in Hell?" She draws Erigan closer to her face, snarling. Intimidation. Her go-to trick when sex won't cut it.

"I don't know," says Erigan. He feels his blood rush to his face. His gasps for breath grow slower, thinner.

"Bullshit," says Lilith slowly, calmly. She lets Erigan drop to his knees yet again and steps backwards. "What did you do?" she asks.

Erigan shrugs. "I was set up," he says.

"You aren't that important," says Lilith. "Hell, you're not even that good in bed. Who would want you out in exile?"

Erigan shrugs. He has an idea, but resists the temptation to say anything.

Lilith smiles. Her teeth are smooth. White. Her lips turn a bright red, reflecting the oranges and pinks of the setting sun. "You do know, don't you?"

She steps forward and extends her hand once again.

Erigan clutches for his own neck and kicks himself backward, away. He crabwalks away from her. Going only away, not caring just what he might run into.

"Who is it?" she says. She catches up to him and stamps on his injured ankle.

Erigan cries out for pain. He tries to grip his foot, to grab her and throw her off, anything. But he can't.

The bolt of pain and ripping in his leg shoots through his hips and to his body. He slams his body backwards, slapping the ground.

"So, who is it?" she says.

"Zeus," he whispers.

It was not the answer she was looking for, Erigan sees. Not by a long shot. She takes a step forwards, raises her leg to stomp on his ankle yet again, and the puts it down.

"What does he want?"

"Revenge," says Erigan. "Lots of it."

"Where is he?"

Erigan shrugs. "He was taken."

Lilith throws her head back in evil laughter. "That's rich," she says. "You damned Greeks are all the same. Stubborn in life and in death." She flourishes her dress slightly and curtseys. "Well, at least you are reliably stubborn."

She snaps her fingers. The sound rebounds off the walls and into the air. Loud enough to make birds take flight and rattle windows.

Then, above, another shadow. First small as a pinpoint. Then bigger. Bigger.

It's falling, and falling fast.

Erigan struggles to move backward as quickly as possible, but it's no use. It's moving too fast for him to notice just where it's going to land.

He looks to Lilith for an answer to what it may be. Some sign in her face.

She only smiles. Her eyes flare with a black flame that dissipates into the air.

That only means pain. And lots of it.

Erigan tucks his arms into his side and rolls over to his side.

Counting his rolls—one, two, three—he stops when he finally hears the hard slap of one hundred twenty pounds of meat hit rocky concrete.

Chapter Fifty-Two

Blood splatters from the explosion to Erigan's tunic and arm. The spots go bright red to dark in a matter of seconds against his skin.

When Erigan looks down to see the extent of his splatter, he notices that his skin is now red, ragged, leathery. His demonic form.

Another heavy shadow grows bigger around the body. Erigan, too shocked to know what to focus on, covers his face and prepares for yet another explosion of corpses.

Instead the ground rumbles.

His heels vibrate against the rocky patch of grass. His body trembles up to his jaw.

Opening his eyes, he's greeted with the bearded smile of his once best friend.

"Let me help you up," he says.

Erigan ignores the offer and slaps away the hands.

The shoulder-length blond hair. The green eyes, now set against a bloodshot sea of red. He recognizes them all.

He's not crying, he tells himself. He's not crying at all. Not for a human.

But he wipes away something from his eyes with the back of his hand. He crawls closer to the corpse and touches the skin.

"Sophie," Erigan mutters. While clutching her shoulders, pulling her closer to him, he shoots an angry look at Lilith. "Fuck you. Fuck you," he stammers.

His arms wrap around the girl. He pulls her body, warm and slick with blood, onto his knees.

The sun sets behind him. The rest of the sky finally turns a solid dark purple. Only a thin strip of pink lines the edges of horizon.

"I don't handle competition well, dear," says Lilith. "You fuck with me, you're stuck with me." She cackles again, this time fading into the darkness. Her voice disappears into only an echo.

Erigan reaches for sand and tosses it at the fading outlines of Behemoth and Lilith. The dirt flies through the outlines, landing on the other side of the walkway.

Erigan looks down, pushes Sophie's hair back and watches as the last bit of life disappears from her twitching cheeks and eyes.

Erigan closes her eyes and holds her hand to his chest. He closes his own eyes as if in prayer. "I'm so sorry," he mutters. "I will get Brad back. I promise you."

Erigan feels the odd sensation of movement around him. His forehead twitches with the sense that he's being watched.

When he opens his eyes, he spots the beautiful, glowing spirit of Sophie.

Erigan drops her hand and struggles to stand up. He presses his hands against the rocky ground and attempts to stand up. His ankle struggles to remain calm, however.

He rests only some of his weight on it, but he cries out and falls back down.

The wall, he thinks. It's the only way he can stand up.

He crawls over the girl's body and struggles to reach the wall in time.

Sophie's spirit—her soul—stands over her body. She looks confused at first, but smiling.

Then, she peers up at the injured Erigan and frowns for only a second, and waves goodbye.

"No," says Erigan. He reaches out for the spirit, but she appears preoccupied with something else around her.

Like a little girl, Sophie's spirit hops on her feet, then skips. The skips then turn to a faster than human run down the streets.

The street is quiet. The air has turned a slight chill, but not enough to make it officially cold.

Erigan knows already where Sophie's spirit runs off to.

She had flirted and bore a child with a known

ex-god, now demon, Zeus. There was no way that she could make it through the Golden Gates of Heaven.

But still, she was a believer of the Greek Gods. She did not fear his confession. If anything, she appeared to be drawn to it, always waiting for someone or something to find her.

For this, her soul will be cast out into Hell.

But first, a coin. Charon's obol.

Erigan's hands claw at the wall until he is finally stand up properly. He hobbles over to the corpse and nods. The empty shell will have to wait.

He has not the power to move it himself.

First, it needs burial rights.

A coin.

He makes a dash for the front door and pulls himself inside. First the front door, then the next set of doors.

The electric lights in the ceiling hum amidst the silence. And this strikes him as odd.

The spell. It has finally worn off.

Erigan turns to the front desk and leans over the counter. "Peggy?"

He looks around from side to side. There isn't a sign of her anywhere, but he hears something rattling around. Movement.

A snake, maybe?

"Peggy?"

Something slaps around again.

Erigan struggles to maybe climb over the counter but stops just short of bringing his injured leg onto the counter.

The thumping of the counter against his bruised ankle tells him that it's not a good idea.

So he hobbles to the other side of the office and opens the door.

On the floor is poor Peggy. She's gasping for breath, lying down and holding the phone in her hand. Her face is as puffy as her brown hair. Red from crying.

"Peggy," says Erigan. "What are you doing?"

Peggy appears to realize that she looks pathetic. Huddled up on the floor, clutching her phone near to her chest. Her face wells up with tears again and before she can get to an explanation, she begins to cry.

Erigan limps over to her and pats her on the head.

He wants to tell her everything will be all right, but he can't. Not now.

"Peggy, do you have any change?" he asks.

Peggy's crying breaks for a moment. She looks up to him from her sitting position. She pats each of her eyes with the sleeve of her power suit. "Y-yes."

"Good," he says. "Where is it?"

Peggy first offers Erigan the phone, but he slaps it out of her hands.

"Where is the money?"

"You're ro-robbing me?"

Erigan rolls his eyes. "I don't have time for this. This is important. Anything. A big silver coin. Maybe a small red one. Copper. Or gold. I don't know."

She reaches into her pocket and hands him two

quarters on a shaky hand. "There's not much you can buy with a quarter," she stammers.

"It is not what I must buy," he says, "but who." He kisses her on the forehead and rushes to the front of the office again. "Thank you," he says on the way out. "You don't know what you've done."

Erigan slams the doors open and pushes right through. His wings flap to speed him up, though it pains him for them to do so.

Each walk floats for a second before landing back onto the ground.

At long last, he's outside, but not alone. A circle of strangers, huddled in their shorts and Hawaiian shirts stand around the corpse.

"What the fuck happened here?" says one guy.

The next points up on top of the building. "I think the bitch jumped or something." He makes a high whistle and then slams one hand into the other in an explosion. "Bam!" he shouts. "Just like that. I saws it."

"Man, you ain't seen shit." A woman comes to the circle and pushes them aside. "Dear god," she says.

Erigan pushes through on the other side of the circle. "God has nothing to do with this," he mutters.

He kneels down to Sophie's mouth and pries the jaw open.

"Mister, you're gonna catch AIDS or something," someone says.

"Shut the hell up, Brian. You catch HIV, not AIDS. Get your ignorant ass back home."

Erigan tries to shut out the voices, but he can't. Though he doesn't want to admit it, it serves as a nice distraction from what he must do next.

Once the mouth is open, he notices some teeth loose in the sides of her mouth. The fall had pushed them out. The body can't fall as far as she did—and as fast—without having some internal damage.

Erigan slides one coin on top of her tongue and closes the mouth. He holds it tight with both of his hands, one on her jaw the other on her forehead.

He presses lightly to keep them closed, then he peers up into the sky and mutters a prayer.

The circle begins to back up at the sound of a high-pitched squeal coming from around the corner.

Erigan waits for the body to hit some form of stasis, for the resistance on his hands to loosen.

Once the mouth decides to stay closed, he takes steps up and walks toward the apartment building. As he does so, each step has him fade closer and closer into invisibility.

The crowd does not seem to notice, or care.

The approaching red and white ambulance is enough to force the group to disperse and let the men with blue coats come in and prepare the body for transport.

As Erigan watches the body get loaded up into the end of the ambulance, he spots a little twitch. Some movement back behind a tree across the street.

There, blinking, waving and—for some reason smiling—is Sophie's spirit watching her body get taken away.

Chapter Fifty-Three

Erigan waits for the crowds to leave before flying across the street to meet with the spirit.

As he follows her closer the spirit runs as if the wind blows against her back.

It was not uncommon for a spirit to hang around for some time after the body was dead. Sometimes it took a little bit of convincing for the ghost to return to Hell— or Heaven. However this one, it seems frightened and excited at the same time.

An interesting mix of scared eyes and a coy, exuberant smile give Sophie an odd expression. One that Erigan himself has been accused of since the day he was born: mischievous.

"Sophie!" he cries out. His ankle wings carry him down the roads and into the forests just outside of town.

The spirit almost seems to glide and float than run.

"Where are you taking me?" he asks, but it's as if she doesn't hear him or doesn't know what to say.

"What game are you playing?"

The spirit goes into the forest, getting lost into the deep darkness within.

Erigan comes to a cold stop. Weighing his options, he can follow the spirit or go back and check up on his father.

He could be walking into a trap. Maybe get captured himself.

No. If they had wanted him, they could have had him by now.

But this spirit. Where is she taking him? What does she know?

Erigan turns head-first into the forest and flies through the branches. They scrape and jab into his sides. His ankle suffers most. Too many of the branches scratch into his feet and ankles that flying at this speed feels more painful than it should.

He tries to slow down when he realizes that Sophie's spirit is within sight. However when the spirit senses he's closer, she speeds up.

Whatever she's up to, she doesn't want to slow down at all.

Erigan tries to play the game and follow closer. Though it is the wings doing most of the work, he finds himself breaking out into sweat, beads tracing down his forehead and into his eyes. The ties he shares with his sandals, it forces him to feel the fire of the injury, the burning pain.

A blessing and a curse, he always thought. Today, more curse than blessing.

The run and flight are mostly silent. Erigan has to keep his sights constantly on her because he cannot hear her here.

The spirit forms do not make noise or touch the physical world unless they wish it.

This new spirit, fresh out of its body, it does not know what it wishes.

Or does it? Its plan and path. It's too specific for it to be just an accident.

Erigan's flight slows down. And so does the spirit. She is leading him somewhere, he realizes, so she slows down so as not to lose him.

But where?

The darkness of the forest begins to give way to small rays of illumination. Bluish white rays emanate from the ground.

Erigan slows down to get a better look.

A cave.

In the New World? Who would but one here?

The spirit disappears down into the cave with a smile.

Chapter Fifty-Four

If someone were to tell Erigan to "Go to Hell", this would be his optimal choice. After all, it was the easiest entrance to find.

Erigan recognizes the low, red rocky walls and intense heat the second he walks into the entrance of the cave.

The entrance had a blurry glow about it. A surefire sign that it did not belong in the mortal realm, but was a gateway for the immortals to go to and from the Underworld.

In this case, it went to Hell. Among some of the Lightbringer's initial plans was to close up or commandeer the entrances to the Underworld. Nearly everything except for the River Acheron was sealed up, apparently.

Buy why the River Acheron?

Dante had written about its existence in *The Inferno*. Surely even Lucifer had known it was down there. This gives Erigan a twisted feeling in his gut. He is being set up. Or worse.

Is someone allowing him to go back?

Feeling strain on his ankle from the weight of walking, his wings lift him into the hot, almost hazy air. From this distance the waves of heat come at him like waves of an ocean. Strong tides first, then weaker ones following thereafter.

He flies deeper, following the spirit. By now he has lost her completely. But he's already done the unthinkable: He's made it back into Hell against their will.

He's going to have to pay through the nose for this.

Deep below he comes across the River Styx: the river of hatred. He searches below for Charon but the docks are empty of boats.

Hundreds of souls push and shove along the docks. Some wailing at each other, or into the ethereal air for whomever will listen to their pain.

They do not move, however, at the sight of Erigan, the Messenger God Hermes, flying above them.

He smiles and nods to the group of impatient, growling, and mumbling souls. One by one, they smile back at him, pressing against each other to raise their arms. No less than fifty of the souls get knocked into the river itself. Their frustrations calm, if only for a moment by his presence.

And as the faces turn to look and smile at the young god, not a single one of them looks like Sophie.

A thought, followed by an empty feeling in his gut, strikes Erigan as he flies over the lost souls.

"Why me?" he wonders. He turns to follow the River Styx down into the center of Hell, the City of Dis. The souls wail and cry out for him as he leaves.

Their words leave no echoes in this tiny closet of a tunnel. The path grows smaller as he passes through it.

Did he do something wrong to have himself in this place? Was he threatening?

At barely the height of a normal North American human, he could barely be seen as threatening at all. If anyone, Behemoth was the real threat.

So then why him? Why be forced into this woman's company and then taken away?

To keep from crying out in pain, he turns his skin into the reddish Hell demon he knows so well. This form is angry, full of wrath and tricks and frustration.

It felt better to be in this form. Down here, the red skin felt as comfortable as home—back when Mount Olympus was home.

He feels the increased heat against his red, leathery skin. The condensed air slows him down as he progresses down the tunnels.

When he gets down into the tunnels and somehow finds his ex-best friend and Sophie, he will rip the ribcage right out of Behemoth's chest. He will shatter the ribs and use them to stab Ba'al right where his heart is supposed to be.

Erigan smiles at the thought of towering over his foes. Victorious. More than the victory, he smiles and grits his teeth in hunger. He needs this anger. This victory. The need to beat and flay and kill the next being that comes his way. And smile at his next opponent while licking the warm blood off his hands.

Erigan shakes the feeling of tension. The tunnels grow smaller still, and he needs to keep his arms and legs tight together to make it through these smaller passages.

No, he thinks. If he makes it to Sophie, he can bargain for her life. For Brad. She was never the target. Zeus was.

And they have both.

And he had nothing. Nothing to bargain with. Nothing to offer them.

They clearly don't want him. He had been "locked out" of Hell for a few days. And Lilith all but had her hands on him.

If he was the target of Hell's wrath, he would have felt it.

Or has he?

His train of thought is temporarily derailed as the small hole finally breaks open into an expansive room that goes on as far as his godly eyes can see.

He had always wanted to set up a signpost here, at this exact spot, maybe in the shape of a finger or a penis. "Welcome to Hell. Hope you brought your sunblock."

The first circle of Hell sits directly in front of him. Sitting on a grassy plateau, these souls wander about without direction around a massive gray castle. This castle with seven gates is the final home of all those who were virtuous non-Christians.

Certainly a luxurious home, but not a great comparison for Heaven, as the angels would say.

He pauses for a moment to search a crowd of souls. The crowd waits in a number of lines waiting for their turn to be sentenced by the great half-man, half-serpent Minos. Technically yet another one of his step-brothers, this serpent use to be a man, king of Crete. It was his creation—the minotaur—that turned into the stuff of legends with the humans.

He searches for blond hair, green eyes and a smile that hints a devilish mischievous mind. He finds no smiling faces. No blondes that fit his friend's description.

Instead he finds all of the souls in the line fear their intended fate. Some whisper amongst each other "How many wraps did he get? Which circle does he to go?"

The lines have gotten longer since he last remembered. More evidence of Hell's perpetual infatuation with bureaucracy.

And while Minos is a serpent, he is now "permitted" to have a dress code. This particular chosen outfit is a long-sleeved white shirt that buttons down the front. He wears no pants because, well, he's a serpent, but his shoulders fill out the shirt quite well, Erigan thinks.

He flies down, lower to within earshot of Minos, but not close enough for him to be in the old king's reaches.

"Have you seen a woman? Sophie?"

Minos looks up and waves at his step-brother. His tails wraps around himself six times.

"Tssk, tssk," says Minos. "You've been extra naughty, heretic. To the Sixth Circle with you!"

Harpies fly out of seemingly nowhere and grab the man by the shoulders. He screams in agony and fear, struggling to break free even though he is now over a mile high into the air.

"Have you seen Sophie?" Erigan screams.

Minos unravels his tail from around his body and seizes another poor soul with his hands. He licks his lips and then looks up to the flying god.

"No, brother. I have not seen your beloved Sophie." Minos rolls his eyes while sizing up this pathetic soul.

Erigan holds out a finger to stop him at beloved, but Minos does not let himself be stopped.

"Ba'al has her in his grips. And some child," he says. "They got a pass to the front of the line, it seems."

One of the souls in the back of the line screams out "Lucky girl."

Minos drops his next soul and snaps his fingers. He laughs as a group of harpies comes to the complaining soul and they rip it to shreds with their razor talons. The evil birds cackles and screech in joy as they tear the soul's limbs from its body and tossed aside.

The king smiles. "Nice to see you again, Erigan."

Chapter Fifty-Five

Erigan flies through the thick and stagnant air of the Second and Third Circle of Hell. The levels of lust and gluttony. Love of people and love of things.

Erigan had seen her apartment. She was a lover of neither, so he flew over the windy plains of the Second Circle and the wretched muddy lands of the third plains.

Down below, someone seems to be swimming amongst the gluttonous as they wallow in their own shit. Some of the souls lie still, sightless and waiting for nothing. Giving up and accepting their fate. Still others, they search around with their hands, slapping the mud with their eagerness to discover just where they are.

He flies into the Fourth Circle—the last one before he gets to Dis—and pays no attention to it.

Again, a circle of greed. And hardly a decent place for Sophie's soul to rest.

Up over the hill is another plateau, this one covered with swamplands. The Fifth Circle of Hell, the circle of anger. The swamp glows a phosphorescent green down in the depths. Erigan doesn't know what grows and lives in the depths of the thick, sludge-like water, but he does know that no one has even tried to count. The sludge worked well as both a barrier and a scene of torture.

After all, those souls who were cast into the Fifth Circle found themselves struggling and fighting each other near the surface as they bobbed back and forth. Everyone with their fists in each other's faces, digging their own claws into the skin of the hapless victims beneath them.

Then deep below, the sullen drown and skulk eternally deep below.

On the edges of the splashing mold-green swamplands is the massive City of Dis. Within its walls likes the rest of the circles of Hell.

On top of the walls, however, a massive legion of dark angels flies to the top of the walls. They hold in their hands spears, wearing dark leather and metal armor that almost seem to absorb the light around them.

They know he is here.

Erigan flies low. He tucks his feet into his chest and keeps his head straight. A cannonball.

The stench of the murky water, now mixed with blood and plant-life growing out of the water, causes Erigan to clench his nose tight. It was rare he'd ever have to fly this close to the waters, but if he wants to avoid detection, this may be the only way to do it.

He flies to the southern end of the walls. His hands rise up to protect his head as he lands. His injured wings feel unsteady. His patience for pain runs low and he knows he's going to crash.

So, he braces for impact.

Erigan curls into a ball and tries to fall with his back to the wall first to protect his legs and ankles.

It works, but the sudden jolt to his body causes him to let out a gasp of breath that could catch someone's attention.

Out of the hundreds of angry, armed angels, one of them was bound to have heard him.

He will have to work fast.

His one good foot digs into the rocky sand the walls were built upon. This served as the plateau peninsula upon which the City of Dis was founded.

An entire city built upon a swamp of anger. Yes, even Lucifer had a soft spot for symbolism, Erigan thought.

A darkened rock comes flying into the air, buzzing past Erigan's ear. The rock smashes into the walls behind him with nothing more than a splat.

He looks back at the wall.

Sod. Bloody, sticky with pieces of green and maroon tube-like stems sticking out of it.

"Who the hell throws sod?" says Erigan. He looks out into the swamps and finds no one paying attention to him. Their hands are busy at each other's throats, their nails slicing and cutting into their opponent's skin.

He looks back at the splattered dirt clump on the wall.

Something looks like it moved when the dirt hit the wall.

He looks back into the swamp one last time. The teeming ocean of anger, and yet not a single person looks as if they had anything to do with the stray ball of dirt.

There are no coincidences, he thinks. Not in Hell.

As Erigan grasps the wall for balance, he realizes he's been here before recently.

The holes in the walls from the wrathful souls in the marsh, everything here looked familiar.

Erigan fans out his fingers and rubs his hands against the wall. Where is that damn spot?

He takes a few steps to his left.

Perfect. A solid gray rock, sharp on the surfaces shows just a hint of movement underneath his pinky finger. Erigan takes a peek around him. No signs of angels, and so far he hasn't been spotted.

He digs his fingers between the holes and digs out the dust and debris from the cracks. Pulling and scratching with his nails, he finally digs the rock out.

He smiles. "Son of a bitch," he mutters. Entrance still sealed.

He looks back at the smudge mark on the wall, where the bloody sod splattered against the bricks. Erigan nods.

If things are being thrown, that trigger would be in

the worst possible spot.

Erigan smiles and nods. Someone's got a sense of humor to put that there in the first place.

Erigan takes the twig from the tunic and adjusts its place. Using magic to keep it still, he thrusts the rock back into the hole and turns around.

Is this what they wanted? Erigan taps the twig in his tunic. Its thorns dig into his skin through the thin leather of his pocket.

Who, exactly, is after this twig? Broken from a random tree in the Seventh Circle, it wouldn't make sense that Ba'al is after this. There was nothing special about it, only that it bled.

But that's typical of the trees in that area. The souls cast into the second ring of the Seventh Circle are suicides, those who gave up their body in violence. As those without a body, they instead become thorny bushes and trees, eternally being fed on by the malicious, bird-like harpies.

Erigan searches the ledge of the peninsula's cliff. There was a hole in here somewhere. A passage back into the city.

Unless they covered it up.

Erigan thinks back to the angels that chased him down the path.

No. Most of the angels are followers, not leaders. Unless they were told to cover up the hole, it's still there. Somewhere.

He digs his hands around and finally finds the

entrance to the tunnel.

When he tucks his right foot into the tunnel, he realizes he is going in without a plan. Only a twig as a weapon.

Chapter Fifty-Six

Beyond the walls of Dis, the black cobblestone streets look relatively empty.

Erigan begins to think maybe a trap. Maybe a lockdown. Maybe dumb luck.

He pats the twig again in the pocket near his chest. For security reasons. It's his only bargaining chip, he realizes.

If something should go wrong, he'll need that piece to keep his hope alive.

But first, he thinks, backup.

He flies among the rooftops to The Pentagram on Grendel Street. Though the streets look particularly empty at the moment, he hears the stomping of cloven hooves and leather boots down the corner.

The soldiers are on march.

Erigan nearly bites his own tongue clean off to keep

himself in this present. Can't think about the future, about making mistakes, getting caught and exiled to the Ninth Circle. The circle of betrayers and backstabbers.

He weighs the different ways he could sell this to Lucifer himself, and bites down harder on his tongue.

The tops of the tallest roofs in the city have about waist-high walls that block one's view from the streets. These were imagined and built because of fear of raids from Heaven. Since the first angel came down from Heaven and forced Virgil and Dante through the city walls, Ba'al has been insistent that they never be caught off guard again.

This is also why they have a watch over the gates. The gates themselves are magical, true, but he knew that Hell was only a realm. If someone wanted to get in bad enough, they shall get in.

Erigan rests on the side of the wall and waits for the soldiers to march past. The small post is led by a large minotaur. It appears to breathe smoke, his wide, muscular shoulders hinting at the immense power those beasts possess.

It was no small thing to go up against a minotaur. Their legs, though small compared to the rest of their body, were powerful and made them fast runners. Hermes, with his flying sandals, was among the rare few who could race a minotaur and live to tell the tale.

The army is filled with smaller fallen angels, whose black wings flap about like capes behind them as they march. Their black armors glisten in the pale light coming from the ethereal around them.

Being granted black armor was a sign of respect and admiration. One had to earn their armor.

Hermes never had the patience nor the respect for the position, so he was placed in the Terror Division. It was a fair job, but a boring one. Lifetimes of being controlled and manipulated through the ages.

Sure it was a Greek god's pleasure to fuck with humans in the worst ways possible. But not like that. What's the fun when the humans aren't free to react and torture themselves? Doing all the torturing for them—it just was lazy and uncreative.

Heaven forbid he should speak up, or he'd find himself on double duty while filling out paperwork—everyone's paperwork—for the next five hundred years.

He has only made that mistake once and once only.

The army disappears down the corner and Erigan takes this chance to fly down and enter The Pentagram. He goes in first as a ghost, transparent to most. Even in Hell, some tricks worked and some didn't.

What Hades had said previous about the gods' power coming from human believers, Erigan had wished it wasn't true. But every few years he felt a deeper loss inside him.

His wings just didn't fly much faster. His strength weakened. His ability to communicate, to travel, to guide—all less than that deserving a god.

At the bar, of course, was predictable Dio. He quaffs a final drink of something light brown and wipes his mouth with the back of his hand.

His blond hair falls down over his eyes and he shuffles it off to the side of his head. "That'll be all," he says. "Thanks."

The bartender nods his horned head and winks. "See ya tomorrow," he mutters.

As Dio gets up from his barstool, he pauses, sniffs. "Who?" he mutters.

The bartender looks to the doorway and shrugs. "Say something?" he calls out.

Dio waves him off. "No, no. Just hearing things. Too much to drink," he says slowly. "You know how it goes."

The bartender nods and grins. He tosses the filthy glass into the trash and pulls another clean one out of a blue fire from a sink.

"Hermes?" Dio says. "Is that you I smell?" He continues to walk toward the door so as to not draw any attention, but he nearly fails when he stops just short of putting his hand on the doorway. "That's you, isn't it?"

"Hey," says the bartender.

Dio and Erigan freeze.

"Make sure that door shuts all the way when you leaves, alright?"

Dio lets out a slow breath and nods. "Sure thing."

Erigan continues his invisibility trick and walks with Dio outside.

Erigan points up top to the ceiling.

Dio nods. "You do know they're looking for you, you idiot?"

Erigan grabs Dio by the left armpit and hauls him up to the top of the building. "You are putting on weight, brother. Might want to watch the beer belly."

Dio slaps his protruding gut and smiles. "Hey, I'm watching it right here." He slaps it again. "What are you doing?"

"That asshole is back," says Erigan.

Dio shrugs. "You'll have to be more specific, Hermes. We're in Hell. Lots of assholes."

"Our asshole. Our father. Zeus."

Dio's mouth drops open. "You're not serious. Where is he? What's he up to?"

Erigan throws an invisible hand over Dio's mouth. "Shut up, okay?"

Dio snorts once and his shoulders relax. Seeing this as a sign, Erigan pulls his hands away from his brother's mouth.

"I think Ba'al has him. Somewhere in the city."

Dio's eyes widen. He sits down on a nearby crate. "That old man finally got himself fucked." He hiccups and adjusts his tunic. "There's really nothing you can do," he says.

"But I have to," says Erigan. "It appears that the boy I was hired to terrify, well, he is our brother. Another demigod."

Dio's eyes narrow and he opens his mouth just a little. Nothing comes out.

"I know, I know," says Erigan. "But the boy is only eight years old, so Zeus has been busy since then. Hades thinks he's trying to get Olympus back."

Dio gasps. "He thinks he can get Olympus back?" he says. "That fucking moron." Dio stands up and points it at Erigan's chest. "You do realize that he would have to wage war with both Heaven and Hell to get it back." Dio runs his hands through his hair. "That man is fucking crazier than I am." He sits back down and crosses his legs. "So then, the question is, big brother, why is the big boss man after you?"

Erigan shrugs. "I am not sure, exactly," he says. "But I think it has something to do with this." He reaches into his tunic.

Chapter Fifty-Seven

"Where did you get that?" Dio runs his fingers over the thorny twig. With his other hand, he catches some of the dark blue blood that drips from the broken end of the tree. "You got this from the Seventh Circle, didn't you?" Dio says.

Erigan nods. "It was another job," he says. "I get the feeling that I have been used all this time. This, then the boy. It must all connected. Probably Zeus all this time."

Dio shrugs. "Beats the hell out of me," he says. He sniffs the blood and sticks a bit of it on his tongue.

"Do not drink this," says Erigan. He slaps Dio's hand away and takes a step back. He places the twig back into his tunic for safekeeping.

"It's human blood, if you wanted to know." Dio licks his lips. "Or was."

"That is sick," Erigan says.

"That is not sick. Now what happened at those Roman Bacchanalias, now that was sick. You have never seen so many uses for a goat's horn."

Erigan raises his hand over his brother's mouth again. "Please, now is not the time."

Dio nods. "Fine. Later then."

"Do you know where Ba'al is now?"

"You do realize what they will do to you if they find out you're back? In Hell? When you weren't supposed to be back?" says Dio. "Do you know what they will do to me and the rest of us?"

Erigan's feet take flight. "I cannot stop now. Father has to be saved from himself. He is going to get us all killed if he is allowed to continue his madness."

"Check his tower," says Dio. "That's where I hear he mostly hangs out."

"Come with me," says Erigan. "I can use the help."

"Pfft," says Dio. "I heard what happens when someone quote-unquote works with you. They get handed to the officials and tortured."

Erigan shakes his head. "That only happened once. And look, Behemoth is perfectly fine."

"He's pissed off at you, that's what happened to him," says Dio. "That's one bad demigod to have against you."

Erigan nods and flies a bit higher, turning immaterial as he climbs into the air. "Very well. Thank you, brother."

"Ya, well," says Dio. He rests one foot over the ledge and lets it dangle over the roof. "Just don't tell anyone that I told you anything," he says. "You know they don't really like me much down here."

"No one would believe me you were this helpful anyway," says Erigan.

He floats upward and turns to his east. At the eastern edge of the city square is one of the three jagged towers that stand watch like onyx sentinels over the city.

The three towers were reserved for the highest and most powerful generals of the Lightbringer's army. Stands to reason that Ba'al would get one of the towers as his own.

He was a conniving pain in the ass as Sisyphus and now he's a pain in the ass in the Christian Underworld. The more things change, the more they stay the same.

Erigan flies to the middle floors of the tower and rests in one of the windows.

Envious of human inventions, most of the buildings in the City of Dis were granted the use of windows and air conditioning. Though only fifty years behind the earthlings in technology, they were welcomed additions to the buildings.

The older souls grew confused at the changes. The tek-nolo-jee was a strange invention. The work of evil.

They never got the irony, stuck in Hell for so long that many of the souls forgot their human lives.

The newer ones welcomed the changes, calling it "just like home" and mourning the fact that they don't get access to them.

And this exactly, is the reason why the towers were

retrofitted with glass windows nearly a century ago.

Erigan thanks Zeus that his mother is part nymph, giving him a smaller ass. He sits almost comfortably on the thin windowsill.

He etches his name in the glass with his black demonic nails. Then smiling, he takes carves out a circle in the glass and presses the oval into the floor.

He waits as the glass lands softly on the carpeted floors inside. He's greeted with a smooth, welcomed wave of air conditioning when he sticks his hand into the window and unlatches the lock.

Within only a few moments, he sneaks inside the tower and looks to both sides of the room.

As luck would have it, it's mostly empty.

Has Ba'al always been alone?

Working for him in the Terror Division has always felt like a punishment worse than anything the first five circles could throw at him.

When confronted with assignments, he was given the worst ones, the most meaningless. When he spoke up, he was given paperwork on top of paperwork. And if he finished early, he got someone else's paperwork.

It wasn't always like this. Last Erigan had heard, this business style was taken from corporate America almost a century ago.

Leave it to the humans to find working conditions worse than Hell.

Erigan flies to the center of the room and searches for a sign of where he may be. He was in the center of the tower, this he knew. But the room looked to be something like a bedroom.

In a tower, however, how many rooms were probably bedrooms?

Following his instinct, he decides to fly to the window and flutter up the sides. His wings grow tired, still weak from the injury but feeling better since he transformed back into his Hellish form.

So he flies close to the outer walls of the tower and grabs a brick in each hand. "Here goes nothing," he mutters, and climbs upwards. His wings push him along, hands pull him up.

Erigan reaches the top of the tower and searches the windows for a way to get in. Each of the windows—four in total—look to go into empty rooms.

Erigan etches another circle into the glass and presses it in. Just as before, he lets himself inside by opening the window and flying in feet first.

He sniffs the air and notices a scent. A familiar scent. Something human. An unwashed human.

Brad?

Erigan rushes to the door, following the musty scent of a sweaty human boy.

Or semi-human. Usually humans were not permitted into Hell. It was physically impossible for them to enter Hell. Against the laws of magical physics set up by God and Lucifer themselves.

So this must mean that Ba'al knows about Brad. Or at least he suspects. He wouldn't have brought him here to

Dis without some suspicion.

Erigan looks down the tower's hallway, looking both right and left. The left hallway leads to stairs going up.

Seemed as good an idea as any.

He rushes to the hallway and floats just above the red low-pile carpeting. Along the edges of the hallway carpets are golden designs—triangles and stars—that seem to point in the same direction—going up.

Erigan does not take the time to notice what's on the walls. It's unimportant. The scent, it grows stronger as he floats to the door.

And as he rests his hands on the door, the knob turns and the door opens.

Chapter Fifty-Eight

"You goddamned runt." Behemoth's massive hand grabs Erigan's face and lifts him from the ground.

Erigan tries not to, but cannot resist smelling the putrid scents on his friend's hand. Was he eating meat? Raw meat?

Air rushes all around him and there is a sudden explosion of light as he is thrown from Behemoth's massive grip.

"Look what I fucking found."

Erigan shakes off the shock of being tossed across the room like a ball and looks to see his friend. He's dressed in a black metal armored chestplate. His feet and hands are covered in leather, his legs in a leather pant with metal plating along the front and sides of each of his ham-sized thighs. Freshly carved and crafted from the ores of the Plutonian cliffs that separate the

Seventh Circle from the Eighth.

The special uniform of Hell's Army.

From the looks of the shiny golden medallion on his chest, he has already received an accommodation medal.

"You fucking traitor," Erigan says between gritted teeth. He spits on the ground and tries to stand up.

His ankle warns him with a shock of pain that feels like Zeus's lightning bolt coursing through his hip and shoulders.

He tries to pull himself up again.

"I was wondering if we were going to have to send a search party for your uppity ass," says a strong, deep voice. Mam'mon. "Too bad you missed the ceremony," he says. Mam'mon's bullhead snorts a tiny snot ball of fire that quickly dissipates in the air. "I'm going to enjoy his," he says.

Mam'mon's grip's on Erigan's neck feels tighter than Behemoth's. His vision narrows, growing blurry along the edges.

His breathing comes to a near stop, his neck almost collapsing under the bull demon's tight grip.

Erigan forms weak fists and bashes at Mam'mon's wrists to break free, but Mam'mon only laughs.

"You're serious?" he says. "This is what Ba'al was so worried about?"

Mam'mon's grip loosens. Erigan grips at his throat to pry off the bull's fingers. Again, he fails.

"You are so lucky that Ba'al wants you alive," he says. "Or you'd already be Satan's chew toy." Mam'mon grips

Erigan's left hand and pulls him upward. He holds him as if eyeing a piece of fish. "You are a little runt, aren't you?"

Behemoth chuckles and closes the door behind him. "Just in case he brought help."

Mam'mon raises an eyebrow at Behemoth's statement. "And just who would he bring? We already have the big man," he says. "As far as this poor guppy is concerned, his family is about to be wiped out for good."

A crooked smile slowly comes to Behemoth's mouth. Was he ready to sacrifice his own father? For what? Zeus is still family.

"Zeus is his father, too," says Erigan. He points at Behemoth across the room, jabbing into the air with his finger. "Are you going to kill your new soldier?"

Mam'mon chuckles and seizes Erigan's other arm, pulling him up by both wrists. "Shut up," he says.

Behemoth's face goes white. The smile remains, but somehow it lost its initial spark of enthusiasm.

"How soon before they come for you, too?" says Erigan. "You know they will."

Mam'mon swings Erigan around in a circle three times and holds Erigan to a stop. "I told you to shut up."

Behemoth clears his throat. "I'll be outside," he says. "Thank you again, sir." He salutes his general and leaves the office.

"Now," says Mam'mon. "What do you say we go for a little ride?"

Chapter Fifty-Nine

Erigan struggles to loosen the black metal cuffs that restrict the movement of his wrists and arms. Another metal circle, shining a glimmering black, joins the two cuffs and a chain that keeps Erigan contained to the back of the red and white chariot.

Mam'mon stands behind the antyx of the chariot, the rim finely decorated with snakes and stars etched into the black marble.

The body of the chariot is large enough for both Mam'mon's massive body and Erigan to stand upright and still move about in either direction. Erigan searches for a place to sit, the ride being too bumpy and embarrassing for him.

The reins that Mam'mon holds on to are made of leather, with a gold pattern of five-pointed stars weaved throughout the length of it. From this vantage point,

Erigan gets the fine view of the rear ends two black horses and one gray one in the middle. At the rear end of each steed is a gray or dark green snake that whips about hissing at Mam'mon's orders.

The chariot travels almost as fast as Erigan's normal flight speed. He finds this impressive, especially down the cobblestone roads.

The speeds keep Erigan just barely able to stand up. Despite this, he determines that it's best to just lay down and not struggle. For now, he is trapped.

And while Erigan sits somewhat comfortably in the chariot, he hears the buzzing of the souls on the streets.

He peers up like a prairie dog from its burrow.

The streets, once nearly devoid of souls and scattered debris is now littered with the crying and cheering spirits of human women and children. The men wave and cheer on Mam'mon and the rest of his army behind him.

A welcoming of the second general of Hell's Army.

Erigan sighs. More evidence that his father is on the wrong path. He couldn't succeed if he wanted to.

The people—souls, rather—were too supportive of the current regime.

It would take miracles to win. The types of miracles that no Olympian could pull off to make the humans to love his family the way they needed to be loved.

As always, it was all up to the living humans to make a difference. A war on souls...down to the humans who know nothing about the war Heaven and Hell wage against them.

When Erigan looks forward, he spots two gray, thick stone towers. As they come up, he sees the top of a wall break just over the horizon. The wall connects the two towers.

Atop both towers and the walls, a line of armor-clad angels, each holding a spear and a shield with an inverted pentagram, etched in silver and gold.

"Where are we going?" screams Erigan over the roaring, welcoming crowd.

Mam'mon does not look behind him when he responds to Erigan. Instead, he throws his bullhead into the air and laughs. "We are going to your execution, runt. Are you in such a hurry to die?"

Chapter Sixty

"Look what the fucking cat dragged in," mumbles Mam'mon.

Erigan hears all of this while he's being thrown—once again—through the air and into a large stone room.

The walls remain relatively bare with the exception of two banners that span the entire walls. The first one looks to be red with silver lines that trace the outer edges. The bottom of the banner is frayed. A broken halo in the center with a three-pronged fork in the middle in black.

The trident of Poseidon, so used in the battle to usurp the throne of Heaven because the Christians had already deemed any Greek gods as pagan constructs. Various aspects of the Evil itself.

Erigan lands on his side at the foot of some steps. They're carved out of stone, block by block placed next to each other and relatively low to the ground.

Peering up, he catches a glimpse of the second banner. This one is burnt at the edges, the charring of the bottom fabric leaves pieces of the original symbolism hard to decipher.

From what he can tell, it's a set of wings and a glowing globe.

This one was brought into battle, near the front lines.

This was the old banner under which Lucifer led his own army of angels.

That must mean he is in His chambers.

A foot kicks Erigan in the back. He pulls forward in the pain and crawls to his hands and knees. He looks up. A huge thigh in black dress pants confronts him.

"Up here, whelp."

Erigan sits backwards on his heels.

Behind him, Mam'mon stands in his general's armor. Behemoth comes into the door and closes it right behind him. He holds something—or someone over his shoulder.

The who or what doesn't move. Dead or succumbing to its fate.

Ba'al's muscular hand grabs Erigan by the nose and pulls him to his feet. "Stand when you're in the presence of royalty."

Erigan tries to turn his head to he left, but is slapped.

"You do not deserve to look at him. Face me."

He does as he is told. His ankle still feels sore, but not injured. Not as it used to. He stands as straight as he can, but the bruises on his back pinch at his muscles when he tries to stand up completely.

Ba'al apparently has no patience for this. He goes around Erigan's pathetic stance and pulls Erigan's shoulders back while punching his lower back.

"I said stand up!"

Erigan drops to his knees again.

Mam'mon laughs and even Ba'al allows for a slight chuckle to leave his lips.

"You never did what you were told, whelp." Ba'al grabs the little god by the hair and lifts him to stand up. He waits patiently for the god to put his feet underneath him. Then for him to stand somewhat on his own.

Erigan grabs for his back, his stomach, his head. Everything hurts, but he knows better than to fall down again.

He doesn't stand a chance if he makes another mistake.

"Better," says Ba'al. "Just a little."

Behemoth tosses the body from his shoulder to the ground. It thumps against the red carpeting, bouncing once and then rolling over to just before Erigan.

He squints his eyes and kicks at the body. "Zeus?"

Ba'al laughs. "The mighty god himself." Ba'al summons up phlegm from the back of his throat and launches it on Zeus's exposed face. "Might god indeed."

The pyre at the top of the stairs sets alight as if by magic. The room darkens.

Then torches and candelabras along the walls are

suddenly set on fire, throwing a haunting red and orange glow across the room.

Ba'al places his forearm against his chest and bows forward.

Looking around, Erigan watches as Mam'mon flourish his cape and kneels on one knee.

Behemoth kneels down as well, keeping his eyes on the red carpet.

Ba'al slams his hands on Erigan's left shoulder. "Kneel," he commands.

A rather large blood red door opens in the back of the room, up on the dais. It opens, slow and creaking, until wide enough to pass an overweight minotaur through. A normal-sized, human figure appears through the doorway, dwarfed by the enormous size of the door frame. He steps forward and comes into the light.

Lucifer, the Lord of Hell.

The most powerful, respected, and feared of the Lords of Hell though you'd never know if you were to meet him. His face is charming, soft features and long blond hair that stops just past his shoulders.

He was an angel first, a thing of beauty. God's right hand man.

For show, Lucifer prefers to walk around in his golden warrior's armor from Heaven. Now it's painted black with the darkened blood of demons and angels alike.

He prefers to walk around without a cape, and so his presence conflicts those who do not know him well. A beautiful face, golden locks set against pale white skin and darkened armor meant for war, for killing.

"You have something for me," says Lucifer. His voice rings like a song in the air, sweet and like a lullaby. His irises, however, are an ashen gray, set against black eyeballs that are small and twitchy.

Ba'al bows once more. "Here, my Lord." He bends over and seizes the chains that bind Zeus's hands together. He holds the chins up to Lucifer's view and drops them.

Zeus's unconscious body lifts and falls down to the floor with a meaty thump.

Lucifer takes a gentle step down one step. Then two. He does this staccato, ghostly and yet full of grace not often seen in the bowels of Hell.

Lucifer reaches the bottom of the steps and comes within spitting distance of Erigan.

Erigan, however, feels frozen in awe. This is the Lord himself. To view him in person was a rare deed, only bragged about by many.

Most of the boasts and braggarts were lies and liars, unfounded and made-up stories to excite those who gathered around the drinking table.

Now seeing the graceful demon in all of his ironic beauty, Erigan is caught—for a change—with nothing to say.

Lucifer lifts his hand into the air and Zeus appears to lift as if by invisible hands.

"Rumor has it you were attempting to take back my

throne."

Zeus's head dangles, unconscious.

Lucifer looks to Ba'al with disappointment.

Ba'al nods and backhands Zeus. The skin on skin contact echoes through the tense air.

Zeus's eyes flutter, then blink open.

"There you are," says Lucifer. His long, white hands grab Zeus's chin with a gentle touch. He lifts it up to meet him eye-to-eye. "I was a little worried that you would sleep through our meeting."

Zeus snorts and spits on the ground.

"And so it is," says Lucifer. He tucks his hands behind him and walks back up the stairs. "Treason is a terrible, terrible crime," says Lucifer. "Punishable by death."

Zeus lifts his head with what little strength he seems to have left. "You cannot kill a god," he says.

Lucifer smiles, his crimson lips like red satin ribbons across his mouth. "Oh, but I can," he says. "When you're in charge of half the known realms, you can do whatever you so desire."

A knock at the door behind them.

Lucifer lifts his head again. His eyes narrow and he snaps at Ba'al. "We have a visitor," he says with a smile. A hint of sharpened white teeth poke through. "Let her in."

Behemoth opens the massive stone door with only one hand. Standing in the middle of doorway is a beautiful, voluptuous woman in black dress. Beside her, a little child. The demoness's black hair falls down one side of her head, and as always, Lilith is always dressed to impress the opposite sex.

"Before you go much further, sire," says Lilith. She curtseys and throws her hand forward. The child falls into Erigan's view. She offers a coy, knowing smile and says, "I think I have something you may want."

Chapter Sixty-One

Brad's body flies into the air, tossed by the invisible magic hand of Lilith. He lands with a thud and a groan of pain.

She takes confident, yet careful steps into the majestic room. Her eyes stay fixed on Lucifer, standing on the dais, but she shoots occasional, flirty glances at both Erigan and Ba'al.

Erigan should be surprised, but isn't. It was only a matter of time before she decided to play every man she could get her claws into.

"Surpri-ise," she sings. Lilith walks to Ba'al's side and stops. She rests her arm around his shoulder and kisses his bicep. The rest of her body relaxes as she leans up against Ba'al's powerful body and, with a wink, she peeks back at Erigan's face.

"Brad," says Erigan. "Are you okay?"

Brad nods, but only half his attention goes toward answering Erigan. The rest of it is divided amongst the various war flags, candles, and weapons around them.

"Where are we?" he asks.

"Welcome to Hell, little one." Lucifer's delicate steps take him to Brad. He offers the little boy a hand up and then dusts off his shoulders. "Are you okay?"

"He's fine," says Erigan. "Leave him alone."

Lucifer rests his arm around the boy's shoulder and smiles. "Why so defensive, Hermes?"

Brad raises an eyebrow. "Hermes?"

Lucifer covers his mouth, pretending that he's surprised by Brad's comment. "You mean he did not tell you? Bad, bad Greek god."

Erigan clenches his fists and feels his heels dig into the carpet. "Lucifer. Don't."

"You see, little one, Erigan here has been lying to you. He's a Greek god. Or rather, *was* a Greek god. Now he's just a little lackey. Sent to haunt you. Maybe kill you. I don't know." Lucifer swishes the air with his hand as he speaks. "That's not even the worst part," he says.

Lucifer waves his hand once more and Erigan feels himself being lifted into the air.

He brings the little god off the ground completely, turning him so he lies face down near the floor. Then, he slides him along the carpet, bringing him eye-to-eye with Brad.

"Brad, meet your step brother. Step brother, meet Brad."

Brad takes a step back. "Brother?"

Erigan tries to look away, but he feels an invisible finger—Lucifer's magic—flick his head back into place.

"You're not my brother," says Brad. "This is all a dream."

Lucifer laughs. His hearty laugh sounds more effeminate, soft and more like a gaspy chuckle. "That is what everyone says at first."

Lucifer snaps his finger and Erigan drops to the floor, landing on his nose.

Brad begins to slap his face, both sides one after another.

Lucifer grabs the boy's head and lifts him into the air with one hand. "Stop that. Really. It's undignified."

Erigan looks up to witness a growing dark, wet dot on the carpet. Something drips down from into the air.

"Did you really wet yourself?" say Lucifer. He tosses the kid toward Ba'al, who snatches him out of the air and holds him at arm's length.

"That is disgusting," says Ba'al. "All of you humans are disgusting."

Lucifer shakes his hands, throwing whatever imaginary human germs may be left on his hands off into the air. He walks to the pyre, silently.

Everyone watches with great enthusiasm each of the Lord of Hell's dignified, graceful steps.

Reaching the pyre, Lucifer stretches his hands into the fire and pulls his head back, relieved. Excited, then calmed.

"Much, much better," he says. "Nothing like cleansing by fire." Lucifer withdraws his hands from the fire. They now glow with a blue flame that lights up Lucifer's face as he speaks. He searches his hands, mesmerized by his own power.

"What shall we do with this?" says Ba'al. He kicks Zeus toward Lucifer. "I trust I'll be handsomely rewarded."

Lucifer smiles. "Sisyphus, pride cometh before the fall," he says. "Believe me, I should know."

Coming down into the steps, he stops just short of reaching Zeus's head. He lifts his flaming hand up into the air.

Zeus's body reacts to the power, lifting up off the ground and turning upwards as if standing on the air.

"I've always wondered about you Olympians," he said. "You were such an interesting bunch. Hiding high above the humans in your mountain. Playing with them for entertainment. Fucking them, leaving them, and then torturing them some more."

Lucifer waves his hand toward his chest.

Zeus's body hovers closer to Lucifer.

"I've always wondered about something," Lucifer says. He holds out his flaming hand, eventually holding out his index finger and pointing it at Zeus's chest.

Zeus tries to shake the spell, but he cannot. His hands begin to turn blue and crackle with electric energy, but they fizzle out as soon as they get started.

Lucifer smirks. "You really do not get this, do you?

Your power is fading. More and more every day. I have the power of Christendom behind me. The world believes in me, and that is all I need to take what I want. Do what I want."

Lucifer's face glows in the blue flame, the shadows of his smooth face dancing across his pale skin.

"But I cannot imagine what it must be like, to be as powerless as you are right now." Lucifer touches Zeus's chest with his finger.

Zeus cries out in pain but then stops.

"Don't try to be brave in front of your son," says Lucifer. He stretches his neck out to see around Zeus's paralyzed body. "I mean you, little one. Not that liar over there."

Brad points at himself. "Me?"

"Indeed," says Lucifer. His lips part to create a toothy smile. "Tell me, Zeus, does it hurt when I do this?"

The first two knuckles of Lucifer's index finger disappears into Zeus's chest.

He cries out louder, tears falling from his eyes and then disappearing into lightning bolts that shoot across the room.

Brad reaches for his ears, nearly falling to the ground.

Erigan winces at the painful cries of his father. Never had he heard a god scream so loudly. With each mournful cry, claps of thunder echo from Zeus's throat. Thin tongues of electricity bolt from his lips, his fingers.

In the ensuing chaos, Erigan reaches into his cloak without anyone noticing.

This might not be the best time, but he needs a distraction. A good one.

He takes out the twig and waves it into the air.

Ba'al releases his grip on Lilith and sniffs the air. He licks his lips at the smell of blood before turning toward Erigan. His eyes widen when he realizes what the little godling has between his fingertips.

"You, give that back to me!" he cries out. "I thought it was lost."

Lucifer watches with great amusement. Zeus crying in pain, his greatest soldier threatening Erigan, the ensuing mess of emotions and plans playing out all at once, it seems to feed Lucifer's smile, the intensity in his eyes.

Ba'al stomps in giant steps toward Erigan, who kneels on the carpet, twig in hand.

Erigan holds it delicately at first, gently letting it wave in the air between his index finger and his thumb. Then, without so much of a warning threat, he holds a tiny branch of the twig with his other hand.

Erigan lets the branch bend slightly as he pushes and pulls on the twig.

"No!" Ba'al commands. He points at Erigan. "Do not dare!"

Erigan shrugs and looks over at Brad, ears covered and crying on his knees. "It does not look like you are in a position to give any orders, general."

Ba'al takes another commanding step toward Erigan. "You will not dare, or I will hunt you down like the dog you are!"

The twig's tiny branch cracks just barely.

But amongst the electrifying cries of Zeus and the crackling explosions of his thunder and lightning, Ba'al still seems to hear the branch's subtle cry for help.

"No," Ba'al says. "I'll save you, I promise."

Erigan raises an eye. "I see now," he says. He snaps a piece of the twig off and flicks it over at Lucifer.

Ba'al stops in his steps. His mouth gapes open and he watches the small chunk of branch launch into the air. It lands on Lucifer's chest.

Erigan covers his mouth, hiding the smile and horror as Ba'al jumps onto Lucifer, scratching at his armor to seize the piece of twig.

"Have you lost your goddamned mind?" cries Lucifer.

The two fall to the ground.

In the background commotion, Zeus appears to fall to the ground with a great thud.

And Lilith, not to be outdone, cries out for Lucifer to kick her lover's ass.

Erigan sees his time. He tucks the rest of the twig into his pocket—he might need it for later—and crawls across the room, propelled by his winged sandals. He seizes Brad's waist and tugs him backward to the entrance.

Lucifer smirks and nods at the attempted escape. "Take care of that, will you please, Ba'al?"

Behemoth stands near the doorway, his arms folded across his chest.

Ba'al sees this and does nothing. Instead he points at Erigan's attempt and says, "Do not let him get away."

Behemoth nods. His shadowy armor glistens for a moment and Behemoth takes a step backwards, preparing for impact.

Erigan picks up speed, rushing headfirst toward Behemoth's stomach.

"Tuck your head in," Erigan tells Brad. He holds his brother's head down with his head to protect him. "This might hurt."

Chapter Sixty-Two

Erigan's momentum carries himself and Brad down the hallways. He spots the last turn he remembered down the hallway and makes it to the top of the steps.

He peers down at Brad, motionless, red-faced and puffy.

"It will be alright. I promise."

Brad groans under his arms.

"Just hang in there."

From behind, Erigan feels the thump of tower moving under his feet. He looks behind himself and watches as Behemoth gets a hairy fist into his face. Erigan shudders at the thought of how much that had to hurt.

"We need to hurry," says Erigan. He grips Brad under his arms tighter and flies down the hallway as fast as his tired body will let him. He feels his toes drag across some of the steps, a feeling that burns his ankle as if it were twisted around Minos's body.

"I think I see him coming," says Brad. He points behind Erigan.

Erigan dare not look. He only tries to go faster but takes a turn down a hallway.

Hoofed footsteps thunder behind him.

Erigan curls his head between his shoulders and presses Brad's head down into his chest. "You can't fly, can you?" says Erigan.

Brad's eyes widen completely. "What?"

They burst through a glass window and flutter, twirling, in the air.

"Just kidding," says Erigan.

His heels kick into full flap as they slow the descent, but only slightly.

And about the same time Erigan feels Brad shaking against his side, his chest rattles from an angry, monstrous roar behind him.

"Can minotaurs fly?" says Brad.

"Shit."

Erigan tries to keep himself higher in the air, but fights a losing battle with the pull of gravity.

"Higher!" screams Brad. "Please?"

Erigan shakes his head. "Not going to happen."

Erigan tucks his feet underneath him and tries to kick upwards, but is halted by a fierce, wrenching grip around his one good ankle.

Brad tries his hardest to kick the monster off, but his kicks are flies at best.

"Mam'mom, get off!"

Mam'mon's lips curl into a crooked snarl. "Not until you and the boy are dead."

Erigan knows it will hurt, but lowers his feet to kick at Mam'mon's bull-like nose. He counts the number of times he kicks, stops at fifteen before he gets tired. And no effect on Mam'mon's grip.

"I can't keep this up," he says.

Erigan and Brad are sent forward by another push. But not from behind.

From below.

"I got him," says Behemoth. His thick hands and sausage fingers grip Mam'mon's waist and squeeze him like an uncooked sausage.

Brad covers his eyes, slapping his forehead. "Are we down yet?" he asks.

Erigan wishes he could say yes. "Trust me," he says, "you will know when we are down."

"That's not very helpful," says Brad.

Erigan feels air escape his chest when Behemoth roars beneath them. The collective weight of everyone— Brad and Mam'mon hanging onto Erigan, Behemoth hanging onto Mam'mon—makes Erigan's waist feel like clay stretched to its limits.

For a moment, he is almost certain he will be torn in half at the waist.

"I cannot do this," says Erigan. His wings give out, his legs struggle to stay onto his body and for the first time, Erigan wishes that he had taken the stairs. "I'm sorry," he whispers to Brad.

The four accelerate to the ground. All Erigan can do is curl Brad up into his arms and brace for the impact. If anything, protect his newfound brother. Protect the future.

Erigan watches as the cobblestones beneath them get bigger, more intimidating.

And then Erigan feels lighter, his legs free.

He peers downwards, past Brad's curled up body. While falling to the ground, Behemoth unloads piston-like punches into Mam'mon's face and neck.

When the two beasts hit the ground, rocks crumble and shatter underneath them. The piercing sound of the cracks command everyone's attention.

So it's only natural that no one sees Erigan and Brad fall to the ground in an ungraceful mess.

The smooth stone road does nothing to soften Erigan's landing. He manages to protect Brad's body from the impact. But just barely, landing on his arm and shoulder instead of his back.

Another appendage down for the count.

Brad rolls out of Erigan's protective grip.

"Wow," says Brad. He holds his head straight and counts how many fingers he holds up. "I think I'm seeing double."

Erigan groans and sits up.

"Are you okay?"

Brad slams his foot down into the ground. A small chunk of the road flips into the air and twirls end on end before landing on Erigan's knee.

"Shut up, okay? I don't want to talk to you. I want my mom."

Erigan lets out a long sigh and averts his eyes downward.

"Where is my mom?"

Erigan's silence bothers even himself. He wants to say something, to apologize. He reaches to grab Brad's hand, but the boy pulls it away with a rapid swing.

"No. What's wrong?" His eyes grow red and glassy. The first tear streams alone down the side of his right cheek along the side of his nose. He sniffles. "Where is she?"

"It's not what you think," he says.

Brad's eyes tell Erigan that everything Erigan is saying—can say—is wrong.

It doesn't matter. Even if it is the truth.

Erigan reaches for his brother's hand once more.

Brad takes a slow step backwards. Then another one.

Something behind Erigan explodes into bricks and mortar.

Erigan covers his head with one arm and reaches out to protect his brother with his other hand.

"Sorry!" shouts Behemoth.

Mam'mon grunts in pain from one of Behemoth's punches.

Erigan's hand slaps around the air, touches the ground. Nothing.

When the dust and debris clears, Brad is nowhere to be found.

Chapter Sixty-Three

Erigan squints and searches down the blood red and black cobblestone road. This part of the City of Dis is unfamiliar to him. It is too far away from the office and his apartment in the lower east side. This has to be, maybe, in the Western Quarter.

The buildings on this side are built larger like ancient mansions compared to the pathetic small buildings everywhere else. A similar theme, though, still declares that you have not left Hell: ashen gray and cracked walls on the outside. Not from earthquakes or time, but from fights and challenged wrestling matches.

The locals in Hell were confident fighters. Not competent, but confident. And confidence plus stupidity often lends itself to severe property damage.

Erigan, being more of a pacifist as of late, left the fighting up to others.

Still, there was an Old World feel to the cracked buildings, the mud-like exterior that reminded him of ancient Greece. Particularly the villages just outside of Athens.

"Brad!" Erigan calls out. He cups his hands around his mouth and shouts, loud and clear. "Brad!"

A voice squeals out, but it appears muted. Maybe not high enough to be a human boy's voice.

Erigan takes a few slow, steady steps down the street. The spirits of people pass by him on the street, paying little mind to the screams and cries of one of their own.

The one thing about Hell that most others could count on—there were always a few crazies, those spirits who believed themselves misplaced or still on Earth.

It was confusion and chaos. And not the fun kind.

The kind that eventually get themselves thrown back into the other circles of Hell.

Those who were considered the good kind of chaotic and crazy, they were chosen by Lucifer himself and granted permission to live in the City of Dis.

These were the people who were not too evil—such as Hitler, Stalin—and not too threatening—like Gaius Julius Caesar—to live in false harmony in the city.

It was a place of demons and angels and only the best, brightest, most moderately evil human beings the earth realm had to offer.

After all, Lucifer would not stand for competition.

And that was what scared Erigan the most at this moment exactly.

"Brad?" Erigan says. Follows the sound of the muted shrieks. "Brad, where have you gone?"

Another muted scream.

Erigan takes a big swallow, takes flight and launches himself toward the sound.

He turns left and right, following the sound down alleys and around buildings until he reaches the gate out of the city.

Erigan stops his flight, landing only his tiptoes on the ground. He rests his hands against the gate and leans forward. He rests the thick metal bars against his cheekbones and screams into the space between.

"Brad!"

The muted cry feels louder this time. Maybe more high-pitched.

"Brad!"

Footsteps come thundering down the alley behind him.

Erigan turns around, taking flight, putting up his hands.

He relaxes them—but only slightly—when he sees Behemoth come around the corner.

"Whose side are you on?" says Erigan.

Behemoth says nothing, but approaches Erigan with a stern look on his face. He is not amused by the sudden display of aggression from Erigan. Behemoth shoves his friend away with a push of his hand and bends open the gates.

The gap between the bars could fit an entire Erigan

standing up in the gates themselves.

"Why?" says Erigan.

"Remember what he said about power? How only those who are believed in have power?"

Erigan nods.

"I needed to join up, become a Christian demon to get more power." Behemoth cracks his knuckles and grins underneath his furry, brown beard. "It was the only way to kick that oversized wannabe minotaur's ass."

Erigan nods. "Thank you. That was very smart of you." Erigan rests one foot through the gate.

"No need to mention it." Behemoth pushes Erigan gently by the shoulder. "Besides, that little boy is my family, too." He rests his hands on his hips. His shoulders and bulging chest make him look like a stone statue, powerful as a monolith. "I guess he is, anyway."

Erigan nods. "And I have to go get him."

Behemoth nods. "I know," he says.

Erigan takes a step out into the salty marshlands of the Fifth Circle.

"And Hermes?"

Erigan turns around.

Behemoth waves and bends the bars back. "Be careful, okay?"

Chapter Sixty-Four

Every step that Erigan makes down the rocky desert of the Sixth Circle is an unsure one. He screams out Brad's name every three steps to ensure that he might be going on the right path.

Because in Hell, everything is deceiving.

He stumbles through a maze of heretics, unfortunate souls who find themselves bound to burning tombs. They remain bound in eternal fire, stuck in tombs—a symbol of death—for speaking and believing against the ruling faith.

The flames burn bright orange and white amongst the craggy desert. The path appears clear-cut and yet contradictory at the same time. Erigan never feels that any path is the right one, each leading turning into a circle and coming upon the same burning casket, the same crying souls.

Souls gasping for air, crying for help. Pleading for truth. For forgiveness. Repentance.

Erigan teases himself with the idea of opening a tomb, finding out who's inside. A fiery present with a surprise marzipan middle.

"Brad," he cries out.

A voice from inside one of the tombs cries out.

Erigan touches the tomb, the flames singing the thick black hairs on his thin, red arm. "Brad?"

The voice cries out again, this time slamming on the tomb. The words are muffled, but give Erigan a glimmer of hope that Brad may be nearby.

Erigan grips both sides of the lid to the tomb. His muscles begin to strain, already tired, as he pulls on the lid.

It creaks open, moving only to rock back and forth on its imbalanced ledge.

"Dammit," he says.

Erigan lets go of the tomb and rests against the inferno of punishment.

"You're not Brad," he says.

The tomb answers back, "Help."

The voice, it's too deep, too dedicated to be helpful.

Erigan slams his fist into the top of the lid and leaves it open. Leaving that own glimmer of hope for the tortured heretic inside. Let him see the outside and know that he'll never get out. Let him burn hopelessly knowing that he'll never see the real outside world.

Erigan's wings pick up speed. He flies above the

tombs, though he feels his wings weaken as he does this. He breathes slowly to focus, but his wings tighten up, straining as he struggles to go higher and higher.

He finally rests on top of a tomb turned on its side. It grants him just enough sight to find the path to the Seventh Level.

Of course, Erigan thinks. This was where he was going. He should have known.

Which means Ba'al has Brad.

But Erigan has the twig—or what's left of it.

In the not so far distance, Erigan spots a sudden downturn of the land. A valley of softer sand-like pebbles that leads to a boiling, blood red river.

"You there!" cries a deep voice. "You will go no further."

Erigan continues down the path and flies upwards into the sky.

An arrow flies past Erigan's shoulder.

"I said you shall not pass the River Phlegethon." Another arrow whizzes past Erigan's ear.

Erigan looks down and spots, at one edge of the river, a large minotaur. Its brown cow-like head turned toward Erigan's direction, but not quite looking up. His eyes are black, narrow. Coal embedded into bristling, matted fur.

"I do not have time for this, Minotaur. You will let me pass or I will have to kill you."

Erigan dodges yet another arrow.

"You talk a good game, little man," says the voice. The minotaur paws at the ground with its human feet.

"But it is difficult to back up such bravado while you're up in the air." The minotaur tosses his bow and arrows onto the ground and takes a spear implanted in the ground near his feet. "Come down and challenge me like a real god."

"What would you say if I had a better challenge for you? One more worthy of your strength?"

The minotaur's spear drops lower. "Go on, you winged freak."

Erigan smiles. Gotcha.

"What if I could hand you the general of Hell?"

The minotaur laughs, a thick glob of spit fires out of his nose and splatters into the ground. It stays round on the sand, not dissolving. "You make jokes, freak." The spear comes back up, pointed in Erigan's direction.

"Surely you saw him run past here already. He is bound for the Seventh Circle."

"He did not run past me. None get past me."

"I wish I could back you up on that, buddy." Erigan drops a bit lower. His wings feeling tired, straining to keep his weight up into the dense, hellfire air. "But the man I'm looking for is right there. And he fancies himself better than you."

The minotaur huffs, another wad of greenish yellow glob launches out of his nose. "Bullshit."

"Nice word choice, my friend. I could not have said it much better."

Erigan looks forward, across the river and into the distant woods. This stubborn bull is slowing him down.

"Come with me and I will show you this offender."

"General or not, none pass me."

Though Erigan lowers his guard—and himself—onto the fiery beach along the bloody riverbed, the spear does not lower.

"If I lie to you," Erigan says, "then you may have your fight with me."

A red tongue sticks out of the bull's mouth, licks its lips. The eyes roll back into its head, as if thinking or dreaming of thinking. Erigan cannot tell which.

"Good. A good deal." The spear lowers and the minotaur offers his hand in friendship. "If you lie, I eat you."

Erigan pauses and shrugs. "If you can catch me."

The two shake hands and continue across the River Phlegethon.

Chapter Sixty-Five

"Are you sure you don't want to give me a ride across the river?"

The minotaur's grip tightens on his spear. As he does this, he looks up at Erigan, eyes narrowing.

"Okay, okay, you win," he says. "But you are going to have to keep up."

"I should not have already abandoned my post," says the minotaur. "It is my duty to protect and guard the Seventh Circle."

"If people are already going into the circle without your consent, then what is the point of you even being there?"

The beast snorts and kicks up dust from the sandy grounds. "Do not make me angry."

Erigan nods and flies faster in the direction of the dark forest in front of them.

It was true and sound advice–do not make a minotaur mad. Especially the one killed by Theseus himself. But for the most part, they were savage, unintelligent creatures. Not stupid by any means. They just were not capable of the amazing mental feats that humble godlings like Hermes were capable of.

That was why Zeus gave them brawn. They needed something to help them survive in the wild.

The same could be said about Herakles up until a few short minutes ago. Just don't ask Erigan to admit it out loud and within earshot of Herakles himself.

"Why do you not help me fly?" says the minotaur in his gravely, rough voice.

Erigan sighs. "Because I can barely fly myself. I'm injured." He looks down at the minotaur and notices a snarl along the minotaur's muzzle, but his eyes do not reveal anger or frustration, but happiness and pride. "You were having a joke, were you?"

The minotaur laughs. Or at least that's what he thinks is laughter. It could have been a stray piece of wood or dust caught in his throat.

All of his time in Greece and beyond, he had never heard a minotaur actually laugh.

Erigan nods and flies forward. "Come along now!"

The minotaur picks up speed behind him.

A dark forest ahead of them is their destination.

"Brad!" Erigan calls out.

"Who is this Brad?" says the minotaur. "Is this the general?"

Erigan raises an eyebrow. "Just how long have you been down here?"

The minotaur begins counting its fingers and the clefs on its hooves. "I do not know."

Erigan shakes it off with a smile. "The general's name is Ba'al now. But he used to go by the name of Sisyphus."

The minotaur's ears perk up. "That sounds familiar."

"He is a royal pain in the ass of Zeus's side. Now he leads an army in Lucifer's name. He has stolen my step-brother and I want to get him back."

"And he has trespassed into the Seventh Circle," says the minotaur between snorts. "He deserves punishment."

"Yes, harsh, harsh punishment."

Erigan smiles with a hint of pride that comes naturally to most Greek gods. It was not difficult to get a rise out of a hapless minotaur, but to turn one against a common enemy?

Well, that was a thing of beauty.

"What is your name, freak?"

Erigan looks down. "My name?"

Perhaps Zeus's blessing and rechristening of Erigan to Hermes the God of Communication and Messenger of the Gods was a sign. A new him. A new future.

Perhaps he can become Hermes once more.

"Hermes," says Erigan. "I am Hermes, Messenger of the Gods, minotaur. A pleasure to meet you."

The minotaur snorts and shoots a wad of thick, gooey snot from his nose.

They come upon the edge of the darkened forest.

The trees stand short and gnarly, not upright and full of green lives like on the earth realm.

Thin black leaves hang, sparsely growing on the trees, off the thorny branches. Up above, a group of harpies coming to feed on these helpless trees.

"Please," says one of the trees, "please listen to my story."

The trees often beg to be listened to by anyone who dares to cross into the forest, for the trees are really the lost souls of people who sacrificed their body through suicide.

The souls' transformation into trees was supposed to be an imaginative way of reflect the thinking of the person when they committed the act itself: Hopelessness, weakness, twisted, painful.

And it's not that Erigan doesn't want to listen, he just simply can't.

Erigan waves the voices and branches away. "No time." He takes his first step into the forest. He had been here a few times before, sent on errands for the upper management.

Not just before, but time and time again.

Pieces were beginning to fall together. Erigan curses himself as he progresses through the thorny bushes and trees. If only he had seen the pieces before, figured out where they fit. He may have avoided all of this before. The death of Sophie. The torture of his father. Losing his new half-brother.

Erigan's steps crackle the broken, half-eaten

branches that litter the dark ground.

No, Erigan thinks. He would not have known about his brother. His new world. The new pantheon that his father wants to enact.

Hope would have been lost, sealed away in a fault of fiery secrets and office paperwork.

Hope is the only thing moving him along. The hope of getting maybe starting over. Of losing his frustrating job and getting to know his half-brother.

And while Hope drives Erigan, the same is not so for his massively bestial friend behind him. The minotaur crunches indiscriminately along the trees. The thorny branches snag along the man-beast's matted fur, and then snap away as the beast charges forward without much thought behind revenge.

If there were anything that Erigan could do about it, however, he would have told the minotaur to slow it down and maybe not break so many branches.

As the trees lose limbs, they cry out for help and for a sympathetic ear.

"Please," they all cry out as the pair moves through the forest. "Please listen."

Each step of his friend sends out a message to the rest of the forest, and Ba'al, that they grow one step closer. Secrecy and hiding, trying to get the upper hand on one's opponents is pointless in a forest of living, crying creatures.

"Erigan?"

A high-pitched boy's voice.

Erigan flies upwards, careful to avoid the waving thorns on the trees. "Brad?" He waits, looking for a sign of movement. Maybe a quick glimpse of Brad himself. "Brad!"

Erigan flies only a bit higher up, but he feels a gush of blood.

"Please!" the tree cries. "Please listen!"

Erigan's concentration and strength leaves him. He feels what little energy he has plummet through him.

He lands in the hands of the minotaur, who seems to have not expected his arrival. "Where did you go?"

Erigan points upward. "Up there. To see."

The minotaur flicks the wings on Erigan's left foot. "You fly with such tiny wings?"

Erigan nods. "Can you carry me?"

"Again, you ask?"

"Please! Just up there. Go forward. Brad is there. I promise you."

The minotaur looks forward, measuring his options.

"And where we find Brad, we'll find the General that slipped by you."

That seemed to be the right amount of words in the right order. The minotaur's grasp on Erigan tightens around his waist. "Hold on," he snarls.

Branches snap, trees and bushes wail, as the minotaur crashes to the center of the second ring of the Seventh Circle of Hell.

Chapter Sixty-Six

Erigan attempts to use his left leg to protect his swollen and purple right ankle.

However Erigan is faced with one truth staring him in the face: the minotaur's charge through the trees is not what most gods would call a "smooth ride."

"Please listen! Please do not hurt us!" the trees wail all around them.

The minotaur's muscular legs plow through the forest at a pace that impresses even Hermes, the fastest of the gods.

"Where is this man, Hermes?"

Erigan looks forward and points. "Up there, I think. Faster."

The man-bull nods and charges faster.

"Erigan!"

Erigan pulls on the rough, bristly shoulder hair of

the minotaur. "Stop, now!"

The minotaur continues to charge forward, but throws his weight into his feet. This attempt to come to a full stop from full speed doesn't work out as planned.

"Stop!" says Erigan. "Now!"

The man-bull, however, cannot stop in time. He crashes forward, rolling and tucking his shoulders inward.

Erigan is shot forward from the minotaur's arms.

He flies through the air, unable to slow his speed or protect his face, everything come at him too fast to react.

The prickly branches of a tree, however, breaks his fall. The small brown thorns jab into each of Erigan's back muscles. He groans and pulls himself free of the tree's twisted grasp.

He falls to the ground in a gasp.

"Brad?" he says and he look up. "Brad? Where are you?"

Erigan looks around and finds nothing more than a surprised Ba'al and the contorted body of a half-man, half-bull hybrid lying on the ground and panting hard.

"Oh no."

The minotaur stands up, wobbly at first, but manages to grab for his spear off his back. He holds it up against Ba'al's face. "You have trespassed," he says.

But underneath the threatening minotaur is a defenseless, little ball of human, huddled together and not moving. Its green and blue striped shirt is mangled and torn, his blue jeans now a rust brown and full of dust.

"Brad," Erigan cries out. "No." He rushes to clutch the boy in his arms. "No. No. No." He forces the boy's head up and opens the boy's eyelids.

The move, twitching first. The blinking.

Erigan smiles and hugs him close to his chest.

"What happened?" Brad says. He reaches up and rubs the throbbing back of his head. "I feel like I got hit by a truck."

Erigan nods. "Close." He points over at the minotaur with his spear against, and into, Ba'al's cheek.

But something about Ba'al's body language catches Erigan off-guard. Ba'al remains on his knees, same as Erigan. In his own massive arms, Ba'al holds the mangled branches of a tree.

At the top of the thickest part of the trunk looks to be a face—eyes and nostrils and a slit for a mouth—carved into its bark.

Ba'al held the tree close to his chest. A tear drops from his eyes, tracing a path down his cheekbones and falling off his pointed chin.

Ba'al looks up at Erigan and says nothing. He just clutches the tree tighter, yet gentler. "You took something from me," says Ba'al.

The branch.

Erigan reaches into his tunic and brings out the shattered pieces of the twig. In small handfuls, Erigan delivers the splintered pieces to the ground.

"This is all I have left."

Ba'al's face turns red, then purple, with rage. "You have destroyed her. Harmed her. Why?"

"What's it to you?" says Erigan. He stands up tall over the kneeling Ba'al. His right ankle bleeds down the ridges of his foot, but for now, Erigan brings the strength to stand up tall in front of his enemy. His tormenter. His brother's kidnapper. "You have destroyed many, many lives since you walked the earth. You think yourself a god? You are no god. You are a coward in onyx armor."

Ba'al rests the delicate body of the tree woman on the ground. The tree's voice whispers something that Erigan does not understand.

With indifference toward the spear, Ba'al stands up and shoves the spear's point away from him.

"You have pissed me off for far too long, whelp." Ba'al makes two tight fists, crunching his knuckles one after another.

"You cannot hit what you cannot catch," says Erigan. He takes flight about as high as Brad's head before falling to the ground.

He winces in pain and grabs his ankle.

Ba'al snatches the spear from the minotaur's weak grasp and snaps it in two.

And in one smooth motion, he jabs the pointed end of the spear into the minotaur's nose and the other he stabs at Erigan's ankles.

"I can bring down a god," says Ba'al. "And in the

process, I can show you what a power a real god should have."

Erigan collapses onto his foot. His wings, his sandals, all a part of who he is and part of his physical being, feel like they send fire through his muscles.

Erigan tries to stand up tall, but feels himself almost fall over.

"I have you." Brad rushes to Erigan's side and catches him.

Erigan shakes his head. "Run," he says. "You have to run, now."

The minotaur rolls away, snorting and bleeding a brownish-black substance in a trail over the ground. Where the bull rolls, he crunches some of the smaller trees just under the forest's canopy.

Then the minotaur sits up and wraps his hands around the spear stuck in his nose. He roars in tortuous pain and tries to pull it out.

The minotaur's roar rumbles in the forest. The trees shake, even harpies caw and shriek in fear.

Erigan looks down, feeling his side starting to tremble. It is Brad's hands, shaking scared of the mournful cries and savage brutality of the circles of Hell.

Erigan holds the boy tight to his side. "It'll be okay," he says.

Erigan tries to fly upwards with his one good ankle. He gets some air off the ground, but not enough to carry Brad.

He collapses to the ground, but lands on his one good foot. "I'm sorry," he says.

Brad hugs Erigan's side. "It's okay," he says. He wipes brave tears from his cheeks. "I'll help protect you."

Ba'al brandishes the tail end of the spear. He flips it around to point the broken, splintered end at Erigan's face.

"You had one fucking job to do," he says. "And you couldn't even do that. I was right. All of you fucking gods think you are so special."

Ba'al's hand begins to glow a bright yellow, then red. The glow travels up the spear and into the splintered end.

He then lets loose a roar that drowns out the cries of the minotaur and rattles the trees around them.

"Please," the trees cry. "Please do not hurt us. Listen. Please listen."

Erigan hobbles backwards. He hopes that he doesn't meet with any thorny branches, no more scrapes. Though he realizes it could be a good thing, to fall down flat on his ass.

The sudden change could catch Ba'al off guard. Maybe give him an edge.

Erigan pushes himself back with Brad at his side. He feels he would go faster without having to coordinate Brad's movements. But he cannot let go.

He will not let go.

"We have to hurry," says Erigan.

Ba'al reaches back with the spear. The splintered tip

glows a bright white. Ba'als eyes let go a black smoke that disappears around the angular ridges of his eye sockets. His lips are pulled back, showing his teeth, his gums, his rage.

"Hurry," says Erigan. He tries to hop backwards but loses his sense of balance.

"No!" Brad cries out.

Ba'al brings the stick down quickly, thrusting downward and forward at the same time.

Erigan flinches from fear, from the brightness, from not wanting to see his new half-brother dead on the ground.

"What is this?" says Ba'al.

Erigan opens his eyes.

Chapter Sixty-Seven

Erigan grabs Brad's shoulders and pulls him from the shattered end of the glowing spear.

Brad's hands glow white hot, absorbing the fire from the spear into himself. But Erigan's fingers burn when he touches the boy's skin.

Brad falls unconscious. His body goes limp, his head falling off to one of his shoulders as if asleep.

"Brad," says Erigan. He knows he will feel guilty for this if it works, but he slaps Brad's cheeks with light taps. "Brad, wake up."

Ba'al holds the spear closer to his face, analyzing it. "So he *is* the son of Zeus himself." Ba'al points the spear toward the boy and Erigan. "That man is setting up fucking deposits around the world, isn't he?"

Ba'al jabs the spear into Erigan's calf muscle and cackles with pride.

Brad wakes up at Erigan's gasping screams. The boy sits up and pulls the spear out of Erigan's leg and tosses it off to the side.

Ba'al grabs the boy by the hair and lifts him up.

"No" Brad screams. He grabs Ba'al's hand, pulling and kicking to break free. "Let go!" Brad says between screams.

Each blood-curdling scream brings Erigan's attention further away from his own pain.

Again, Erigan tries to stand up, but he struggles, falling down while Ba'al grabs Brad's head and squeezes with both hands. His fingers press against each of Brad's eyeballs, turning white from the pressure.

Erigan can already see the bruises around the boy's face, blood vessels popping in the boy's head.

He's a demigod alright, thinks Erigan. He's shown his bravery, his ability to fight.

But he is not strong enough to take down a general of Hell. Not now.

Brad's fingers scrape along Ba'al's hands. Clawing away with weak scratches.

But Ba'al only laughs, shaking the kid so his legs flail about.

Erigan tries to stand, but his head spins. His legs ache and demand he stay on the ground.

Hi heart pounds to escape his chest for Erigan can only watch and listen. And wait for the inevitable end of his brother. An act of bravery turning into his own undoing.

Ba'al's face tenses up. His attention goes into this hands, his strength squeezing has hard as he can.

"Trespasser!" The minotaur stands tall, though he hunkers forward, lurching toward Ba'al. With the sharpened end of the spear in hand, he thrusts it through Ba'al's shoulder and snaps the handle off of it.

Ba'al drops Brad and falls to his knees. He cries out first, then breathes in, pulling in the pain, inhaling the dense, humid air of the hellish forest.

Ba'al collapses backward. He holds the spear in place. Rather than pulling it out, he caresses it. Almost admiring it as one would admire a trophy, an award.

"So it is," says Ba'al.

He pulls himself backward to his tree-like wife. "Merope," he whispers and clutches her shattered, gnarled body next to his.

Meanwhile Brad rushes to Erigan's side and helps him up. "Are you okay?" he asks.

Erigan nods, though he is not quite sure if it's the truth just yet. "Yes," he says. "Thank you."

The minotaur lands on his knees, then falls to his side. His chest feels heavy, heaving up and down, each breath taking in less and less air.

"Can we go home?" says Brad.

Erigan nods and smiles. He secures his hands to stand up, but feels the energy rush from his body and waist. He's too tired to move.

He pulls Brad's head in closer to his chest.

"I want to find my mom," says Brad.

"Soon," he says. "I need rest."

Brad looks at Erigan's ankle and touches his calf muscle. "You're hurt. Bad." Brad looks around. "Can you walk?"

There's a long pause. Erigan nods first, "Yes." He pauses again, then shakes his head. "No," he says. "No, I cannot."

"But that means we're stuck here." Brad points at Ba'al. "With him."

"He's not going anywhere," says Erigan. "Not for a long while."

A voice calls out to Erigan from beyond the trees. "Every time I leave you alone, you seem to get in more trouble."

Chapter Sixty-Eight

Erigan looks up and smiles at his friend Behemoth.

"Herakles," he says. "You found us?"

Behemoth drops an injured and somewhat unconscious Zeus onto the half-eaten shards of thorny trees scattered about. "I figured this is where he was running," says Behemoth. "When I saw the branch."

Erigan offers a weak smile and points at his friend. "Again, smarter than you look, you big ox. What happened to our father?"

Zeus moans and rolls over. He appears to know he's in a place surrounded by people, but he does not react to his name.

"I found him, flying through the air. Out of a window." Behemoth acts out the scene, extending his hands out and then pretending to catch a heavy person in his arms. "When he landed, he landed right here."

Behemoth smiles. "I thought maybe he won his battle with Lucifer, so I ran to find you guys."

Erigan grabs hold of Brad's hand and tries to pull himself up. "He's a traitor and a suicidal megalomaniac," says Erigan. "He was better off dead."

A puff of purple smoke appears amongst the trees. Something crunches the branches, stomping about the roots and dried debris on the ground. "I wouldn't worry about that. That's my job." Lucifer appears through the branches with a graceful smile.

Behemoth throws himself between Lucifer and Zeus. "Stay back."

Lucifer wipes away the charred layer of skin that sits wrinkled on his face. With a swipe of the back of his hand, Lucifer looks brand new, baby-faced and dangerously charming.

"Get out of the way, beast."

Behemoth kneels down into a fighting stance.

Erigan slaps at the ground to get his brother's attention. "Stand down."

Lucifer looks over at Erigan and nods. "At least some of you have a bit of common sense. It's so rare in your species."

Lucifer waves his hand in the air in front of him.

As if moved by a giant invisible fist, Behemoth is tossed to the side and into a grove of wailing bushes.

"Thank you," says Lucifer.

He approaches the wheezing King of Olympians and kicks the body. "You have been a very, very bad god," says Lucifer. "It's time that you are cast away. He bends over and grabs Zeus's chin.

He lifts Zeus into the air and eyes his wounds on his face. Zeus's electric blue eyes amidst his charred and disheveled white mane appear to pull in the attention of everyone near them.

Even Brad cannot seem to turn away.

"You traitorous, jealous dog," says Lucifer. His voice grows soft yet solemn. "I cast you into Judecca, the Fourth Ring of the Ninth Circle of Hell. There, you shall be eternally chewed by Satan, suffering an agonizing death over, and over, and over again."

Lucifer's grip on Zeus tattoos a black mark—something of an upside-down cross—upon Zeus's cheeks and chin.

Erigan watches with some fascination at his father's body wobbling in Lucifer's deceptively powerful grip.

A shapeless shadow comes over the skies, screeching and crying out into the cold, darkened skies.

A flock of harpies, those twisted female angels.

They come to the ground, but never land, and seize a small part of Zeus's body. It takes a total of fifteen of them to grab a part of Zeus and haul him away into the air.

Erigan watches with fascination—never pity—as his father disappears as a black dot into the skies.

After his enemy disappears, Lucifer turns his attention Erigan. "You are the messenger of the Olympians, are you not?"

Erigan nods, though he doesn't know if it was a rhetorical or direct question.

Lucifer kneels down and pinches at Erigan's chin.

"Good," he says in his soft whispering tone. "Then I have a message for you to relay for me."

Lucifer stands up and extends his hands off to his side, forming the shape of a cross with his arms and his torso. He looks at Erigan, but his eyes, his voice, his hair crackles with electric fire.

"I will spare you so you can run and tell the rest of the gods that if they are to be challengers, then they must come prepared for death. I will not suffer fools or traitors. Hell is, and forever will be, *my* realm."

Ba'al's unconscious body lifts into the air. He grunts. His arms slap the ground and he dangles as if being pulled by his waist.

"Speaking of which," says Lucifer. His bright, white smile consumes the bottom of his face.

Chills run down Erigan's spine. While Lucifer may be smiling, everyone knows that he has something horrible planned for the poor bastard.

"And this pretender to the throne," Lucifer says. He waves his hands closer to him, pulling Ba'al's body near him. "For your traitorous actions, you deserve nothing less than spiritual death."

Lucifer looks into Ba'al's eyes, almost lovingly. His fingers caress the sides of the face and for a moment, Erigan forgets that Lucifer is pissed beyond belief.

Something crackles in the air. The sound of rocks,

trees, or bone shattering.

The Lord of Hell rests his hands against Ba'al's head and rips it off. Pieces of throat and dark red muscle hang from the neck hole. They dangle, dripping blood and thick pieces of pink tissue onto the ground.

"Here," says Lucifer. "If anyone should doubt my words, perhaps this will convince them." He tosses the head over to Erigan, who steps back and lets the head drop to the ground. It rolls over to its side and stares at Brad.

Erigan steps forward and kicks it to face the other way.

Lucifer's clothing flutters in the wind and the skies grow dark, cloudless, starless.

In a flash, shadows consume Lucifer where he floats like an angel in the sky.

The sound is quick like a puff of air or a quick breath.

The trees cry out, "Please, please. Listen, please."

Their branches crackle and snap underneath the pressure of the giant hands of Behemoth. He sticks his head out of the grove of trees and into the clearing where Erigan and Brad sit. "What just happened?"

Chapter Sixty-Nine

The trio reaches the edge of the City of Dis once again.

Behemoth, however, holds his thick arm out to keep Erigan and Brad from just waltzing into the streets.

"Hush," he says. Behemoth listens, resting his hand against his ear to catch any echoes of noise.

"It sounds quiet," Brad whispers.

Erigan nods. "Is that a bad thing?"

Behemoth shrugs. "I don't know," he says. "It's as if Lucifer's Citadel was never attacked." He takes a cautious step forward and pauses, then waves the other two in. "It's eerie."

Brad nods. "Mom?"

Erigan squeezes Brad's hand for safety. "We'll find your mother, I promise." He looks over to Behemoth. "Do you know where Sophie could be?"

Behemoth shrugs. "If she was a believer, then she'd

be down here somewhere."

Erigan kneels down to Brad's level. The boy's face fights the urge to cry. His mouth turns downward, his eyes red and puffy. Streaks of tears, traced in the dirt that was windblown into his face in the Sixth Circle of Hell, tell Erigan that the boy is not as brave as he would seem.

But he's trying.

"Brad," Erigan says. "Do you know if you and Mommy ever went to church?"

Brad shakes his head. "No, Mom never liked church. Said it was supersilious."

"Superstitious?" says Erigan.

Brad shakes his head. "Ya, that's what I said."

"No, you said—" Behemoth begins to speak, an effort that is ended when Erigan stamps onto his foot.

Erigan smiles for Behemoth to take the hint. "Okay, then buddy. I think I know where to look."

Behemoth grabs Brad by what is left of hi shirt and hoists him onto his shoulders. "Hang on tight," he says. Brad's fingers clench onto the armor, his knuckles digging into the Behemoth's thick skin.

Behemoth nods and begins running toward the Gates.

Erigan follows as fast as he can go, but the injuries slow him down too much to catch up.

Behemoth disappears out of sight down the street.

Erigan, however, struggles to keep going forward. He limps, drawing his right leg along the floor like a dead stump. He groans and winces, grabbing his thigh and pulling himself forward.

When Erigan looks up to measure just how far he has to go until reaching the gate, his view is blocked by a pair of round tits in a black dress.

"Get out of the way, Lilith."

"So should I consider this your two weeks' notice?" says Lilith. She adjusts her breasts, jiggling them in Erigan's plain view.

"Understatement, bitch."

Lilith sighs and adjusts her tits back into her dress. "Fine. Have it your way. If you're looking for the girl, she's in Limbo. She was apparently never baptized." Her lips turn a cold blue across her mouth, smiling though not meaning it. "In case you were looking for her, that is."

Lilith turns to walk away, but stops when Erigan calls out her name.

"Why?" says Erigan.

"I told you. Never baptized."

"That's not what I meant," says Erigan. "Why help me? Why help the boy?"

Lilith flips her hair with a coy smile. "What good is having a man if he loves you? Half the fun is taking him away from someone else." She laughs in her black dress, buckles along the edges dragging across the black cobblestones. "Erigan," she calls out.

"It's Hermes now," says Erigan.

Lilith's open mouth freezes and it turns into a seductive, evil smirk. She nods with approval. "Here," she says. She snaps her fingers.

Erigan is consumed in a flash of light. It blinds him completely, feeling lost in it. His body, his mind, his form all lost and jumbled around him. His mind feels ripped to shreds, torn from the inside out.

Erigan grabs his head and then it stopped. Seemingly as quickly as it appeared, the pain pulls out of his body.

Out of exhaustion, Erigan falls to the ground. He searches the cobblestoned road for clues. Is this real? Fake? Was that a dream?

He pats himself down, his chest, his shoulders, his legs.

"What's he doing?" says a familiar voice.

"Brad?" Erigan rubs his eyes. The faint vision of a green ripped shirt comes into view. Slow and gentle, it comes together into a solid form—Brad and his green shirt. "Brad," say Erigan. He falls backward.

"What happened to him?" says Brad. He pokes at Erigan's shoulder, jabbing him with his index finger.

Behemoth chuckles. "Who knows."

"What happened?" says Erigan. He tries to stand up, but cannot without the help of Behemoth's massive leg.

"You were teleported," he says.

Erigan's head falls forward, his neck too weak to hold it up. "Lilith," he says.

Behemoth looks down the streets. "She's not here."

"She was. She let us go. Told me where Sophie is."

Behemoth slaps Erigan's back, throwing him forward. "Sorry for you, but that's great for us. Where is she?"

Erigan lets out a quick breath. "Limbo."

Chapter Seventy

With the help of Minos, a path is cleared for the three to the Asphodel Meadows, better known as Limbo, the First Circle of Hell.

Minos untwists his serpentine tail away from his still human body, extending it straight out beside him and he tenses the muscles.

"To one side, please," says Minos. His strong hands wield the tail as if an axe or morning star, and he twirls it around. "I said one side!"

He brings the tail down to the peninsula upon which the souls wait for their judgment.

The souls split into groups, some falling into the River Acheron, clutching to the sides to keep from being swept away by its violent tides.

Minos bows and offers the path to the Erigan, Behemoth, and Brad.

Erigan catches a glimpse of Brad inhaling, but not letting it out. Brad clasps his hands together and looks back. "It's pretty," he says.

Behemoth chuckles and ushers the boy along.

"Comparatively," Erigan says.

The three look out upon the muted greens and grayed whites of the Asphodel Meadows.

"This is Limbo," says Erigan. "Where we should meet your mom."

Brad taps onto Behemoth's leg. "Pull me up."

Behemoth lifts the kid with one hand and rests him on his shoulder, extending his bicep for a larger perch. "See anything?"

Brad points over near the massive stone castle with seven doors. Nearest to the fifth door, closest to the east sits a makeshift stone table, with three figures sitting around the oblong tabletop.

"There, I think."

Erigan starts off in a quick sprint but falls to his knees, clutching his calf muscles. "Not yet," he mutters.

Behemoth lifts his friend off the ground and hauls him over the other shoulder.

Together, the three push aside the contented faces of the wandering souls.

Brad runs to the side of the woman sitting at the table. "Mom?"

Sophie takes a casual glance at her son. The glance turns into a wide smile, her face turns into a deep red.

"Mom?" says Brad again. He grabs her hand and hugs

her arm, nearly pulling her off the stone she uses as a chair.

"You found my son and followed my clues," says Sophie. Her eyes look red, glossed over, but she cannot cry. Limbo is an emotionless realm. Everything muted, made lesser than it should be.

The punishment for being good, but not believing in Heaven.

Erigan finally arrives at the table and bows. "Gentlemen."

Virgil, nods and smiles. His short brown hair is pushed to one side of his narrow brow. "Hermes," he says.

The other stands up with his arms open wide. "Hermes, my old friend," Orpheus says. His arms clasp around Erigan's arms and shoulders, nearly pushing the air out of his chest.

"Careful," Erigan wheezes.

"Brad," says Sophie. "I'm so glad you're okay." She kisses his temples, on both sides, and then pulls his head close to her shoulders. She squeezes hard enough to get Brad to push her away.

"Mom, I'm a god?" he says.

She looks up to Erigan and Behemoth. Both of them look away, then at each other. Erigan cannot answer, even if he knew what to say.

"I—" she says. "I'm so sorry." She hugs her son, letting him sit on her lap. "What do we do now?"

"She is in a state of temporary death, son," says

Virgil. "Do not worry about her."

"That is good news to hear," says Erigan. He pulls Sophie to stand up. "We are taking her out."

Brad smiles at the idea. "Can we?" He appears to bounce from his knees.

Virgil stands tall in front of them. His white robe falls down over his knees and into the pale green grass. "It can be done. Yes," he says.

Orpheus nods his blond head. His baby blue toga falls carelessly over his body. An orange shawl drapes over his shoulder and falls deep down his chest to his stomach. He is a not a strong spirit, but his smile captivates many who see him.

"Aye, but there are some things you need to know first," Orpheus says to Brad. He kneels down and presses Brad's head away from his mother's face and to his own. "Do you hear me?" he says.

Brad nods, paralyzed. Unsure.

"Good," says Orpheus. "You are permitted to leave if you want. You are a demigod, are you not? You have more freedoms, more abilities, than the normal man." Orpheus takes Sophie's hand and pats it lightly. "But she is not a human, and therefore if she is going to go, you are going to be asked to do something very hard to do. Very difficult. Do you understand me?"

Brad nods his understanding again, but his eyes look toward Erigan for answers. He receives none.

"You have great power," says Virgil. "We cannot see the present while down in Hell, only the future. But your future is bright. You can save worlds. Many, many people, young Brad."

"Really?" Brad whispers.

Orpheus smiles. "Yes, really. Are you prepared?"

Erigan takes a long breath. "If you want to save your mother, it can be done, Brad. Because you are very, very powerful."

Brad's lower lip sticks out. "But?"

"But you must walk in front of her. And you are not permitted to look back at her until you both are in the over world."

"Permitted?" says Brad. "What does that mean?"

Behemoth kneels down. Even kneeling down amongst the others, he still towers over Erigan. "You cannot look back at your mom. You must trust that she is here. Always."

Brad nods. He musters a smile that pulls out the dimples hidden deep in his cheeks. "Okay."

"Good," says Erigan. "And when we reach the surface, she should come back to her own body, and remember herself."

Brad grabs his mother's hand. "Stand up, Mom."

Sophie stands up as her son commands. "Did you understand that the nice man said, honey? You cannot look at me. Not until we leave Limbo completely." Sophie fights back tears while stroking her little boy's face.

Brad pulls on his mother's hand. "Yes, yes, I got it," he says. "Let's go."

He starts pulling in the first direction he sees.

Sophie pulls him back, offering resistance. Her eyes widen and she lets out a snicker when she realizes that it's impossible to fight back. "He's strong," she says.

Chapter Seventy-One

Behemoth leads the way. Erigan hangs tightly on to his back, pulling his arms together around Behemoth's rather bull-like neck.

Directly behind him, Brad. His hands lay buried in his pockets. Any temptation to reach back and grab his mother is a temptation to lose her forever.

He can't risk that chance.

Sophie's spirit is close behind, following last and managing the rocky terrain much easier than her mortal companions.

Erigan searches back, looking for the rest of the group. "Slow down, Herc. I think Brad needs help."

Behemoth holds on tight to Erigan's legs and swings himself around. "Are we okay back there?'

Brad sticks both his thumbs up and smiles. "Yea!"

Sophie nods and steps onto another large rock.

The roads up ahead continue to grow rockier, with larger boulders blocking the edges of the path. Looking further still, the path turns into something of a cave, but with a cracked ceiling, letting in some of the stars and light from the celestial bodies above.

The boundary where all realms coexist at once.

This was a path that Hell often refused to allow its messengers to take.

Because of this, the Port Division was created, allowing only those with the Legion's blessing access to and from the mortal world.

Paths like this were, therefore, abandoned years ago. Little upkeep meant that everything dangerous could— and usually did—hide in here.

"Are we allowed to help her?" says Behemoth.

Erigan grabs both sides of Behemoth's head and pulls it backward. He looks directly in his eyes and shakes his head. "This is not our battle. This is Brad's."

"But that's not fair," says Behemoth. "I'm starting to like the little guy."

"A little guy that you sold out just so you can kick Mam'mon's ass."

Behemoth turns and walks slower, grabbing a rock and pushing it out of the way with one shove. "You say that like it's a bad thing."

"When it goes against me and my family, it always is."

"You know we're part family, too."

Erigan whistles, then stops. "What was that? I wasn't paying attention."

"I said that we are—"

Erigan kicks Behemoth's side. "Hey look, Brad's coming along nicely. How are you doing, buddy?"

Brad stops and grabs his sides. "How far do we have to go?"

Erigan leans over Behemoth's shoulder and pats him on the head. "Not far. We just have to pass that river up there."

"Are you sure?" says Brad. "You said not far a little while ago. Are you lying to me?"

"He's got you pegged," mumbles Behemoth.

Erigan shoves his heel into Behemoth's side. "Shut up, Herc, you are not helping." He rubs Brad on the head. "I promise you. Once Charon helps us across the river, we are good as home."

Sophie looks as if she wants to open her mouth, offer some words of motivation, but she quickly closes it. Any words she says, Erigan can see, Brad will turn around to see her.

It's a child's natural reaction, to look at his parent when they speak.

And Brad is only eight. Hardly old enough to be an ignorant teenager just yet. He still wants to please. And it's because of this need to please his mother that he sacrifices his closeness to her—even just temporarily—to save her from living in Limbo for eternity.

Something cracks from underneath them.

"What was that?" Brad asks. His weight shifts to his back leg. His body begins to turn.

Behemoth snatches Brad's shoulders with both hands and lifts him up. "Whoa, there buddy. You can't do that."

Erigan feels his heart beating in his ears. His heart wedged somewhere in his throat. "We must be careful."

"I'm trying," says Brad. His eyes turn red and watery.

"No, don't cry." Behemoth pats him on the head.

He looks over his shoulder, where Erigan has managed to squeeze himself. "We can't do this," he says to Erigan.

"Shh," says Erigan. "He can hear you you know." Erigan slides off the lion skin on Behemoth's shoulder and onto the ground. He breathes in sharply for a moment, pausing to let the pain shoot through is body. "We can get through this. We will. I promise you."

Brad wipes his eyes. He closes them tight, then opens them. "Promise?"

Erigan grabs him with a big hug. "I promise."

Brad smiles and wipes away more tears.

From behind, Sophie climbs up a few more rocks and comes just behind Brad. She rests her hand on his shoulder. "It's just me, honey. We're good. I'm good."

Brad smiles and runs off ahead.

"Please be careful!" Erigan says.

Behemoth offers him a lift but Erigan pushes his friend's massive hand away. "No, I shall walk for a moment. It will do me some good."

They take another small step to the river when something cracks underneath them again.

"Behemoth?"

"Hermes, it isn't me."

Sophie holds her hands up. "Not me." She looks down and the ground ruptures underneath her.

The cracked ceiling of the caverns become clouded with black feathers and bloody screeching.

"Harpies!" Erigan screams. "Get down, Brad. Now."

Brad drops to his knees and covers his head with his hands.

The flock of harpies begin their attack, razor sharp claws slashing everyone in the group without discrimination.

Everyone, that is, except Behemoth, who swipes back.

Erigan rushes to Brad's side and covers his body with his own. "Stay down, buddy."

Brad nods. Sniffles come from underneath his huddled mass.

Erigan can only imagine how scared he must be. He had never been in this situation.

Hell, when he was just an infant, he was pulling pranks on his brother Apollo. Thank the Gods Zeus had a sensible sense of humor.

Who knows where he would have been.

Erigan peeks backward to check on his friends.

Behemoth has two harpies in his fists, one each, using them as clubs to swipe at the other harpies.

Erigan smiles. "He always did know how to dole out a fine beating."

Behemoth roars with joy. He casts off his armor and

roars again. "Come!" he says. Behemoth slaps his bare chest. "Come at me!"

More roars of laughter.

Sophie slices with her open hands at the birds.

They grab her hair with their talons. Their human-like faces screaming at their prey, hissing and slapping with their wings.

And all Sophie can do is crunch herself into a ball and try to walk forward.

Erigan holds both of his hands on Brad's head to keep it still. "Herc!" he calls out. "Get Sophie. Get her out of here!"

Behemoth roars again. While the black bird demons dig their talons into his shoulders and back, Behemoth digs his hands into the ground and rips the ground out from underneath them.

The ground ripples upwards like someone ripping off a bandage. A huge, rocky, million-year-old bandage.

Holding the rock overhead, Behemoth tosses it into the air at the harpies.

Erigan holds his breath.

"What's happening?" Brad asks.

"Nothing, Brad. Nothing."

"Liar."

"We don't have time for this," Erigan groans. "Stay still."

The rock flies over Sophie's direction, nearly missing her head.

"Careful, you oaf," Erigan whispers.

"What?" Brad says. He lifts his head and, seeing the birds come flying at his face, covers it again.

Erigan swipes away at the birds with one hand, keeping Brad protected with the other. He lays still on top of him.

He must be the shield, he thinks. His body can stand the attacks. Brad's can't.

This is it, Erigan decides. He must do it.

"Are you ready?" says Erigan.

"For what?" Brad peeks up.

Erigan nods. "Good." He snatches up Brad into his arms and huddles him. "Keep your eyes closed. With your hands."

Brad does as his step-brother commands.

Erigan's steps are high into the air, any attempt to try to fly against his own leg's wishes.

When he reaches the edge of the river, his grip on Brad loosens up.

"What happened?" he asks.

Erigan picks up Brad but then winces, falling to the ground. "Take him, Charon."

Charon sits on the boat, a short, bearded man in a cloak that drapes over his body like a loose rag. His face remains hidden in the brown, ragged hood that covers nearly all of his body except for his hands and feet.

Erigan points to Brad. "Take him to the other side. Do not abandon him."

Brad begins to kick Erigan's hands away. "No!" He reaches out for Charon's hands and holds them still. "I can't leave you. Don't leave me."

Erigan freezes. "I have to, buddy. We need to save your mom."

Brad seems to realize the truth in Erigan's words and he stops fighting. His body remains still, frozen even, allowing Charon to find a place to seat the boy in the low, wooden boat.

"Can you do this for me, Charon?"

The hooded figure nods and takes the large pole at his side. He pushes it into the river and shoves off away from the edge of the river bed.

Brad keeps one hand over his eyes, but with the other, he waves back at Erigan.

Not knowing if he's peeking or not—he had better not be—Erigan waves back. "I'll be back," he says. "I promise."

Chapter Seventy-Two

Erigan uses the last ounce of his strength to fly back to Behemoth.

His friend's gigantic fists hold a flock of harpies each by the tail feathers. They screech and yell at Behemoth, clawing at him with hidden talons on their wings.

"Remind me to eat chicken when we get out of here. It sounds really good right about now." Behemoth smiles.

A claw come across his face. A trickle of blood drips down his cheekbone.

"That hurt, you bitch." He slams the flock of harpies into the ground, smearing them around as if putting out a cigarette.

"Where is Sophie?"

Behemoth tosses a harpy into the air like a spear. "What?"

"Sophie?"

"I don't know." Behemoth rips the group of harpies into two and tosses their black, oozing pieces to the side. "Where are these things coming from?"

"They're here because of Sophie. She's not supposed to leave Hell."

"Why didn't anyone tell us this?"

"I didn't want to scare you."

"You knew?" says Behemoth. He turns to Erigan's side and catches another harpy with his bare hands. He pulls back on its wings, snapping them in half and then tosses them both out into the wild again.

All if this, while keeping his eyes on Erigan.

"You could have told us, you know."

"Not in front of the boy," says Erigan. "Now where is she?"

Behemoth nods. "There, I see her."

Behind a rock at the edge of the road. Sophie, hiding and stabbing at a harpy with a sharpened rock.

Erigan sighs and flies toward her. He puts his strength into keeping into the air, not landing.

He promised Brad they would make it out alive.

Erigan picks up a rock and chucks it at the harpy.

The bird deftly avoids the rock and then grabs hold of Sophie's arm with gray, sharpened claws.

The harpy screeches at her flock. She has caught her pray.

The piercing screams cause Erigan to smash his teeth together.

He runs to the Sophie's side and wrestles the harpy's talon off of Sophie's arm. She bleeds through the three scratches on her arm, deep enough to separate the skin from her muscles.

"Cover with this," says Erigan. He takes the tunic off over his shoulders and wraps it around Sophie's arm. "They are after you. You are not supposed to leave."

"Then maybe I shouldn't endanger you."

Erigan pauses and stares directly into Sophie's eyes. "I promised your son. You will come with us, am I clear?"

Sophie nods, but she does not smile.

But as far as Erigan is concerned, she doesn't need to smile, she needs to follow directions. Get themselves out of there and think about Brad first.

Erigan grabs Sophie's other hand and tries to make a run for it.

"Come," he says. Sophie cannot keep up with him, dragging him down so he adjusts his speed. He's already running slower than he wants to, but his injured leg is too much.

"We are almost there," he says.

"Up there?" says Sophie.

Erigan nods. He pulls Sophie up in front of him and pushes her forward. "Go," he commands.

Sophie runs harder, but falls into the jagged white and gray rocks that make up path to the River Acheron.

"No," says Erigan. "Get up."

Erigan falls, too, tripping from trying to go too fast

with a swollen ankle. His leg shoots a level of pain he hasn't felt before. Too much strain. Too much work.

But not enough to save them. He must go further. Faster.

A harpy snatches Sophie's arm and screeches again. "We got you," it screams to her sisters.

Sophie kicks and pulls at the harpy, but it flies upwards enough to bring Sophie's toes off the ground.

"Herakles! Help!" Erigan cries. He pulls himself to Sophie's legs and latches on.

His swollen, bleeding leg sits in a pile of sharp, jagged stones. Each one of them stabs at his ankle, the bruises and cuts opened up.

"Please, Herakles, hurry up." Erigan feels his hands slipping from Sophie's shoe.

He, too, feels the ground pull away from him. He will get carried away along with her.

"Herakles, where are you?"

Erigan's question is answered with a slam to the face. The ground meeting his nose and jaw. His skin feels hot from the bruises. His nose, probably broken.

He looks up at Sophie's shoe. She is still in it.

"Herc! You did it!"

Behemoth snatches up both Sophie and Erigan in his hands and starts running at full pace.

"Did you miss me?" he says.

Erigan groans from the pain and Sophie remains unconscious, but breathing.

Erigan closes his eyes. Everything has turned into a

distraction from something else. His legs a distraction from the harpies. The harpies a distraction from his oath to protect Brad. His oath a distraction from his job.

Circles and circles.

"Hold on," say Behemoth.

Erigan feels the air rush all around him and he looks up. The dark blue Acheron River is underneath him, smaller, and passing by.

"You jumped the whole river?" says Erigan.

"Did you want to wait?"

Erigan feels Behemoth land on the other side, a jolt of suddenly stopping rattles his bruised jaw.

He gasps and Behemoth freezes still. "What?"

Erigan throws his hands out in front of him. "Brad! Cover your eyes."

Brad raises an eyebrow and then slaps his face with both hands to cover his eyes.

"We're not out of the underworld yet," Erigan says. "But soon. I promise."

Behemoth lets down both Sophie and Erigan and then grabs Brad's hand. "Come on, let's get a head start, okay?"

For the rest of the path, the light creeps in through the cracked ceiling. More and more, the ceiling disappears, covered with the far-reaching branches of trees inside and outside of the caverns.

"Is that crickets?" says Brad. He pulls on Behemoth's hand. "We're outside!" he cries out. "We're outside."

His body turns to see his mother, but Behemoth lifts

him up and holds him still. "Not yet. After all, she's not out of the cave just yet."

Erigan emerges from the dark, dank caverns and takes a deep breath. The air tastes thick, humid. Hot. The sunshine pokes through the leaves and holes in the canopy above.

"I'm out," he says. He holds out a hand at the edge of the cave.

Sophie's hand emerges from the cavern and takes Erigan's into hers. She smiles, which quickly turns into laughter and then running toward her son.

She snatches up her son and kisses his forehead.

"Mom? We're safe?" he asks.

Sophie allows her tears to drop onto her son's shredded green shirt. "Yes, honey. And you were so, so brave." She kisses him on the forehead.

Erigan takes a few steps, sliding his leg behind him, to Behemoth.

"I am truly sorry, Herc," he says. "For sacrificing you so I could escape. And, you know. For everything."

Behemoth slaps Erigan's back. He loses his balance and stumbles forward. The only thing that keeps him from landing on the ground is his quick and tight grasps of Behemoth's long arms.

"Ow," he murmurs.

Behemoth lifts Erigan up and allows him to stand on his own two feet. "It's fine. You're an ass," he says. "But I get it. Just don't get me wrong. You pull that shit again, and I'll kill you where you stand."

Behemoth's large finger presses deep into Erigan's shoulder, shoving him down.

"Am I clear?" says Behemoth through his thick beard. The sun reflects off the sweat on his forehead and shoulders.

Erigan nods. "I understand."

"Hey guys." Brad steps forward, but still holds on to his mother's hand. "Where are we?"

Erigan sniffs the air. "Pine," he says. "This one's familiar."

Pine needles and dry scattered leaves crunch underneath Erigan's gentle, light footsteps.

"I've been here."

"Where is here, exactly?"

Erigan takes another step forward and points east. "That way," he says.

"We are 'that way'?" Sophie grabs her son's hand and takes to Erigan's side. She holds her hand over her eyes and peers out. "What is out that way?"

"You don't recognize it?" he says. "You were the one who showed me this path."

Sophie looks up, searching for a memory of sorts. "No, I didn't."

"Maybe souls have a mind of their own?" says Behemoth. He takes a three large steps and shoves the branches off to the side.

A car drives by, honking at Behemoth's attempt at walking out into the street.

"Hey, guys. I think we're home."

Chapter Seventy-Three

With his leg up on his leather couch, he flicks through the television.

"Are you sure you want to stay?" Sophie's voice calls in from the kitchen. She comes in with a cup—grape juice since there was no more wine in the condo—and a bowl of crackers.

"I have nowhere else to go," Erigan says. He takes a cracker and lets it dissolve in his mouth before washing it down with sweetened purple grape juice. "Lucifer himself said we are not to return."

"So you get *him* as a roommate?" she says.

Behemoth comes running out of the hallway, all elbows, his massive arms bumping into the handles and doors of the hallway.

"You got me!" he shouts. He cups a pretend wound in his chest and then falls to the ground.

From out of the hallway comes Brad, also bare-chested. He climbs on top of Herakles's chest and flexes each bicep. "I defeated the monster."

"Again, I don't have much of a choice just yet."

Sophie smiles and kisses Erigan on the cheek. "Thank you," she says.

Both Brad and Herakles run to the kitchen. Brad pours them both a small glass of grape juice.

Herakles sniffs it first and wrinkles his nose. He slurps up a tiny sip. "Not bad," he says. He smacks his lips together.

"It was something I had to do," says Erigan. "For myself. For him. For my father."

"Will your father be okay?" Sophie sits on the opposite end of the couch and lifts Hermes's foot up with another pillow.

"Probably not. He's in the Ninth Circle, so he's suffering eternally." Sophie sighs and pretends to watch the muted television on the wall. "He is Sophie's father, isn't he?"

Sophie nods and wipes away a tear. "I wanted to tell him."

"Well that cat is already out of the bag," says Hermes. He pulls himself to sit up, but feeling pain, relaxes back down. "And you know what, he'll adjust. They always do."

"Have you ever seen an Xbox?" says Brad.

Herakles nods. "I think so. I think my friend Pandora had one."

Brad shrugs. "Have you ever played one? Hey, Mom, can we go play Xbox?"

Sophie waves them off and they both leave for next door. The door slams behind them, shaking the walls and tilting a picture of a mountain set against a stormy sky. Hermes had not noticed it before when he moved in.

Left here by Zeus, no doubt.

"I hope so," says Sophie. "I really do."

To be continued in Book II of **The War of Souls** Series

Reign of Heaven

Hell's recent shake-up thanks to Hermes and his friends, Heaven declares victory in the War of Good and Evil and lays claim to the Earth Realm. Meanwhile Sophie is shot trying to save her son Brad, leaving Hermes with a mess as he deals with Lillith's sudden arrival. As if things couldn't get worse, the angels declare war against humans on Earth and Brad is the Earth's only hope.

About David Gearing

David writes and teaches in Arizona. He lives with his partner and his loveable, but very fluffy, cat. Having studied psychology and law in university, his stories explore the darker side of the human mind, with a bit of a supernatural twist. Not much of a surprise since his favorite authors are Kafka, Hawthorne, and Poe.

He has recently committed to the idea of "genre hopping" and writing whatever comes to his mind.

Check out his books at www.akusaipublishing.com

www.ingramcontent.com/pod-product-compliance
Lightning Source LLC
Chambersburg PA
CBHW030542260626
47157CB00006B/2152